DANGEROUS BEAUTY

"Are you afraid of me, Noble? I'm not holding a gun on you now."

His voice deepened, his eyes fastened on her mouth as he stared at her with fervent intensity. "You are far more dangerous now than when you held the gun on me." He searched her eyes. "You have not been with a man, have you, Rachel?"

She was beginning to enjoy herself because she was making him uncomfortable. "No. I haven't. Do you want to be the first?"

He groaned. "Hell, yes. And therein lies the trouble, Rachel. You are the kind of girl who should save herself for her husband."

She lunged forward, taking him by surprise. Their bodies came together, caressed by the soft water. A shock coiled through her and she was momentarily stunned by the way his body welcomed hers. The hardness of his body held her as if she was bound to him.

TEXAS PROUD

CONSTANCE O'BANYON

LEISURE BOOKS   NEW YORK CITY

A LEISURE BOOK®

March 1999

Published by

Dorchester Publishing Co., Inc.
276 Fifth Avenue
New York, NY 10001

ISBN 0-8439-4492-7

The name "Leisure Books" and the stylized "L" with design are
trademarks of Dorchester Publishing Co., Inc.

Printed in the United States of America.

When you were born, you brought such joy into my life. I held you so tightly, reluctant to let you go, but knowing that you had to try your wings. Now, your gentle, loving hands help bring new life into the world. With your kind commitment to others, I can imagine the comfort you bring to so many new mothers. You are my real heroine, my daughter, Kim.

To Todd Melton, who saw a precious jewel, and took her for his wife. (Hfo)

Lenore Ambergis, thank you for allowing me to use your beautiful poem. Poetry shared is a precious gift.

In the sultry heat
our bodies play.
He wants my happiness
above all else.
My God . . . He loves me.

—Lenore Ambergis

TEXAS PROUD

Prologue

The rifle rose slowly and a feminine hand lightly touched the stock to take deadly aim at the man the woman intended to kill. With lethal accuracy, Rachel Rutledge swung the barrel downward until it was dead center on Noble Vincente's heart. The rifle followed him as he dismounted and led his horse to the creek to drink. Her finger touched the trigger as hatred burned within her, almost cutting off her breath. She silently shifted her position so she could steady her aim, all the while watching Noble's every move. There was no hurry. She had waited five years for this moment; a little while longer wouldn't make any difference.

11

Her lip curled in anger. Noble Vincente was only a trigger away from being the last Spanish grandee of Casa del Sol.

Noble Vincente pulled the brim of his black hat lower across his forehead to shade his eyes against the sun's glare. But there was no escape from the heat that beat down upon the parched land like fire on an anvil. He untied his neckerchief, dipped it in the water and wiped his face. His gaze swept across muddy Deep Creek past a clump of mesquite trees to the craggy cliffs that looked as if they had been forcefully rammed through the earth by a long-ago earthquake. The land had no continuity; there was an intermingling of canyons, shallow gullies, mesas and long stretches of flatland. The never-ceasing wind rippled through the straw-colored grass, giving the appearance of waves upon an ocean, while a lone hawk circled widely in the blue sky, riding the wind currents, its eyes ever watchful for prey.

A rattlesnake slithered among the cactus and coiled on a rock to bask in the sun. With its violent beauty, Texas was a harsh, inhospitable land and not for the faint of heart. It was a land of contradictions, the merging of cultures: Indian, white, Mexican, Spanish, all interwoven like a patchwork quilt—yet united in one respect. They all loved Texas.

Memories, emotions, old hatreds saturated Noble's mind and twisted his heart. Rage was never far from the surface, but he controlled it by sheer strength of will. He'd seen so much killing in the war—senseless killing. Many of the dead had been only boys, too young to die. Hell, they hadn't even begun to live.

For two years following the war, Noble had wandered with no particular destination in mind— he knew only that he could not go home. Without any conscious thought in mind, his wandering had taken him to Mexico, where he'd blended in with the vaqueros on a horse ranch. He'd become a faceless, nameless being with no past and no future. In the beginning, he'd forced himself to get up in the mornings, trying to find some reason to go on living. Revenge, perhaps. Hatred, maybe. Two months ago he'd realized that he could never free himself from the tangled past until he came home.

Noble's nostrils flared, and memories unwound in his head as he inhaled the familiar pungent odor of cedar mingled with the fragrance of multicolored wildflowers. There was no use lying to himself—even though he'd sworn never to return to Texas, the land had called him back. This land was in his blood, in every fiber of his being, in every intake of his breath.

Unaware that death stalked him, Noble allowed his gaze to turn westward in the direction of his family's ranch, Casa del Sol. If he rode hard, he'd be home before dark. But even now a part of him

13

wanted to mount his horse and ride away and never look back.

No, he thought angrily. This time he would not allow the hatred and suspicion of others to matter. He was going home.

Years of war had honed and shaped Noble; he was no longer the young man who had left five years before. He had come home to erase the tarnish from the Vincente name, and he would not leave until that had been accomplished.

Rachel's aim followed Noble when he bent down and cupped his hands to drink thirstily from the creek. She was attuned to his every move, and her finger was never far from the trigger. The heat left her breathless and jabbed through her like a dagger, perspiration plastered her clothing to her body, and she could taste the dust like grit in her mouth. Every breath scorched her throat. She was so thirsty that her tongue stuck to the roof of her mouth, and even though her canteen was within reach, she must endure the thirst because any movement on her part might give away her hiding place.

She continued to observe Noble through her gun sight, wondering what he was thinking at that moment. Her gaze moved across his strong jawline. He hadn't changed much; though perhaps he looked a little older than she remembered. His coal black hair curled damply at the nape of his neck, and sweat molded his shirt to his chest and emphasized the broadness of his shoulders. He wore black leather Spanish trousers that outlined his long, lean body. She watched him remove his hat, toss it carelessly across his saddle, and brace his back against a cottonwood tree as if he hadn't a care in the world.

Suddenly Noble glanced in her direction, and Rachel could almost feel the heat of those dark eyes. His eyes were what she remembered most about him. When he'd laughed, they seemed to dance with mirth; when he was angry, his eyes became an intense, swirling tide that could consume and burn whomever he chose to single out. She also remembered his silent arrogance, and the way he'd hidden his true feelings behind a mask of indifference.

Rachel suddenly felt faint. With effort she dragged air into her lungs, speculating whether the sensation was caused by dread or expectation. Reverend Robinson had once preached a sermon on how Satan came disguised in beauty, and Noble Vincente was certainly a man created in beauty, and surely Satan's own disciple. There had not been a day since Noble had left that she hadn't thought of him and prayed for his death. Damn him, now she would see her father avenged at last!

Rachel rested her cheek against the stock of her rifle, licked her dry lips, and cocked the hammer. No one would blame her if she killed Noble. Few people from Madragon County would mourn him, and most of them would probably thank her if she ended his miserable life.

All she had to do was squeeze the trigger and he would be dead. So why, then, did she hesitate? It was what she wanted to do, had dreamed of doing for years.

Noble continued to stare in her direction. Although Rachel was well hidden, she had the strangest feeling that he could see her. Her hand trembled and she gripped the rifle tightly against her body to steady it.

The jingle of Noble's Spanish spurs jarred her back to reality, and once more she aimed her rifle dead center at his heart. Yet she felt frozen, her fingers stiff, her heart hammering in her chest. Taking a steadying breath, she watched him mount and ride his gelding in the direction of Casa del Sol.

Slowly she lowered the rifle, feeling sick.

It wasn't as easy to kill a man as she'd thought, even Noble Vincente. She would let him live today because only a coward would shoot a man when his back was turned. She had given him the chance he'd never given her flesh and blood. She would force Noble to admit that he'd cravenly shot her father in the back. Then, with him facing her, she would shoot him. She wanted to be the last image he saw before he closed his eyes in death.

Chapter One

Noble approached Casa del Sol with a strange detachment. After being away for so long, there was no feeling of homecoming and no feeling of belonging. His mother had died ten years ago; his sister, Saber, had been only a child when he'd left to join his unit. He'd had no contact with his father since the day he rode away from Casa del Sol. Perhaps his father wouldn't welcome him back, since he'd brought so much trouble down on their heads.

When Noble rode through the gates of Casa del Sol a sudden gust of wind caught the sign hanging above the entrance, and it made a ghostly sound as it rocked back and forth on rusty hinges. Glancing up, Noble could hardly read the name of the ranch because the sign was so weatherworn. His senses became alert—all about him was evidence of neglect and devastation. With the eyes of a rancher, Noble took inventory of his surroundings. The north pasture, where once a thousand head of cattle had grazed, was now deathly quiet. The evidence of drought was all about him—the buffalo grass was strawlike, and tumbleweeds were carried frivolously about by the hot, torturous wind. The lone trill of a mockingbird broke the eerie silence, and the call of a raven was lost on the wind.

Noble's father had once told him that Texas was not a land for the faint of heart, and he'd been right. The land had almost claimed Noble as a victim, and it still might, but not without a fight.

As Noble drew near the hacienda, uneasiness gripped him. The stately oak trees that lined the roadway to the house were almost dead from neglect. Their branches dipped and sagged as if in sorrow; most of the leaves were autumn colors, and it was still high summer. As he rode beneath the arched branches, fallen leafage sounded dry and brittle beneath his horse's hooves. His mother had brought the oaks to Texas as saplings from her native Georgia when she'd arrived to marry his father.

Noble spurred his horse forward until he reached the slight incline where he could look down on the hacienda that had once been the showplace of Texas. Sam Houston had frequently been a guest at Casa del Sol. His father's friendship with Houston went back many years. They'd fought side by side at San Jacinto. Later, when Houston had become President of the Republic of Texas, he'd attended many parties there. Now Sam Houston was dead and a part of Texas had died with him—the part that was courageous and exciting. Casa del Sol stood like a ghostly reminder of graceful living—a time that belonged to the past and that was gone forever.

Noble was relieved when he saw that the hacienda was still standing, even though many of the red roof tiles littered the ground. His horse's hooves clattered against stone as he rode through the fountain courtyard. The ponds were filled with dead leaves, and water no longer flowed from the beautiful marble fountains that had been imported from Spain when the house was built.

Something was wrong. The place was deserted. Casa del Sol had once employed over a hundred vaqueros and servants. Where were they now?

He dismounted and walked through the broken tiles that crunched beneath his boots. Taking a deep breath, he climbed the steps and shoved open the massive front door, only to hesitate before entering. It was dark inside, and the aroma of dust and decay permeated the air. When his eyes became accustomed to the dim light, he saw that the imported furniture and valuable paintings were gone. His boot struck broken glass, and

19

he bent to pick up a broken vase that had been in his father's family for generations.

"Father, I am home." His voice resonated through the house, echoing against the high vaulted ceilings and through the unfamiliar emptiness.

He heard no reply.

He went into his father's office, but it was empty like the other rooms.

"Father, where are you?"

With dread in his heart, Noble raced across the entry, up the stairs and down the darkened corridor to his father's bedroom. Slowly he pushed the door open and stepped quickly inside.

Empty.

"Father!" He cried out in agony as the significance of the silence hit him full force. "I'm home," he whispered, knowing no one would hear him.

Heaviness settled on his shoulders as he stood there imagining the room as it had once been, with the warmth of a loving family, smelling of lemon oil, seasoned wood and leather.

After a time he slowly walked downstairs.

Had his father died? Had Don Reinaldo Vincente, *Patrón* of Casa del Sol, suffered because of his only son's disgrace? Where was his sister, Saber?

Without thinking, he went into his mother's music room. He leaned against the wall, hardly daring to breathe. His mother's piano was gone; it had been a wedding gift from his father. Noble closed his eyes, remembering when this room had been filled with music and laughter. If he concentrated, he could still see his mother sitting at the piano, her nimble fingers dancing across the keys.

He shook his head as if to clear away the ghosts of the past. But there were too many ghosts and too many memories left to haunt him. Loneliness pressed in upon him like a heavy weight. Perhaps his father and sister had gone to visit relatives in Spain—but no, a *patrón* would never leave his ranch while such a destructive drought endangered his cattle.

Beautiful little Saber, blessed with her mother's china blue eyes, had been only a young girl of thirteen when Noble had left. She'd be eighteen now, a young lady. He felt shame because he'd given her so little thought over the years. Now he had the strongest urge to see her, to know that she was all right.

"Raise your hands, señor—slowly. Do it now if you value your life."

The man spoke in Spanish, and Noble could feel the gun jammed against his ribs.

"Turn around, señor, and do not make any sudden moves. I shall have no regrets if I am forced to kill you."

Noble raised his arms and turned slowly, a smile tugging at his lips when he recognized the familiar voice of Alejandro Salazar. A member of the Salazar family had held the title of *gran vaquero* of Casa del Sol for three generations. Alejandro had been *gran vaquero* for as long as Noble could recall.

"Would you shoot me, *amigo*?" Noble asked.

Noble watched astonishment cross the old man's wrinkled face, followed by an expression of disbelief and then joy. Alejandro was tall and slender, and his hair was as white as his mustache; his eyes were so dark that they were almost black.

"Señor Noble! God be praised. You have come home at last!"

Noble answered in Spanish. "Is this any way for you to welcome me home, Alejandro? Would you mind if I lowered my arms now?"

The old man's leathery face was transformed by an expression of happiness, and he pushed a shock of white hair out of his face, while his once brilliant eyes glittered with tears. "I waited for you each day. I never gave up hope that you would return, *Patrón*."

Noble laid his hand on the *gran vaquero*'s shoulder as the significance of his words hit him hard and confirmed what he'd suspected but didn't want to believe. Alejandro would never address him as *patrón* unless his father was dead.

His took several deep breaths before he could speak. "Where are my father and my sister, *amigo*?"

Alejandro sadly shook his head. "I am grieved to tell you that your papa has been dead these last two months. He was very ill for a long time." Alejandro wiped a tear from his cheek. "*Patrón*, he tried so hard to stay alive so he could see you again, but he was too weak. It was almost a blessing when he no longer had to suffer."

Grief knotted inside Noble like a fist twisting, turning, pounding against his heart. He tried to speak, but it took him a moment to find his voice. "You were with him until the end?"

"*Sí, Patrón.*"

Noble wanted to strike out at the injustice of it all. He should have been with his father in his final days, but he'd been too consumed by his own troubles. Self-loathing coiled like a poisonous viper inside him. "Did he ask for me?"

"Every day, *Patrón*, while his mind was clear. At the end, he spoke only to your good mother as if he could see her in the room with him. I like to think they are together now."

"And my sister?"

"When your father became ill, he sent Señorita Saber to your great-aunt in Georgia. She begged your papa not to send her away, but he would not give in to her. It is good that she was not here to see his decline. It would have broken her heart."

Noble tried to imagine what his Saber would look like as a young woman. She was the only family he had left, and he needed to see her.

"Señorita Saber should be sent for, *Patrón*," Alejandro said as if he'd read Noble's mind. "This is her home and she needs you."

"Does she know about my father's"—Noble

could hardly bring himself to say the word—
"death?"

"*Sí, Patrón.*"

Noble made a gesture around the room. "There isn't much for her to come home to, *amigo*. It looks like thieves took whatever they didn't destroy. But you are right, Saber must come home. I shall post a letter asking my Great-aunt Ellen to make arrangements to send her home. But not right away."

"Señorita Saber will be so happy to see you again. She did not want to leave, fearing you would come home and she wouldn't be here for you."

"How can I allow her to come home to this?" Noble said dispiritedly. "I must make the house habitable before she can return."

Alejandro managed to smile, and said with satisfaction, "*Patrón*, the looters who came to Casa del Sol did not take so much, although they tried. When your papa became confined to his bed, he had me hide the valuables. Much of the furniture is in the hayloft—some in the bunkhouse."

"My mother's piano?" Noble didn't know why that was so important to him when there were many things that were more valuable than the piano. He could see Saber as a child, climbing up on the piano stool with her chubby legs dangling and her tiny hands banging away at the keys.

"It is safe." The old man shook his head. "Men— drunken men bent on mischief—came many times, shooting out windows and rummaging through the house. But when my sons and I returned their gunfire, the cowards came no more. They rustled most of the cattle, though. We saved less than a hundred head, and they took all but five horses." Alejandro lowered his gaze. "It is my shame that I failed you."

Noble felt a rush of affection for the man who had stayed at Casa del Sol when everyone else had gone. He could only guess at the difficulties Alejandro and his family had faced. His voice caught when he said, "You did more than anyone could expect. I am indebted to you and your family, Alejandro."

"You are home, *Patrón*, and that is thanks enough for me. My wife, Margretta, kept your room just the way you left it." Alejandro looked somewhat unsure. "You are going to stay?" Fervent hope shone in his dark eyes. "You will not go away again?"

Suddenly Noble felt the weight of his responsibilities, and knew what his father would expect from him. "No, *amigo*. I am home to stay."

"We will make Casa del Sol great again," Alejandro said with a wide smile. "When the other vaqueros learn that you have come home, then they will return, *Patrón*." The *gran vaquero* watched his *patrón*'s eyes take on a tortured look.

"I can't pay them wages, Alejandro." Noble swallowed hard. "I can't even pay you."

Alejandro's expression became indignant. "Pay!

What are these words coming from you? This is my home, as it is yours! I was born here and my papa before me, and his papa came from Spain with your grandpapa. It is the same with many of the others. They will return because they have always worked for the *patróns* of Casa del Sol."

Noble turned away and stared through the jagged glass of the broken window, wishing he could express his gratitude but unable to speak for a moment. Finally he said softly, "It will not be easy, Alejandro."

"You have but to tell me what to do, and it shall be done."

Noble pivoted, meeting Alejandro's questioning gaze. "First we need to rebuild the herd. We will also need horses, and that takes money."

Alejandro grew sober and nodded in agreement. "Your papa wrote you a letter. Perhaps there is something in it that will help you."

When Alejandro hurried away, Noble moved to the window and stared out at the dusty courtyard. How would he ever take his father's place? He was not wise or dedicated as his father had been. But he owed his best to the Vincentes, who had died carving this ranch out of the wilderness. He owed it to his father to save Casa del Sol.

Alejandro returned, puffing to catch his breath. "Here is the letter, *Patrón*. Read what your papa said to you. Everything will be good again—you will see. They can't beat you; you are too much like your papa to let anyone defeat you."

Noble looked about the dust-covered room, trying to imagine it as it once had been. "I hope you're right."

"There are many who will try to stop you," Alejandro warned.

"Let them come; they have already done their worst." Pain cut through him, which he tried to conceal by concentrating on opening his father's letter. He was determined never to be taken unaware again, and he would never, never trust a woman.

His father's handwriting was shaky and the paper was splotched with ink. Noble had trouble reading the scribbled words.

My son,

If you read this I shall be dead. Do not grieve for me, but take your rightful place as *Patrón* of Casa del Sol. Hold on tightly to what belongs to you, and let no man take your heritage away from you. I have placed money in a bank in New Orleans. Contact attorney-at-law George Nunn in New Orleans. He is a man of integrity, so put complete trust in him. Mr. Nunn has a copy of my will and he will direct you in any of your needs. Send for your sister as soon as you feel it is safe to bring her home. Keep together what is left of the family. My body and soul have left this earth, but my heart walks with you.

I love and honor you, my son.

27

Noble stared at the page a long time. He felt as if his father had spoken to him from beyond the grave; it fired his blood and gave him the courage he needed to do what had to be done.

He wondered why his father had chosen to deal with an attorney in New Orleans rather than in Texas. He slipped the letter into the envelope and placed it in his breast pocket.

"Who can I trust to go to New Orleans for me, Alejandro?"

The *gran vaquero* didn't hesitate. "My eldest son, Tomas, can go for you, *Patrón*. He is very responsible."

"Send him to me at once. I shall draw up the necessary papers for him. Can he leave within the week?"

"*Sí, Patrón*. You give the order and he will obey."

Noble shook his head. "I hope I can be the man my father expected me to be, Alejandro."

"*Cada quien construye su propio destino, Patrón*."

"*Sí, amigo*, we do make our own destiny."

Chapter Two

Rachel dismounted and tossed her horse's reins to Zeb, the old cowhand who had worked for Broken Spur Ranch for over forty years. As much a part of the ranch as the land itself, Zeb was bent and aging, his hands misshapen and gnarled. When it had become impossible for him to keep pace with the younger cowhands, Rachel had put him in charge of the horses, which suited him just fine. Zeb loved horses, and they responded to the gentle care administered by those misshapen hands.

Zeb gave her a wide grin, which showed that most of his teeth were missing. Long white hair touched his shoulders when he respectfully removed his dusty hat, slapping it against his bowed leg. "Sure is a scorcher today, Miss Rachel." He patted the rump of her lathered horse. "Looks like you've been riding hell-bent in this heat." There was no reproach in his voice; he knew if Rachel had ridden her horse hard, there must have been a good reason. "I'll just give Faro a good rubdown and cool her off slow-like."

Rachel's mind had already settled on other matters, and she gave Zeb the merest nod before entering the ranch house. Winna Mae, the housekeeper and cook, came out of the kitchen, wiping her hands on her apron.

Rachel had been twelve the winter her father had found Winna Mae by the river, half-frozen, severely beaten, and with horrible burn scars on her arms and hands. Her father had brought her to the ranch house to recover. When Winna Mae had regained her health, it seemed only natural for her to remain at Broken Spur as cook and housekeeper. Her hands were never idle, and she ruled the house as though it was her domain. Few people ever dared to tangled with her.

Not much was known about Winna Mae's past. No one questioned her about it, and she never volunteered any information. Her dark skin and high cheekbones suggested that she could be half Indian. Her black hair was streaked with gray, and she wore it in a tight bun. Her face reminded Rachel of the map hanging in the back of the schoolroom—the lines reflecting the hard life she'd led, the sadness she'd known, the pain she tried to hide.

To Rachel, Winna Mae was invaluable, and she didn't know what she would have done without her, especially in the months following her father's death.

Winna Mae nodded toward the narrow staircase. "Your sister's here. Said she's resting and don't want anyone to bother her."

Rachel removed her gloves and hat and dropped them onto a leather settee, disdainfully rolling her eyes and wishing she didn't have to face her sister today of all days. "Delia never comes to Broken Spur unless she's displeased about something or she wants something."

Winna Mae merely nodded and made her way back to the kitchen.

Rachel knew why Delia had come all the way from Austin in this heat. For the last two years Delia had been pressuring her to sell Broken Spur to Delia's husband, Whit, and she'd probably come today to renew that argument.

Reluctantly, Rachel climbed the stairs, berating herself because she'd had Nobel in her gun sights and had allowed him to just ride away. Her shoulders sagged with weariness. She had broken the promise that she'd made at her father's grave site. Gathering her composure, she knocked on the door of the bedroom that had been her sister's before she'd married Whit Chandler and moved to Austin—a room always kept in readiness for Delia's infrequent visits.

An irritated voice bade her enter. Rachel found

her sister, stripped down to her petticoat, lying across the bed and fanning herself with a silk and ivory fan.

"Why is it so hot?" Delia asked plaintively as she flipped tresses of golden hair from her face. "I can scarcely draw breath."

Rachel walked to the heavy green curtains and forcefully jerked them aside, then shoved open the window. "If you'd let in some fresh air, it wouldn't be so hot, Delia."

"I'm accustomed to servants doing that for me. Winna Mae never sees to my comfort. I don't know why you kept her here after Papa died. I don't like looking at her scarred hands—they're horrible and make me shudder."

"Winna Mae has more things to do than see to your comfort, Delia. And you know that I keep her because I need her and this is her home. As for her hands being scarred, have you no pity? Something dreadful must have happened to her."

Delia frowned. "She never did like me, and I don't care for her either. And no, I don't pity her; she has you to do that for her."

Rachel gathered her thoughts before she answered. "Winna Mae treats everyone the same. You just don't understand her."

Delia eased herself to a sitting position while gazing disapprovingly at the way her sister was dressed. Rachel wore a dusty green shirt, chaps and scuffed brown boots. Her red-gold hair, which she'd gotten from their father, was wind-blown and tangled about her face.

Delia realized for the first time that Rachel was pretty, almost beautiful with her unusual green eyes and delicate features. Of course she was tall for a female, and if that didn't chase the men away, her temper or her manner of dress certainly would.

"Why do you insist on dressing like a man, Rachel? For God's sake, can't you take a little pride in yourself? If you don't care what people think about you, you might at least consider me and Whit. After all, everything you do reflects on us, and could affect his chances to run for governor when the time comes."

Rachel took in an impatient breath and scoffed, "With a Yankee military governor sitting in the capitol building, and Texans unable to vote, I'd like to see how Whit accomplishes that feat."

"Well," Delia said irritably, fanning herself with renewed vigor. "When Texas is admitted back into the Union, which it will be, Whit intends to be the first elected governor since that awful war ended."

"Texas is nothing more than a Yankee stronghold," Rachel stated with distaste. "I'm not so sure we'll ever be free of Washington's yoke, or if we'll see free elections in our lifetime."

"That's what little you know. Whit has culti-vated the friendship of the right people. Our friends believe that Texas could be readmitted to the Union as early as three years from now. Whit intends to lead Texas into a bright new future when that happens."

Rachel could almost hear Whit spouting those words to anyone who would listen to him. "I never was quite sure if Whit was a Yankee sympathizer or if he was loyal to the Confederacy." There was a stilted pause before Rachel said, "He never quite makes his loyalties clear, does he?"

"That's called politics, sister dear. You play one side against the other and you go with the winner." Delia skillfully turned the conversation back to Rachel. "The last thing Whit needs is his sister-in-law flouting convention and riding about the countryside like a hellion."

Rachel had heard this argument before; undaunted, she walked to the other side of the room and shoved open another window to allow a cross breeze to circulate through the room. She was in no mood to be lectured today.

"A ranch the size of Broken Spur doesn't run itself. Papa made it my responsibility, and if the way I dress offends your husband, I just don't care!"

Delia yawned and stretched her arms over her head. "Whit's still willing to take the responsibility of the ranch off your shoulders, but you're so determined to do everything yourself. Look at you; you're as brown as an Indian—browner than Winna Mae."

Rachel dropped down on the bed beside her sister, trying to see her through the eyes of a man.

Delia was incredibly beautiful, with golden hair, a creamy complexion and big, cornflower blue eyes. She'd inherited their mother's soft beauty as well as her slender and petite form. Rachel felt clumsy compared to her sister, but she didn't envy her—she loved her too much.

"If only I could make you understand how I feel about the ranch, Delia. Papa put his heart and soul into Broken Spur—he and Mama are buried here. It's my home, and I won't sell it to anyone. Not even your husband."

Delia studied a broken nail with a pensive frown. "I don't understand or forgive Papa for leaving the ranch to you. It's a humiliation that I'll never get over, and neither will Whit."

"Papa knew how much you hated the ranch and how much I loved it. It's as simple as that, Delia. He left you the house in town—which you sold— and most of his other holdings. As I recall, when his will was first read, you were happy enough about the arrangement."

"Maybe, but since then, Whit has convinced me that Broken Spur is the jewel in the crown." Delia's eyes became misty. "Papa always liked you better than me, Rachel—you know he did. That's why he left you Broken Spur."

Rachel had a sudden rush of affection for her sister, who could be so childlike at times, needing everyone's approval and attention. Their father had made no secret of the fact that Rachel was his favorite. "This will always be your home, Delia—

you know that. You can come here as often as you like and stay as long as you want."

Delia's expression hardened. "I resent your stubbornness, Rachel. Wouldn't you like to be free of tiresome obligations that go with running a ranch this size? Just think—you could do anything you desired. You always said you'd like to travel. You could visit San Francisco. You could come to Austin and stay with us. You would be a sensation! There isn't a woman in town who can match your beauty. You could have your pick of beaus."

"Try to understand, Delia; I don't want to leave here. If I sold Broken Spur to Whit, it would be like selling a part of Papa, and I'll never do that."

Delia gripped her sister's shoulders and said heatedly, "Let the dead go, Rachel. I have."

"Never!"

Seeing the anger reflected in Rachel's green eyes, Delia released her hold. Rachel had a fiery temper to match her red hair, and it wasn't wise to provoke her—not if she was ever going to convince her to sell Broken Spur.

"How can you even suggest such a thing?" Rachel asked passionately. "I won't rest until Papa's murderer lies six feet under." She sprang off the bed and walked to the door, then paced back to her sister.

"He's back."

Delia was puzzled. "Who?"

"Noble Vincente."

Chapter Three

Delia leaped from the bed, her heart thundering. "Noble's home? Are you sure?"

"Yes. I saw him."

"I knew he'd come back." A smug smile curved Delia's lips. "I knew Noble couldn't stay away from Texas for much longer."

Rachel studied her sister closely: Delia's eyes were bright and her face was flushed with excitement. At one time Delia had fancied herself in love with Noble, and that was the beginning of all the trouble that had led to their father's death.

"I could have killed him today. I had him in my rifle sights, and I just let him ride away."

Delia gripped Rachel's shoulder and swung her around so forcefully that Rachel winced in pain.

"I don't want Noble hurt—do you understand me?" She shook Rachel hard. "Remember that any scandal that touches this family will ruin Whit's chances to win the election."

Rachel pushed her sister away and glared at her. "You are the last one to worry about scandal after what happened between you and Noble. You're fortunate that the gossips didn't find out, or Whit's political career would be over before it started."

"You're cruel to bring up the past, Rachel. I don't want to think about it."

"Be warned that when the time is right, I'll bring Noble Vincente to his knees. Just how I accomplish that is for me to decide." She smiled secretively, suddenly aware that she was baiting her sister, and worse still, that she was enjoying it. "I might let Noble live and wound him to the heart. He always had an eye for a pretty girl—maybe that's the weapon I'll use against him. What do you think, Delia: am I pretty enough for him?"

Delia laughed scornfully. "*You*, pitted against Noble? I don't think so, little sister. What will you wear to entice him—your usual male attire? Noble wouldn't even notice you as a woman." Her eyes swept over Rachel. "Besides, you know nothing about a man like Noble, and he surely wouldn't be interested in someone like you."

"As I recall, he wasn't too interested in you either." Rachel watched the color drain from her sister's face. "He smiled at you, flirted a little, and you fell into his arms, giving him everything he wanted. Noble didn't love you or he would have married you when he learned you were going to have his baby."

Delia lowered her lashes, looking like a wounded bird. "I made a mistake but I've paid for it. God knows I've paid and paid."

Rachel felt a rush of pity for Delia and softened her tone. "Noble didn't care about you or the baby. Even now he probably wouldn't even care that you lost the child."

"You don't understand; it wasn't his fault."

Rachel had tired long ago of Delia's defense of Noble. "You should be thinking about your husband. I don't like Whit much, but at least he married you and made sure that no one knew about the baby."

"And you are too quick to condemn Noble for our father's death, when the law found no evidence that he shot Papa."

Rachel looked thoughtfully at her sister. "Most of our friends are convinced that Noble killed Papa. Fortunately for you, they believed that the quarrel was over water rights to the Brazos."

"Our friends and neighbors have always hated the Vincentes because of their wealth and power. Most of them would latch on to any excuse to drag the Vincente name through the mud."

"Noble is guilty," Rachel stated forcefully, her eyes like green fire. "I don't want to talk any more about him. Especially not with you."

Delia dropped her gaze and said, "It's not Noble's fault that Papa's dead—it's mine."

Rachel was rapidly losing patience. "Never defend him to me. If you think he's innocent, keep your thoughts to yourself."

Delia's shoulders slumped and she looked miserable. "I loved him so much that I was sure he'd love me too. But he didn't." She shook her head. "If you only knew how kind he was to me at the time."

"There's another word for what he did to you, and it isn't kindness. For my part, I prefer his hatred to his love. And he will hate me passionately before I'm finished with him."

Delia grabbed both of Rachel's wrists and dug her nails into the soft flesh. Her eyes took on a faraway look, and her voice was so faint it was almost inaudible. "Noble is *not* like other men. If only Papa hadn't died, I believe Noble might have married me. He has a good heart."

Rachel yanked her hands free, staring at Delia as if she were seeing her clearly for the first time. "My God, your love for Noble has made you blind to his villainy! I'm astonished at just how far you'd go to defend him."

Delia dropped down on the window seat and drew up her legs, resting her chin on her knees. "You have no idea how far Noble went to protect me. If you only knew—" Her voice broke off.

"If I knew what?" Rachel demanded. "Let's take the facts as they happened that day. First, you told

Papa that you were going to have Noble's baby, so he went to Casa del Sol to confront him. Second, Papa's body was found on the Casa del Sol side of the Brazos. Third, Noble's gun was found beside Papa. If that doesn't add up to his guilt, what does? Tell me, Delia—what more proof do you need?"

Delia tossed her golden mane defiantly. "Let's look at more truths, Rachel. One, there would have been no reason for Noble to kill Papa, because he could refuse to marry me and leave the state, which he did. Two, Noble is too smart to kill a man and leave his gun behind as evidence to be used against him."

Rachel had never fully forgiven her sister for the part she'd played in their father's death, but she'd buried her resentment deep, since her sister was the only family she had left. And Delia needed her at times. Like now. Rachel knew that her sister's marriage to Whit was not a happy one, and whether Delia admitted it or not, when she came home to Broken Spur it was to find peace.

"Come on," Rachel cajoled, hoping to end their discussion about Noble. "Get dressed and we'll eat supper on the porch, where it's cooler. You know you like Winna Mae's cooking."

Delia didn't appear to be listening. She seemed locked in her own hell. "It's not my fault that Papa's dead. I was young, in love and foolish. If only . . . if only I could go back and change everything."

41

"What you should have remembered at the time is that the Vincentes never married out of their class—you were not of their social standing. Were you ever invited to any of the grand fiestas that were held at Casa del Sol?" She shook her head. "No, you weren't, nor were you likely to be." Rachel's tone became harsh. "The Vincentes spring from Spanish nobility, and you were only a poor rancher's daughter, not fit to polish their fine black boots."

"As I recall, Noble liked you. He always singled you out and showed marked attention toward you," Delia countered pettishly. "He even had a pet name for you." She bit her lip, trying to remember, and then sighed. "I've forgotten what he called you."

Rachel closed her eyes and tried to keep her thoughts from going back to a time when she'd adored Noble. He had called her Green Eyes. She didn't want to admit that she'd once been among the hordes of females who'd fallen victim to Noble's formidable charm. She'd been only sixteen the summer she'd first thought of him as a man. She had buried those memories deep, unwilling to examine them too closely. All she wanted to remember was that he'd impregnated her sister, deserted her, and killed their father.

Delia's voice fell to a whisper. "You seem to forget that Noble was never convicted of Papa's murder."

"Did you expect that he would be? People like

42

the Vincentes don't hang or go to prison for killing a small rancher. But Papa has a lot of friends, and they would have lynched Noble if he hadn't run away like a coward."

Delia caught and held Rachel's gaze. "There are things that you don't know about, so don't go rushing off and doing something foolish. Just leave Noble to me."

"If you really thought he was innocent, you'd have spoken up long before now. You know only what your heart tells you to believe." Rachel's voice grew cutting. "As ironic as it sounds, Delia, you are probably Noble's only friend."

Her sister shrugged. "He was kinder to me than you will ever know. Even after . . . after—"

"Of course he was kind to you—it got him what he wanted from you, didn't it? Thank God Whit loved you enough to cover for Noble's little mistake."

"Love was not a consideration when Whit married me. But we're alike, Whit and I," Delia added forcefully. "We're both ambitious and we'll do anything to get what we want." Her expression suddenly grew sad and she said softly, "Rachel, there must be justice in the world, because I wanted children so badly and have never been able to conceive since I lost the baby."

"You may still have children," Rachel said gently. "Just be patient a little longer."

"You don't understand. Whit says we don't need children. He says Texas will be our child."

Disgust rose within Rachel like bile. "Sounds like a match made in hell." She opened the door and glanced back at her sister. "Don't get in my way, Delia. I intend to destroy Noble Vincente, and I'll do it—you know I will."

"You're just like Papa," Delia warned. "And you know what happened to him. If you aren't careful, you'll end up dead too!"

"I'm not afraid of Noble Vincente."

"No?" Delia laughed sardonically. "Maybe you should be."

Rachel grew weary of the conversation. There was no reasoning with Delia on the subject of Noble because she was still in love with him. "Take this for the truth—no one is more dedicated to Noble's downfall than I am!"

Delia's quick retort was laced with malice. "Take heed that Noble doesn't cause your downfall. Beware that you don't fall victim to his charms, as I did." She moved closer to Rachel, her eyes suddenly soft. "Noble is like the Texas wind that soars above us all. You cannot hold the wind in your hand any more than you can hold Noble."

Rachel grasped the doorknob. She had to escape; the room was stifling and smelled strongly of the rose fragrance Delia always wore. "I'll bring him down," she muttered to herself, and took the stairs two at a time, hurrying out the front door. "Somehow, some way, I'll make him pay for what he did to Papa."

Chapter Four

Delia pressed a quick kiss on Rachel's cheek before she climbed into her private coach and settled back into the plush softness of the leather seat. "Think more on Whit's offer to buy Broken Spur."

"There is nothing to think about. My answer will always be the same." Rachel stepped back. "Have a safe journey, and write me." She watched the brown-and-yellow coach jolt into motion, and waved until it was out of sight. Then, with relief, she went to the barn, saddled Faro, and rode toward the Brazos River.

After riding for an hour, she reined in her mount and watched the way golden sunlight vaulted across the clear blue sky. Her gaze moved to the buffalo grass that was perpetually stirred by the relentless, blistering wind. She loved this land because, to her, it represented her father. She could never sell to anyone, not even Delia and Whit.

She hadn't intended to ride toward Casa del Sol. Her instinct just seemed to guide her in that direction. For a time, she galloped parallel to the Brazos River, which was the border between the Broken Spur and Casa del Sol. Both ranches had benefited from the Brazos's bounty in the past, but this year the water was low from lack of rain. In places it was so shallow that she could ride across without wetting her horse's girth.

Without thinking, she plunged Faro into the mud-colored river and rode up the bank to the other side. Her mind took her to a place of reveries. Her reflections were of dark, flashing eyes— the eyes of a killer, Noble Vincente's eyes.

He'd dominated her thoughts since his return to Texas. Just like now, when a memory out of the past flowed through Rachel's mind even though she fought vainly to suppress it. She didn't want to remember how she'd once adored Noble. But the memories would not be denied. She could almost hear his teasing voice calling her Green Eyes.

Although Noble was only half Spanish, his mother being from an old and respected Southern family, his complexion was dark like his father's, and he chose to wear the traditional Spanish attire, as had his father. When Rachel thought of

Noble, he was always wearing black leather with silver trim. Just as he had that day his image had been stamped forever in her memory.

Rachel's attention was yanked back to the present when a jackrabbit jumped in front of her, causing Faro to rear. With a firm hand on the reins and soothing words, she calmed her horse.

Again the unwelcome past invited itself into Rachel's thoughts. She was being drawn back, against her will, through the curve of time. She remembered the day she had accompanied her father to Casa del Sol to buy a breeding bull from Don Reinaldo Vincente. She'd been sixteen at the time and as vulnerable to Noble's charms as any woman in Madragon County.

When they'd arrived at the Vincente ranch, her father had driven the wagon to the corrals, where several of the vaqueros had been breaking horses.

Happily, she had scampered out of the wagon while her father had conversed with Don Reinaldo. She'd hurried to the corral and hooked the heel of her boot in the fence, hoisting herself up to watch. She recalled her father smiling indulgently at her; he never berated her or objected to her wearing britches and boots and riding astride like a man. He'd prided himself on the fact that his youngest daughter could stand toe-to-toe with any man and beat him at his own game.

Rachel's mind had opened up, and she was flooded by more memories. As she rode beneath the scorching Texas sun toward her destination, she visualized that day so long ago when Noble first unleashed emotions that had awakened her virginal body. Her thoughts tumbled, spinning out of control, backward in time. . . .

Sam Rutledge conversed with Don Reinaldo while sixteen-year-old Rachel watched a vaquero trying to slide a leather halter over the head of a spirited black mare. To her surprise Noble came from the stable, his silver spurs jingling with every step he took. He propped his booted foot on the fence, tightened the strap of his spurs and then gave the silver spike a spin. He nodded to the vaquero, who was gripping the waiting mare's ears and holding her firm. Then, with catlike grace, Noble bounded onto the back of the exquisite animal, whose coat shone like polished ebony.

For a moment, man and beast stood perfectly still, but Rachel knew what was to come. The mare's ears were laid back in defiance; she was wild, untamed and ready to challenge the man who would try to master her.

With a suddenness that startled Rachel, the horse took a tremendous leap toward the sky, carrying Noble with her. The defiant mare resisted gravity and bounded upward again and again. She spun and bucked in an attempt to dislodge the man on her back. Yet Noble's muscled legs hugged the horse's heaving sides, and he refused to be unseated.

He was power and grace, indomitable. Rachel's

heart pounded with excitement while the vaqueros yelled out their approval. She held her breath when the horse reared, kicked, twisted and turned, but still was unable to throw Noble. Time had no meaning as she watched him master the horse. His firm brown hands held the reins steady, his long legs issuing their own commands. Rachel felt glad that he used his spurs sparingly, knowing just how much pressure to apply without breaking the beautiful animal's skin.

At last the mare halted, her sides lathered and heaving, her graceful head bowed as if in surrender to the man who had conquered her. But she remained spirited even in defeat.

While the vaqueros shouted out their praise, Noble seemed as calm as if he'd been on a pleasure outing. His composure impressed Rachel more than anything else.

Seeing her, he rode over to the fence on the now docile mare. Noble stood up in the stirrups and swept her a bow, saying, "Señorita Green Eyes, you are growing up to be a beauty. With those eyes you will surely break every man's heart in Madragon County, including my own."

His smile made her heart skip a beat—in fact it skipped several beats—and she struggled to regain her composure. When his electrifying gaze settled on her, Rachel tightened her grip on the fence post to keep her balance.

"Noble, you were magnificent," she said timidly,

wondering why she should suddenly feel so shy with a man she'd known all her life.

He reached out and gently touched her cheek. "Careful, Green Eyes; you should never look at a man like that."

She was confused as she shoved his hand away. "I don't know what you mean."

"Do you not? There is fire in your eyes that would stagger the strongest man."

Her face flushed and she tried to hide her embarrassment by saying flippantly, "That's not so, Noble Vincente." She groped for words. "I was merely admiring your horsemanship. I have never seen such a mare—what breed is she?"

He laughed and dismounted, tossing the reins to a vaquero. "I won't tease you anymore, Green Eyes. My throat is dry. Walk with me to the well and I will tell you all about the black mare."

She accompanied him reluctantly, wishing that her heart would stop fluttering. A new sensation tightened the muscles in the pit of her stomach and left her feeling breathless, a sensation that she didn't like at all.

"You said you would tell me about the horse," she reminded him. She pressed her palm against her heart because it was beating so fiercely she feared he could hear it.

He chuckled and ruffled her hair. "All right, inquisitive one. The mare was bred by Carthusian monks at a mountainous monastery in southwestern Spain."

"Noble, I have never seen a horse with such a shiny black coat. She has such strong leg muscles and must be over fifteen hands high. You may have broken her to the saddle, but you didn't break her spirit."

"I would not want to break her spirit," Noble said with a meaningful smile. "Neither a horse nor a woman should ever have her spirit broken."

Rachel tossed her head and gave him an impetuous glance. "How like you to compare a woman to a horse. That mare should have thrown you."

He gave her a look that sent her foolish heart reeling. "Perhaps. And yet I broke her to my will. From now on, the mare will be a gentle mount."

"I saw very little gentleness in her."

He smiled, flashing strong, white teeth. "She merely had to learn who is her master. Is this not so with all females? Is it not so of you?"

Before Rachel could retort, Noble raised his hands in surrender. "A man should never tease a woman who has hair the color of flame, and the temper to match. Am I forgiven?"

His tone was deep and compelling, and she felt it echo through her head. She nervously intertwined her fingers, clasping them so tightly that her knuckles whitened, so she held them behind her. Everything seemed to take on a new significance. She stared at the ground, where his shadow loomed above hers, until he moved, making it appear as if his shadow consumed hers. "Are you

51

comparing me to a mare?" she asked, at last finding her voice.

He took her hand and placed it against his heart. "You, my little beauty, are incomparable."

She jerked her hand away as if burned. Why was she behaving so oddly? she wondered frantically.

By now, they had reached the well. Noble took the dipper and scooped it into a bucket, handing it graciously to her. She shook her head, still dazed by his compliment. He had called her beautiful. Was she? She'd never thought of herself in that way—not until today. Suddenly she wanted very badly to be beautiful, and to be older, because Noble still thought of her as a child.

He raised the dipper to his lips and she watched, fascinated, as several drops trickled down his chin to disappear in the dark mat of hair on his chest, just visible below his unbuttoned shirt. A flash of warmth spread throughout her body, and she found herself wanting to slide her hand over the same path the water had taken. She remembered the arranged marriage between Noble and a woman in Spain, and she felt as if the point of an invisible knife was buried deep in her heart.

Why had her feelings for Noble taken such a sudden change? She'd always thought of him as a godlike person who teased her and made her laugh. Now she was no better than all the other simpering women she had scorned for idolizing Noble to the point of making fools of themselves. Today she had found his conversation tantalizing, and his nearness unsettling. Seeking comfort, she gazed at her father, who was still deep in conversation with Noble's father.

"Sure you don't want a drink, Green Eyes?" Noble asked. "It's a hot day."

"I—Yes, please."

He thrust the dipper into the bucket and handed it to her, his hand brushing hers and sending her foolish heart soaring again. Her hands trembled when she lifted the dipper to her lips, and she drank quickly, dropping the dipper back into the bucket so there would be no chance of touching him again.

"What will you do with the mare?" she asked, trying to swing her thoughts to the horse and away from Noble.

"Faro is a horse for a lady."

"Faro?"

"Yes, that is her name." Noble gave Rachel a slow smile that wrenched her heart. "The lady who rides Faro must have spirit to match the mare's. Perhaps I shall give her to you, Green Eyes. Yes, I think she should belong to you."

He started walking toward their fathers, and she had to run to catch him. She'd never wanted anything as much as she wanted that mare. "No—no, Papa would never allow me to accept such a gift from you."

His expression grew suddenly serious as he slowed his long strides to match hers. "The horse is mine to give or keep as I choose."

53

Rachel stood beside her father now, needing his strength to calm her erratic heartbeat.

"Mr. Rutledge," Noble said with his eyes on Rachel, "I have just made a gift of a horse to your daughter, yet she says you will not allow her to accept it. I hope to change your mind."

Sam Rutledge looked startled for a moment while Noble's father only laughed. "Do you speak of the mare from Spain?"

"*Sí*, that is the one, Father."

"Then you should accept her, Señorita Rachel," Don Reinaldo urged jovially. His spoke with a slight Spanish accent, but Noble and Saber had no accent at all. "We had her shipped over for my daughter, but Saber prefers a smaller, more docile mount. The mare should go to someone who knows and appreciates good horseflesh."

"I'll buy the horse from you," Sam offered. "It's not my habit to be beholden to any man. How much for the mare, Noble?"

Rachel lowered her head so her father wouldn't see how badly she wanted the mare. He could ill afford such a magnificent animal, and they both knew it.

"It is easy to see where your daughter gets her perseverance," Noble said, half serious, half joking. "The mare is not for sale. She is my gift to Green Eyes. And there is no owing between friends."

For a long moment the two men stood eye-to-eye until Sam lowered his gaze. "I'm sure my daughter will take good care of the mare. But I still say it's too generous. The horse is a thorough-bred."

Noble's voice grew soft. "As is your daughter."

Rachel squinted against the sun, the memories fading. That day had been her last day as a care-free, innocent girl. Every moment after that, she'd thought of Noble with a powerful longing that only a young girl could feel for her first love.

Yes, she had loved him then, as much as she hated him now.

Chapter Five

Rachel glanced at the great hacienda of Casa del Sol. She hadn't been there since her father had been murdered, and she didn't know why she had come today.

She halted her mount and patted the mare's sleek black neck. Even though Noble had given her this mare, and she now despised him, she couldn't bring herself to part with Faro.

Rachel heard footsteps, and she watched as Noble emerged from the trees and walked past the corrals. She knew instinctively that he was going to pay his respects to his dead father.

She dismounted and moved forward, taking care to stay hidden from his view. From her vantage point behind a cedar bush, Rachel watched

Noble kneel beside Don Reinaldo Vincente's grave. She could plainly see the pain on his face. She knew what he was feeling, because she'd suffered the same loss with her father's death. She wished she could find satisfaction in Noble's grief, but she could not. Even a cowardly murderer was allowed to mourn the death of his father. She was amazed to feel tears hovering just behind her eyes, burning and stinging. She blinked her eyes to keep from crying. Not one tear would she shed for Noble Vincente. He deserved everything he got and more.

Noble removed his hat and bowed his head as grief tore at his heart like thorns from a thistle. He wanted absolution from the torment within his soul. His chest tightened with a familiar pain. He should have been with his father to comfort him in his last hours. The knowledge that his absence had probably hastened his father's death was added to the guilt that he already carried within him.

His gaze moved sadly to his mother's grave, which was choked with weeds. On the other side of her was the grave of an infant brother who had died at birth, and other Vincentes who'd been born and died on this land. Loneliness pressed in on him like a physical pain. The prayer he wanted to utter was locked in his heart and he could not give it voice.

Noble's head came up when he heard a twig

snap. In a quick, fluid motion he rose to his feet, turned in the direction of the noise and drew his gun. "Come out slowly," he said, aiming at the cedar bushes to his left. "Do it now!"

Rachel stepped forward, her head high, her gaze meeting his haughtily.

"Who are you?" He holstered his gun, as if he had nothing to fear from a woman. "Do I know you?"

It disturbed Rachel that Noble did not recognize her when she had thought of him every day since he'd gone away. She took several steps closer to him before she spoke.

"I never knew you, Noble Vincente, although I once thought I did."

A flicker of recognition flashed through him, and he could hardly believe his eyes. Although there were differences, he should have known her immediately. Her hair was now a richer red-gold, and she was taller. A slight frown furrowed his brow. "So it is you, Green Eyes. All grown up and still wearing trousers."

Despite the fact that she was trembling all over, she faced him with courage. Stepping onto the overgrown path, she planted her booted feet wide apart. "I'm no longer the child you once knew. You stole my childhood. Why did you come back to Texas when you're not welcome here?"

His gaze touched on her flaming hair before moving to the blouse that was stretched taut across the gentle swell of her young breasts. Her waist was tiny and her hips softly curved and tantalizingly outlined by her trousers. There was little evidence of the young girl he'd once adored and teased. The woman standing before him was beautiful and cold, and naked hatred burned in her eyes.

"Green Eyes, there was a time when you would have welcomed me as your friend."

"Fool that I was." Her gaze knifed into his. She remembered when those dark eyes had danced with laughter. Now they were dull, lusterless and unreadable. Power radiated from him, and she knew instinctively that he was making an effort to keep that power under control. She did not fear him; she merely hated him. "It seems that you are the Don of Casa del Sol now, Noble."

"I will not be referring to myself as a don. For me, the title died with my father. This is not the Texas he knew, and I am not the man he was."

"I agree with you on both points. I once thought you had the same honor that your father possessed, but you don't."

"Now you want to see me dead." This pronouncement came with little emotion.

Rachel had just looked into his soul and found torment churning there. "Yes, I do," she admitted. "I could have killed you the day you returned," she continued, her voice flat and without feeling. "I had my rifle trained on you when you drank from Deep Creek."

He flinched as if her words had wounded him.

"Yet you didn't shoot me." He raised his hands to show there were no bullet holes. "I'm still alive. I wonder why?"

She moved closer to him, gathering courage. "If you were dead, you would no longer feel, and if you couldn't feel, you wouldn't suffer for what you did to my father."

He stared at the tips of his shiny black boots. "Perhaps I have suffered, Green Eyes."

"Don't call me that! Don't ever call me that again!"

Suddenly there was unspeakable sadness in his fathomless brown eyes as he met her gaze. "How can you believe I killed your father? I liked and respected Mr. Rutledge."

"You can deny it all you want. I know you murdered him. And I know why."

His gaze slid away from hers as if he could no longer look into those cold green eyes. With effort, he glanced at his father's grave. "And you came here seeking satisfaction by witnessing my pain."

She bent down and pulled a weed near Don Reinaldo's headstone, tossing it aside. "I take no pleasure in your father's death. He was a kind and honorable man." She stood. "These graves are shamefully neglected. I would never allow this to happen to my family's graves."

Noble drew in a deep breath and exhaled. "I didn't kill your father, Rachel. I don't care if no one else believes me, but I hope that you will come to know the truth."

She moved away from him. "I could hardly expect you to admit it, could I? You're the only one with a reason to kill him. Everyone else liked my father. He had no enemies, save yourself."

His tone was soft when he said, almost to himself, "Why did it have to be you?" Then his lips thinned and his gaze slammed into hers. "Why have you set yourself up as the instrument of my punishment?"

"Because you are a Vincente the law wouldn't do it, so it's left to me." Her growing courage took her a step closer to him. "How shall I punish you, Noble? I could have shot you—I didn't. I still could, but I won't." She tossed her head and met his eyes. "How shall I extract justice? You tell me."

Noble stared at her for a long moment, and she knew he was confused. Was he looking for the little girl who had adored him? Well, she was no longer that girl, and he would find no pity in her. She saw the anger burning in his eyes, but she did not realize the danger until it was too late.

He grabbed her and brought her forward until her face was level with his. "Nothing you can do will touch me in my hell, Rachel."

She was so near she felt the heat of his body. Every muscle in her tightened. "No? I know what you are feeling at this moment, Noble, because I felt it with my father. You stand over your father's grave, wondering if there's been some terrible mistake—can he really be dead? You'll walk away from the monument that was erected to his memory, feeling as if you've left a part of your life behind. Then you hurry to the house, feeling bereft, thinking he'll be there, but he won't be. You will never see him again. Death, you see, is so final, Noble, and that will be your torment."

His fingers bit into her arms and he jerked her against him, sweeping her forcefully into his embrace. With his free hand he lifted her chin, and their gazes locked. "What if you are wrong?" he asked in a raspy voice. "What if you are to be my final torment?"

He lowered his head, seemingly preoccupied with the shape of her mouth. As she held her breath, his lips brushed against hers, and she went limp in his arms. Then his mouth became hard, punishing, and ravished her tender lips. The kiss was not prompted by affection or even desire; it came from anger, frustration and futility.

Rachel wanted to shove him away, but he was drawing all the strength from her body. All she could feel was the hardness of him, the hand that supported her head, the mouth that ruthlessly plundered hers. Against her will, her lips softened beneath his and she returned his kiss. She moved forward, pressing her body more firmly against his, feeling almost faint with longing. She tried to remember why she was there. Suddenly she envisioned her dead father's face and struggled to be free.

Noble released her immediately, amusement in his expression. He knew how his kiss had affected her. "I don't know if you realize it, Green Eyes, but you have issued a challenge—which I shall accept."

Rachel stared at him for a long moment. She hadn't challenged him. She rubbed her hand across her lips as if she were wiping away the taste of his mouth, but knew she could never erase the memory of that kiss. She had hoped to find his weakness, and instead he'd discovered hers.

"I will prove you killed my father, Noble." She hated the fact that her voice trembled—her whole body trembled, for that matter. She had to forget the sensation of his lips against hers and remember that he was her enemy. "Soon, all of Texas will hear about your guilt. Then Sheriff Crenshaw will be forced to arrest you."

He seemed to be ignoring her when he bent down to pull weeds from his father's grave. Then he glanced up at her. "Do your worst, Rachel. I always thought you were different from Delia, but perhaps I was wrong."

Fury erupted within her. "How dare you speak insultingly about Delia! You haven't even asked about her or the baby. How can you be so heartless?"

He closed his eyes and then stood. "How is Delia? How is her baby, Rachel?"

She felt a lump in her throat and feared she would cry. "Delia lost your baby."

"I'm sorry."

"Are you sad about the baby? Don't you care

63

about what Delia has suffered? Have you nothing more to say?"

"Nothing I said at the moment would make an impression on you. You have judged me guilty without asking me if I fathered your sister's child."

Suddenly his eyes were profoundly sad, and weariness was reflected there, as if he'd witnessed too much and valued too little. With a suddenness that startled her, pity for him rose like a well-spring inside her.

Noble's gaze slid away from her and just as suddenly the sensation of sadness vanished. He had retreated behind an unreadable mask, leaving Rachel confused and shaken.

Without a word he walked away, leaving Rachel alone with her troubled thoughts. Her earlier confidence had been vanquished by a pair of probing brown eyes. He'd won the first confrontation, but she was not beaten. They would meet again; she'd make certain of it.

She found Faro where she'd left the mare, mounted and galloped toward the Brazos. Like some inexperienced young girl, she'd allowed herself to be captivated by Noble's obvious maleness. He would not find her so vulnerable the next time they met.

With her troubled thoughts as her companions, she rode home, a part of her holding on to the memory of that dashingly handsome Spaniard who'd conquered the wild mare. Then there was the sad stranger she'd met today.

"Which one is the true Noble?" she whispered to herself. And her lips formed the words, "The one who killed your father."

She bent low in the saddle, riding homeward and away from the man who occupied the hacienda of Casa del Sol.

Chapter Six

Tascosa Springs, Texas

Like many towns that had sent young men off to fight for the South, Tascosa Springs had fallen on hard times. And the residents realized that the times would only get worse, because the conquering North had become the ruling authority in Texas.

The town itself was made up of several weather-beaten buildings, the exception being the new red-brick tax office that stood beside the bank. McVee's Mercantile stood next door to Baker's Hotel. Further down the partially rotted board-walk, the Crystal Palace Saloon was adjacent to Goodies ranch supply store, where shovels and rakes leaned against the wall beside the door. Across the dusty street the sheriff's office was located beside the two-story structure that served as an apothecary on the first floor, and the doctor's office upstairs. At Tuttle's Blacksmith the contentious clanging of the smithy's hammer was accompanied by the acrid smell of Tuttle's stoked fire.

The sun was white-hot and the wind raked over exposed skin like searing particles of grit. Still, a knot of people had gathered in front of McVee's, watching Noble Vincente dismount and loop the reins of his horse around the rickety hitching post. Men who'd known Noble all his life watched him scornfully while their wives put their heads together, elbows nudging and whispering among themselves.

Noble nodded curtly as he passed the group, but didn't break his stride as he entered the store. Anger boiled inside him, but he kept it under tight control. Clearly his neighbors still believed that he'd killed Sam Rutledge. Nothing he could say would change their minds, and he didn't care to try.

The storekeeper, Jess McVee, broke away from the others with a sour expression on his face, and followed Noble into the store, where he stood disapprovingly.

Noble studied the storekeeper, thinking he hadn't changed in the years he'd been away. Jess was a small man, with hair the color of dirty well water. His small, mouselike eyes darted nervously about the store before they rested on Noble. "I need supplies, Jess." Noble shoved a list at him. "Will you have these items delivered to Casa del Sol for me?"

"I gotta say this or I'll choke on it. If I didn't need the money, I'd tell you what you could do with your order," Jess stated, his breath coming out in panting gasps.

An impatient intake of breath expanded Noble's chest, and he regarded the man silently. When Noble spoke he didn't raise his voice, but his words were delivered with the intensity of a whiplash. "It's good to know how low a man will sink for the sake of money, Jess." Noble turned away and deliberately counted out several bills atop the scarred counter. "Put whatever is left over on my account. Have the supplies delivered to Casa del Sol today."

Jess swallowed his resentment because there was something about a Vincente that demanded respect. Whatever that something was, it ran strong in Noble. Jess nodded reluctantly. "I'll see to your order, and it'll be delivered today."

He watched as Noble departed. The younger Vincente's aristocratic head was held high, his back ramrod straight, his strides long.

The women who had been pressing their faces against the window to get a glimpse of Noble now rushed inside, anxious to hear every word Noble

Vincente had uttered. Their questions flew fast and furious.

"Where has he been all these years?"

"Is he back to stay?"

"Did he marry that woman from Spain?"

"Did he bring a wife home with him?"

"Will he bring his sister back from Georgia?"

"Do you suppose Rachel Rutledge knows he's back?"

Jess McVee brushed their questions aside as he watched Noble cross the street, walking in the direction of the sheriff's office. He shivered, remembering the fierceness of those cold brown eyes. "I wouldn't want to be the one to make him mad," he told the others. "You can do what you want, but the next time he comes into my store, I'll be more respectful."

Harvey Briscal was slumped over the desk, almost asleep, when he heard someone enter. He raised his head and yawned, ill-tempered because his nap had been interrupted. "Sheriff's not here. If you've got business with him, come back later."

The man was a stranger to Noble. He took note of the man's shaggy brown hair, thin face and hooded eyes, then looked at the deputy's star pinned to his stained leather vest. Noble grasped a rickety wooden chair, turned it around and propped his booted foot on it. "If the sheriff's not here, I'll talk to you."

Noble watched the deputy lean forward, shaking his head to come fully awake.

"You certainly aren't from around here, stranger," Harvey observed. "Not one of the ranchers or cowhands I know." His sleepy gaze fastened on Noble's crisp, white shirt and buff-colored leather pants with a dark brown stripe down the legs. Envy crept into his eyes as he took in the ivory-handled six-gun that hung about Noble's waist. It wasn't difficult to tell that this stranger was a man of importance. "What's your name?" Harvey asked.

Noble's eyes were hard and probing. After the incident with Jess McVee, he was in no mood to suffer fools. "You first," he said forcefully. "Tell me who you are."

Harvey puffed out his meager chest and said with pride, "I'm the deputy sheriff."

Noble's lip curled in distaste. "I already guessed that. What's your name?"

Harvey's mouth formed a sneer. He shifted his slight weight and straightened to his full height, which was a head shorter than the Spaniard. He tugged at pants that were a size too big for him, and adjusted them about his waist. "I'll be asking the questions here. State your business."

Noble turned the chair around, slowly and deliberately. He then sat down and crossed his long legs. "I'm Noble Vincente. Mr. Vincente to you."

The deputy gawked at Noble for a moment, immediately recognizing the name. He hooked his hands about his waist because his trousers were beginning to slip down his slender hips again. His tone was surly when he spoke. "You're one of the Vincentes that own Casa del Sol. I've heard of you—didn't know you'd come home, though." His eyes gleamed like polished copper. "I've just been here for seven months, but I recall hearing talk that you was suspected of killing a man some years back."

Noble stood, towering over the man. "Be warned, Deputy, that I've had a bad morning, and I don't intend to waste time on an *imbécil*."

Harvey looked blank. "I don't speak Mexican. What's that im—Uh, whatever you said?"

Noble decided that there was some doubt that the deputy spoke English. "Let's just say the term means less than brilliant."

Harvey's face colored with indignation. "You can't say that to me! Just who do you think you are?"

Noble took a step forward, and the deputy took a step back. "Is Crenshaw still the sheriff?"

Harvey saw danger in Noble Vincente's swirling dark eyes. He swallowed several times before he said, "Y-yep. But he's getting on in years. I 'spect I'll be the sheriff soon enough."

"God help us if that happens," Noble murmured under his breath. "Tell Sheriff Crenshaw that I stopped by and I'd like to see him at his convenience."

Harvey followed Noble outside, watching him

cross the street and mount his horse. Jess McVee joined Harvey and they stood silently watching Noble disappear in the distance.

"He won't find any friends in this town," Jess stated flatly. "Sam Rutledge was well respected 'round here, and there are those of us who still think Noble Vincente back-shot him. Did it, and got away with it."

"I didn't know Mr. Rutledge, but I surely like that pretty daughter of his. I'm kinda sweet on Rachel Rutledge, but I ain't told her yet. It's not right that some rich bastard got away with killing her pa."

Jess glanced at the deputy in astonishment. Did the man really think that Rachel would be interested in the likes of him? He grinned, trying not to laugh. "Rachel would probably look kindly on the man who puts her pa's killer away." He was baiting Harvey, whom he'd never credited with having much gumption. " 'Course, Sheriff Crenshaw never believed that Noble killed Sam. At the time, he said there wasn't enough evidence to take to court. The circuit judge agreed with him. I figure if you'd been sheriff at the time, things woulda been different." He continued to bolster the deputy's ego while planting numerous seeds of ideas, wondering if they'd take root inside Harvey's simple mind. "I always wondered how much Don Reinaldo paid the judge to get him to let his son go free."

Harvey felt a stirring of excitement as he

thought what it would mean to his standing in the county if he got rid of that Spanish bastard. "There's other ways to give justice a little push." Cunning brightened his eyes. "Sometimes you just have to step outside the law."

The heat beat down with punishing force as Noble rode toward home. He clenched his jaw, still angered by what had happened in town. He should have been prepared for the hostile attitudes today—but he hadn't been. Damn them all! Why should it matter what they thought of him?

But strangely enough, it did.

He detoured around the main gate to Casa del Sol and guided his horse toward the river. When he got there, he dismounted and walked to the water's edge, staring into the muddy depths. He'd always loved the Brazos, which snaked its way through hundreds of miles of Texas. It was here, beneath this very cottonwood tree, that he had fished many times with his father, here that he'd learned to swim and dive off the high banks. But boyhood memories brought no comfort to him today; they were part of a past that was dead and gone.

"It's been a hell of a day," he observed aloud. He picked up a stone and skipped it across the water, watching it sink into the murky depths. "And worst yet, I'm beginning to talk to myself."

On a sudden impulse he unbuckled his gun belt and draped it across his saddle. He then proceeded to remove his boots, and stripped off the rest of his clothes, dropping them into a careless heap. Naked as the day he was born, he took a deep breath and plunged into the river.

The water felt cool and soothing as it closed over him. It was peaceful and serene, so he plunged deeper until he reached the riverbed. He allowed the swift current to carry him downstream without ever coming up for air. He wondered what it would feel like never to come up. His chest felt tight and his lungs begged for air. Above him was the real world awash in sunlight and pain—here, there was silence, forgetfulness.

Then, uninvited and unwelcome, a pair of green eyes invaded his sanctuary—eyes that had once danced with laughter, but now reflected cold hatred. He shot upward toward the light and, gasping, dragged air into his starving lungs. His first breath was painful and he quickly took another, and another. When he was breathing normally, he looked around him, determining that he'd been swept some distance from where he'd left his clothing. With strong strokes, he swam against the current until he rounded a bend in the river.

As if his thinking about her made her appear, Rachel sat upon the bank, her trouser-clad legs stretched out before her. Her red-gold hair shimmered like fire in the sun, and her slender form was outlined by the green shirt she wore. She balanced his pistol in her hand, casually spinning the cylinder.

Noble treaded water, trying to stay in place because the current was pulling him downstream. "Hello, Green Eyes. You'll excuse me if I'm less than formally dressed. You see, I wasn't expecting a visitor."

Rachel glanced down at Noble's clothing. "So I see." She hoped her presence made him feel uneasy. She certainly felt tense knowing that he was naked, but she chose not to show it. Without meeting his eyes, she said, "Nice gun—ivory and gold handle. Hmm, England-made by Wevley-Fosbery." She whistled through her teeth as if impressed, then spun the cylinder. "Smooth. Certainly not a gun of the line." She ran her finger down the polished barrel. "A specially made instrument of death."

"It was my grandfather's."

She met his gaze. Again she spun the cylinder. "I never did understand why a man would carry such an ornate weapon. Of course, myself, I prefer a rifle. I can shoot a silver dollar out of the air before it hits the ground—did you know that?"

He was growing fatigued. His legs and arms ached from the constant paddling against the current. "If you'll turn your head so I can come out and get dressed, we'll discuss my gun and your marksmanship at length."

She slowly shook her head. "I like it this way." She leveled his gun at him. "Good balance. Most definitely a gentleman's weapon." She pulled the trigger and it clicked on an empty chamber.

Noble didn't blink. In fact, he stared boldly back at her without showing any emotion or any sign of fear when she cocked the hammer and pressed the trigger once more. Again it clicked on an empty chamber, and she pressed the trigger again and again, until the cylinder had advanced six times.

She opened her other hand, displaying the bullets she'd removed earlier. "You are trusting. You couldn't have known I unloaded the gun. I'll say this for you—you've got grit."

While his tone was cool, his voice was somewhat breathless because of his constant paddling. "Rachel, you're the damnedest woman I've ever met."

She arched an inquiring eyebrow at him. "How did you know I wouldn't shoot you?"

"I reasoned that you wouldn't kill me while I'm undressed." Humor crept into his voice. "How would you ever explain my naked body to the voters who are considering your brother-in-law for governor?"

Rachel slowly, deliberately, loaded the gun and turned her attention back to Noble. "You place your faith in such a thin hope." She pulled back the trigger. "It's loaded this time. And I don't give a damn if my brother-in-law ever becomes governor of Texas."

Noble merely stared back at her. He wondered how much longer he could keep his head above water. His arms and legs were throbbing and ach-

76

ing. "You're doing all the talking and you're holding the gun. Why don't you fire?"

And she did. Rachel fired six times in succession, hitting a branch that was suspended just above his head.

He didn't flinch.

"I like a man who doesn't scare easily," she purred. Grudgingly, she felt respect for his steady nerve. Would such a man shoot someone in the back? she wondered. She nodded to herself—this man would, and had.

"I know your game now," he said laughingly, seemingly unruffled by her exhibition. "You intend to stay here until I am too tired to tread water, and then you'll watch me drown."

"What an appealing notion." Rachel slipped his gun back into its leather holster. "How long do you think you could stay afloat before the current drags you under?"

"To tell the truth, I'm getting tired already. I'm coming out."

"I'm not leaving."

"Suit yourself."

She watched him swim toward shore, and despite her resolve to stay calm, she scampered to her feet and took several steps backward. "You wouldn't dare come out."

Noble raised himself half out of the water. "Wouldn't I?"

Rachel was momentarily mesmerized by the water that streaked down his shoulders to his waist. She noticed that the dark hair on his chest narrowed to a line that ran down his taut stomach in a vee. Although she was trembling inside, she refused to turn away. This time she would be in control—she had to be.

"Come out if you dare," she said with much more bravado than she felt.

Noble paused with his hands on the bank. "I have a better idea. Why don't you come in?"

The word *never* was forming on her lips, but she quickly reconsidered. If she was going to defeat Noble, she must control her emotions, at least make him think she was in control. "Why not?" She wanted to run away, but she planted her booted foot against the ground. With shaking hands, she pulled her shirt free of her trousers and lifted it over her head, hoping that she would find the courage to meet his challenge.

Noble eased himself back into the water. "Rachel, don't do this. The game is over. Go home."

Rachel stood before him, naked to the waist, her gaze fixed just above his head, not quite meeting his eyes.

Noble seemed to have no control over himself. His gaze left her face and fell to her creamy breasts. He sucked in his breath at the rosy circles surrounding her nipples. His hand fisted, and he could almost feel her creamy skin beneath his exploring fingers. He wanted to touch her so badly, and he hated himself for wanting her. A part of him didn't want to admit that she was grown up, while another part of him delighted in her womanhood. He wanted to scold her, to order her to put her shirt back on—he wanted her to leave so he could catch his breath.

But most of all, he wanted to clasp her in his arms and press her against him until his body stopped trembling.

Chapter Seven

Heat spiraled through Rachel's body as Noble stared at her with a pained expression. Then his expression changed, and his dark eyes burned into hers. She watched him turn away and she could almost read his mind. He was troubled because she was a woman and not the young girl he'd once known. She heard him exhale abruptly.

"The game's over, Rachel." His voice was gruff, with an edge to it. "You've won today."

As Noble turned away, she gazed at his profile, which appeared to be carved of stone. The muscles in his neck were taut because of the tight control he kept over his emotions. She smiled, enjoying his discomfort. It gave her the courage to continue with the charade. "But you invited me to swim with you," she persisted, amazed by her own boldness. "Have you changed your mind, Noble?"

He still wouldn't look at her. "Let's just say this river isn't big enough for the two of us. Go home."

She merely tossed her head, acting on a daringness she was far from feeling. She summoned all her courage as she unbuttoned her trousers and pushed them over her shapely hips. "It's a hot day. I'd enjoy a swim."

Noble's reluctant, hot gaze fastened on her breasts, moving to her narrow waist to the red-gold hair nestled between her long, shapely legs. She was the most beautiful creature he'd ever seen. But one thought kept pounding in his head—this wasn't right! She was his Green Eyes.

Rachel felt his gaze on her, and had the sensation that he'd actually touched her. She went as far as to reach for her shirt to cover her nakedness, paused, and then forced a smile to her lips.

"Make room. I'm coming in."

Noble wanted to look away, but he couldn't. He tried to separate the child she'd once been from the daring beauty who stood before him now. Seeing the blush on her cheeks, he knew she was an innocent, and pure, and completely unnerved by her own nudity. His lashes swept over his eyes but he could see her in his mind, beautiful and naked.

"You don't have to do this, Rachel. It won't prove a thing, and it might complicate matters between us even more."

He opened his eyes and watched as she poised her body in a graceful arch and plunged into the river, surfacing within inches of him. Water beaded on the tips of her eyelashes and slid down her cheeks. He was relieved that only her bare shoulders were visible above the waterline.

"All right, Rachel, you've shown me that you are a woman grown. And I will admit that your body is magnificent. I'll just swim downstream now so you can get out and put on your clothing."

She felt perplexed by his sudden detachment. Now that most of her nakedness was covered by water, he was the one in control. She had been so certain he'd found her desirable. If only she were more experienced. Her feminine instincts triumphed and she dipped her head backward, wetting her hair so it would stay out of her face.

"Isn't it too late for modesty? You have already seen me the way God created me. And I might remind you that this fork of the Brazos River belongs to Broken Spur as much as it does to Casa del Sol. I have as much right to be here as you do."

He swam a safe distance away from her. "Have it your way, Rachel. But none of this is necessary."

She lunged toward him, her naked body brushing deliberately against his side. She saw his dark eyes dilate, and delighted in the gasp that escaped his lips.

"Don't, Rachel," he warned, swimming backward a few strokes in a desperate attempt to escape from her. He was confused by her actions, because the last time they'd met she had wanted to see him dead. He fought the urge to crush her in his arms. He must not think about smothering those sensuous lips beneath his. He doubted that she was aware of the consequences that might come from taunting him. There were already complications between the two of them—he didn't need more.

Rachel gleaned his thoughts. He was dismayed because of his desire for her. This knowledge made her grow even more bold; she would entice him with a promise of what he could never have and then swim away.

"Do you want me, Noble?"

He stared past her. "I once desired a whore in New Orleans, but I was able to resist her."

She smiled, knowing that Noble was insulting her, hoping she would leave. "Are you afraid of me, Noble? I'm not holding a gun on you now."

His voice deepened, his eyes fastened on her mouth as he stared at her with fervent intensity. "You are far more dangerous now than when you held the gun on me." He searched her eyes. "You have not been with a man, have you, Rachel?"

She was beginning to enjoy herself because she was making him uncomfortable. "No. I haven't. Do you want to be the first?"

He groaned. "Hell, yes. And therein lies the trouble, Rachel. You are the kind of girl who should save herself for her husband."

She lunged forward, taking him by surprise.

Their bodies came together, caressed by the soft water. A shock coiled through her, and she was momentarily stunned by the way his body welcomed hers. The hardness of his body held her as if she were bound to him.

Noble could no longer resist her. His arms went around her and he drew her even closer.

How foolish she'd been in thinking she could arouse his desire and swim away unaffected. A rush of feelings opened up inside her, and she was too unworldly to resist. Her skin tingled and she wanted to draw even closer to the forbidden male hardness that pressed between her thighs. Breathless, she felt as if her body were on fire. The hair on Noble's chest tickled her breasts, and she could feel his every intake of breath. She felt the swollen heat against her grow harder, and her body became liquid—every fiber of rationality unraveled— all resistance gone.

She was lost.

Noble's iron control snapped and he was almost beyond reason. In a last attempt at rationality he groaned, "Rachel, you must go while you still can. You don't know what you're doing to me." But he did not push her away; he kept her pressed against him.

"Yes, I do," she said, as her hand slid up his taut shoulder and rested there while she met his eyes. "I know exactly what I'm doing."

He was like a man possessed. He could no longer control the rising tide of passion that ripped through his body—it was too late to stop now and he knew it. He wanted to drive into her, deeper and deeper, losing himself in her sweetness. To find release within her for his tormented soul. Like a man dying of thirst in the desert, his mouth sought hers and her lips opened to him.

Noble plunged his tongue deep, and Rachel thought she would faint from longing. She stiffened in surprise, then surrendered against him with a groan. She slid her hands around his shoulders and up his neck, before sliding them through his wet, midnight hair, wanting him to go on kissing her and never stop.

She was unaware that Noble had guided them to the shallows. His feet were now planted on solid limestone, but she was dangling in his embrace.

Noble's voice was deep and husky with passion. "I knew you were going to be trouble the minute you came back into my life. I knew it, and I wanted it."

She threw back her head when he lifted her up, his hand sliding sensuously across her breast. He lifted her higher, and his mouth closed over a nipple, which hardened against his tongue.

For the moment Rachel forgot she was in the arms of her enemy. She felt no shame in being held against his strong male body. Noble was passionate and he was tender and he stirred her blood and brought new pleasure with each touch of his hand.

Noble lowered her to fit against him, kissing her

brow, sweeping his mouth across her cheek to her lips. "Damn you, Rachel, for making me want you and for making me feel again."

She clamped her hands behind his head, drawing his wonderful lips to hers once more. When he gently nudged her legs apart and slid against her, his intimate hardness swelled and throbbed, firing her desire.

Somewhere in the back of her mind a small voice warned, *Fool, fool, you are in his trap—he'll break your heart.* She felt as though a large fist had clamped inside her stomach and was squeezing the life out of her. She gazed into dark, passion-filled eyes and trembled from a force that rocked her body.

No! she answered the voice inside her head. *He's fallen into my trap. I'll make him love me, and then I'll break his heart.*

The water gently lapped against her skin and all thought of resistance dissolved. With a soft groan she surrendered herself to him completely. Noble supported her weight with one hand while his other hand moved across her flat stomach. Her head fell forward to rest against his shoulder when his hand moved downward to her thighs, then glided between her legs.

Unleashed desire sang through her, and she knew that she'd sink to the bottom of the river if he weren't holding her. His mouth covered hers, stealing her breath as effectively as the river would have if she had slipped beneath the surface.

Neither of them heard the shot ring out, not consciously, but the force of the bullet struck Rachel in the chest and ripped her from Noble's grasp.

She felt hot, searing pain; then a sudden weakness washed over her. She reached out for Noble just before she slid downward, the water closing over her head. Too weak to fight her way to the surface, Rachel was sure she was drowning.

Noble thought Rachel might be playing another game, but when she didn't surface right away, he dove under the water, grasping her shoulders and propelling her upward. He still didn't know what had happened, but when he saw blood oozing from her chest—enough blood to color the muddy water red—he knew. He'd seen enough bullet wounds during the war to know that she'd been shot. But how—who?

Rachel struggled against the darkness that seemed to hover over her. She tried to focus her gaze on Noble, but she was too weak. Her head fell against his arm and she murmured, "Noble, why? Why did you do it?"

Then she lost consciousness.

Noble lifted her in his arms and moved toward the shore, his eyes and ears alert for any motion, any sound. Rachel's assailant was probably lurking nearby. He heard a horse galloping away, but he wasn't convinced that the danger had passed.

He stepped onto the bank and laid Rachel gently upon the grass, then quickly draped his shirt across her nakedness. She looked so small and helpless, so pale, that he feared she might die. He had to act quickly if he was going to save her life. She was losing too much blood.

Primal instinct flamed to life inside him. He was a man who had witnessed death and had killed, but the sight of Rachel's lifeblood soaking into the grass enraged him beyond reason. He was like a man possessed, a predator, protecting what belonged to him. He wanted revenge against whoever had done this to Rachel.

His gaze scanned the immediate area and then beyond to the trees that lined the river, but he saw no one. Reaching forward, he grasped his gun—it was empty, thanks to Rachel's playful exhibition. He tossed the weapon aside and turned his attention back to Rachel. Quickly examining her wound, he frowned—it was bad.

At no time in Noble's life had he felt more helpless then he did at the moment. Dammit, he wasn't a doctor, but he knew she could die if he didn't get help. She lay so still, maybe she was already dead. He breathed a little easier when he saw the faint rise and fall of her chest.

He quickly slipped into trousers and dropped down, examining her carefully. The bullet had lodged in her chest, and it was close to her heart. He tore a strip off his shirt and tightly bound it around her, taking care not to move her more than necessary. With each movement more blood oozed from the wound.

He gently draped her shirt about her, lifted her into his arms and laid her across the saddle. With a fluid motion, he thrust his foot into the stirrup and mounted his horse, gathering her to him. With pressure from his knees, he nudged the animal forward into a slow walk. His first instinct was to ride fast so he could get help for Rachel, but common sense warned him that any jarring motion would only aggravate her wound. He made his way slowly home, praying that Rachel would not die.

The sun had dropped low on the horizon like a dark, ominous shroud when Noble finally reached his hacienda. He glanced down at Rachel and saw that fresh blood had seeped though the makeshift bandage. She was still unconscious, her dark lashes lying still against her pale cheeks.

She would not die! He wouldn't let her.

When Noble reached the front of the house, a puzzled Alejandro rushed forward, his dark face creased in worry, his eyes filled with questions. He opened the door for Noble and followed him inside.

"What has happened, *Patrón*?"

"Miss Rutledge has been shot. Ride into town as fast as you can, Alejandro. Don't spare the horse, and fetch Dr. Stanhope. Tell him to come at once."

Alejandro was too well trained to ask why the *patrón* and Miss Rachel were soaking wet, or why they both wore very little clothing. A *gran va-*

quero was trained to obey his *patrón* without question. "*Sí*. I shall ride very fast and bring the doctor right away."

Rage tore at Noble like thorns, ripping and chewing at his flesh. Why had this happened to Rachel? Someone had made a deadly mistake when they shot her.

No matter how long it took, he would find the bastard and make him pay with his life!

Chapter Eight

Noble hurriedly carried Rachel up the stairs to his bedroom, since it was the only room that was furnished. Alejandro's wife, Margretta, raced ahead of him, opening the door and following him inside. Noble gently laid Rachel upon his bed, thinking she looked even paler against the white sheets.

Hours passed with Noble sitting beside Rachel, often replacing a blood-soaked bandage with a fresh one. Margretta lit the lamps to chase away the darkness. Still Rachel had not regained consciousness.

Noble glanced at the mantel clock that ticked away the minutes as if they were hours. It was nearing midnight. Why hadn't Alejandro returned with the doctor? Where were they?

He refused the food Margretta brought him and hovered next to Rachel, feeling a helplessness that verged on panic. If Dr. Stanhope didn't come soon, Noble realized, he'd have to remove the bullet himself. That thought scared the hell out of him; the bullet was deeply embedded in her chest, and only a doctor had the knowledge to operate so near the heart.

Night passed, and predawn light filtered into the room. Noble rose from the chair to extinguish the lamps, stretched his cramped muscles, then returned to his vigil beside Rachel. Panic lingered on the edge of his mind. If she died, it would be his fault because he knew in his heart that the bullet had been meant for him.

Rachel moaned in her unconscious state, and began tossing and fretting. Noble pressed her back onto the mattress, forcibly restraining her to keep her still. Already fresh blood soaked through the bandage he'd applied only moments before.

The morning breeze stirred the curtains, and soon bright sunlight streamed through the open window. Noble steeled himself for the inevitable. He could no longer wait for the doctor. He'd have to remove the bullet or Rachel would probably bleed to death.

Alejandro's wife, Margretta, poked her head in the door. She was a tiny woman with even features and looked ten years younger than her actual age. She didn't look strong enough to be the mother of five strapping sons. Her dark hair was braided and wrapped at the nape of her neck. Her soft brown eyes were filled with concern and pity. She advanced into the room and laid her hand on Noble's shoulder. "Will you let me sit with her now, *Patrón*, while you rest? You have not left the señorita's side all night."

Noble glanced down at his hands, which were trembling—in fact he felt as if he were a mass of trembling flesh. He drummed his fingertips against his leg, knowing what he must do and rebelling against it. "I have to remove the bullet, Margretta. Bring me the sharpest knife you can find—one with a good point—and lots of boiling water, whiskey and more clean linens."

"*Sí, Patrón*," she said with understanding. "It is very bad, is it not?"

"*Sí*, very bad."

Margretta hurried away to accomplish her appointed task, while Noble removed a blood-soaked bandage and examined the wound carefully. "The bullet is less than an inch above her heart. Unless it's lodged at an angle; then it could be even closer." He felt his palms sweating and he dragged air into his lungs. Involuntarily his hand went to Rachel's hair, which was matted and tangled. He softly touched her cheek, now flushed because she was feverish—another bad sign.

It seemed to him that hours passed before Margretta returned, her arms laden with the items he'd need. He moved a small wooden table next to the bed. Without being told, Margretta laid a clean strip of linen across the table, then arranged the knife, hot water and bandages in a neat row.

Noble looked at Alejandro's wife, trying to gauge her character, and wondered if she was strong enough to assist him. "I'll need your help," he told her. "Can you do it?"

Margretta looked somewhat apprehensive, but she nodded without hesitation. "I will not fail you, *Patrón*." She crossed herself, and her lips formed a quick prayer before moving to Noble's side.

Noble reached for the knife, his grip tightening on the handle the same way his insides were tightening. He'd dug bullets out of people before, but never this deep, never so close to the heart, and never a woman—God, help him, not just any woman but his Green Eyes. All it would take was one slip of the blade to finish what the unknown gunman had started. Noble doused the knife with whiskey, wishing he could have a drink to get him through this ordeal, but his hand must be steady, so he resisted the temptation.

"I need more light, Margretta. Bring more lamps." He was stalling and he knew it. He glanced out the window that faced the front of the house, his eyes searching the road. "Dammit. If only that doctor would get here."

Rachel chose that moment to open her eyes. She saw Noble gripping a hideous-looking knife and she tried to raise her head, but she was too weak. She fell back against the pillow, the room spinning. "Kill me," she said weakly, licking her dry lips. "I don't care."

"Rachel," Noble said softly, laying the knife aside, "do you recall what happened to you?"

She felt so helpless, and her voice seemed trapped in her throat. Why did her chest feel as if it were on fire, and the rest of her felt ice cold? Why couldn't she move? "Where . . . am I?"

"Rachel, you are at Casa del Sol. I brought you here after you were shot—do you remember?"

She tried to think past the nausea that rocked her in waves, and past the throbbing pain that sapped her strength. Shot—had he said she'd been shot? Her eyes widened and terror iced through her veins. She flinched when Noble reached out to her. She wished she could get up, move, run! But when she tried to rise, Noble's hand came down on her shoulder to hold her in place. It didn't take much effort for him to subdue her, because she was as weak as a newborn baby.

His voice came to her muted, as if he were speaking to her from a deep cavern. "Rachel, you've been shot and—" he started to explain.

"You . . . shot me." She licked her lips. "And now you want to finish me off?" Her eyes fell to the knife and deeper terror took possession of her. "Go ahead—I can't stop you."

Noble felt sick inside because she feared him. How could she think he'd harm her? He remembered her at the river, beautiful, tantalizing, irresistible, and he spoke to her with gentleness. "You mustn't distress yourself. Try to remain calm." He wanted to wipe away her fear. "I only want to help you, Rachel. You should know that I would never do you harm."

Rachel tore her gaze away from Noble's and looked for help from the Mexican woman who seemed to be studying her with compassion. "H-help me, señora . . . he . . . he will—" Darkness hovered over Rachel like an ominous bird of prey, circling, circling until there was only a tiny pinpoint of light. Her instincts were sharp, but her body was encumbered by weakness. Her hope, like the light, was quickly being swallowed by darkness, leaving her powerless to defend herself. Rachel allowed the blackness to win. She floated on an endless sea where there was no pain—a safe, dark place to hide.

If this was what it felt like to die, she thought, it wasn't so bad.

Noble took a deep breath and gripped the knife handle, nodding at Margretta. "It's a blessing that she's lost consciousness again." He crossed himself, a prayer lingering on his lips. He needed God's help to guide his hands on his quest to save Rachel.

Rachel awoke in a state of confusion. She felt as if a weight were pressing down on her chest, and when she attempted to move, searing pain made her head spin, and bile rose in her throat. She gasped for breath and was finally able to take air into her lungs. After a moment, she turned her head to stare at the lamp flickering on a nearby table. The feeble flame lent very little light to the darkened corners of the room.

Everything was unfamiliar. She had never seen the massive hand-carved wardrobe that was in her line of view. Inch by inch she turned her head to puzzle over the double doors that stood open, allowing a slight breeze to circulate through the room. She surmised that the doors led to a balcony, because she could see the treetops.

Where was she?

As she became more alert, she could hear the mumbling of male voices just outside the door, but they weren't speaking loud enough for her to hear what they were saying. And did she really care? She was so weary, she just wanted to sleep.

Suddenly the door opened and Noble stepped into the room, his dark gaze going directly to her. "She's awake," he said to someone behind him.

Vague memories flickered through her mind. She remembered now—she was at Casa del Sol. She took a deep breath, allowing air to rush into her lungs. Bits and pieces of memory fell into place. She'd been swimming naked with Noble. She clutched at the sheet, remembering how wantonly she had thrown herself at him. But after that everything was a blank. No matter how hard she concentrated, she couldn't recall how she got to the Casa del Sol.

Rachel cried out with relief when Dr. Nathan

Stanhope came into the room. Calm settled over her and she was comforted by the presence of the doctor who had brought her, and most of the babies born in Madragon County, into the world.

Rachel tried to rise but she didn't have the strength. She tried to speak but her throat tightened and she couldn't utter a word. She wanted to tell Dr. Stanhope that she was in danger in this house. Again she tried to move but it felt as though she were pinned to the bed. Her eyes were pleading as she said in a raspy voice that was hardly audible, "Please . . . take me away from here, Dr. Stanhope."

The short, wiry, slightly balding man bent over her, his soft gray eyes reflecting serenity. His broad brow wrinkled as he smiled at her. Rachel knew that his profession was his life. He'd never married, so his devotion was to the babies he'd brought into the world. Rachel looked into his calming eyes, knowing she'd been rescued.

"I'll have to examine your wound, Rachel, so I can determine if you can make the trip to the Broken Spur."

Rachel's eyes went to Noble and then back to the doctor, her heart contracting with fear. "I want to speak to you . . . alone, Dr. Stanhope."

He turned to Noble. "Wait outside while I examine her. I'll call you if I need anything."

Noble nodded grimly and left, closing the door quietly behind him. He leaned against the wall outside his bedroom, waiting for the doctor to tell him Rachel's condition. He hoped that by removing the bullet, he hadn't done her more harm than good.

Rachel's tongue darted out to moisten her dry lips. "You have to get me away from here." She paused to catch her breath. "Noble will . . . kill me."

Dr. Stanhope's voice was compelling, his eyes sympathetic. "Rachel, it just doesn't make any sense to me that Noble would put a bullet in you and later remove it."

She closed her eyes, feeling more helpless than she had at any time in her life. When she opened them and looked at Dr. Stanhope, she tried to sound composed and not like some hysterical female. "I saw him with a knife."

He nodded and patted her hand gently. "You saw him with the knife he used to remove the bullet from your chest." His winsome smile dug deep crevices in his face as he dropped a spent rifle shell into her hand. "The souvenir that Noble removed from you."

Rachel stared at the shell in confusion. "Are you saying that Noble took this out of me?"

"Yes, he did." Dr. Stanhope set his black bag on the bed and opened it, removing his scissors. "Noble sent his foreman, Alejandro, to town to fetch me. Unfortunately I was delivering Helen Simon's baby and couldn't come right away. Her delivery wasn't an easy one." While he talked, his scissors deftly snipped at the bandage. "However, mother and baby are doing fine, and Gilbert is now the proud papa of his seventh son."

Rachel scarcely heeded the news of Gilbert Simon's seventh son. She was trying to reach back into her memory so she could keep a grasp on reality. "I still think Noble will try to kill me. There was a woman here with Noble, a Mexican woman—ask her what Noble tried to do to me."

"That would be Alejandro's wife, Margretta." Dr. Stanhope made the last snip in the bandage and pulled it away. After a moment he nodded in satisfaction. "And a fine job Noble did too. I couldn't have done better myself."

Why wouldn't Dr. Stanhope listen to her? "You don't understand. Noble has his reasons for wanting me dead."

The doctor spoke to her as if he were speaking to a child. "What reason would that be, Rachel?"

"He . . . I despise him. I swore to avenge my father's death. He knows I'll do it."

"Hell, Rachel. Noble had the whole Yankee army shooting at him. Do you think he's worried about one small woman?"

"He realizes that I . . ." Her voice faded away. She couldn't think clearly, and she couldn't think of a solid reason why a man like Noble would want her dead. "Some people don't need a reason to kill, Dr. Stanhope."

"And you believe that Noble is one of those people?"

"No," she said truthfully. "But it seems to me that—"

"Do you want the truth?" he asked kindly.

She nodded, trusting Dr. Stanhope as she had trusted her own father.

"Noble probably saved your life by removing the bullet. It missed your heart by less than a quarter of an inch."

She shivered at his words. She searched her memory carefully, feeling as if she viewed it through a fragile veil. Noble couldn't have shot her because he certainly hadn't been concealing a gun at the time she'd been shot. They were both naked in the river! Distress filled her mind. When she tried to move, pain shot through her as if it were tearing at her flesh. She lay very still, gasping for breath.

She wouldn't try that again anytime soon.

"You will have to remain quiet, Rachel, if you want the wound to heal," Dr. Stanhope told her sternly while he patted her hand. "Try not to upset yourself."

Rachel hardly heard him because she was still trying to sort out her thoughts. "If Noble didn't shoot me himself, he could have had one of his men do it."

"Who?" Dr. Stanhope asked, with a slight edge to his voice. "Kindhearted Alejandro? He would die for Noble, but he wouldn't kill a woman for him. Perhaps you think Margretta did it—or one of her sons. Understand this, Rachel. Noble didn't shoot you, and he didn't have anyone else do it either."

"One of the vaqueros could have done it."

"No. They all left after Don Reinaldo died."

"So they deserted Noble," Rachel said with satisfaction.

The doctor nodded while he applied healing ointment to her wound and then rebound it. "I have a gut feeling that most of them will hightail it back when they hear Noble has returned. The vaqueros of Casa del Sol have a strong loyalty to the Vincente family."

"Well," she said, changing the subject, "someone shot me, Dr. Stanhope. I certainly didn't do it myself."

"That much is true." He studied her for a long moment. "Noble didn't tell me any of the particulars. He just said that the two of you were together when you were shot. Would you care to tell me what you remember about the incident so I can relate it to Sheriff Crenshaw?"

Her face reddened and she looked away. She couldn't tell anyone, especially not Dr. Stanhope, that she'd been swimming naked with Noble Vincente. "I don't remember . . . very clearly." With effort she raised her hand to her chest, feeling the bulkiness of the bandages. "When can I go home?" she asked, wishing she could leave with him.

"Not just yet. I don't want you moved for at least a week. You've lost a lot of blood, and I can't take a chance on your rupturing the wound."

Rachel had been so terrified of Noble when she thought he was going to kill her. Now she no longer feared him, but she was deeply ashamed because of her brazen conduct at the river. How could she ever face him again after he'd seen her naked?

Dr. Stanhope took her silence as consent. "You will have the best of care here, Rachel."

"You never believed that Noble shot my father, did you, Dr. Stanhope?"

"Nope. I've known Noble all his life, and a cowardly act would not be in his nature. Like his father before him, Noble's a man of honor." The doctor offered her a spoonful of some foul-smelling concoction. "Take it like a good girl," he said, smiling.

She wrinkled her nose just as she had when she'd been a little girl and he'd coaxed medicine down her throat. "What is it?"

"Just something to take the edge off the pain so you can sleep."

Reluctantly she allowed him to lift her head and spoon the liquid into her mouth. With a satisfied nod, he eased her head back against the pillow. "Do you want me to send for your sister?"

"No!" She almost shouted the word, and then quickly said in a softer tone, "I don't want Delia to know what happened. Not until I'm able to go home."

Dr. Stanhope picked up his black bag and ambled for the door. "Suit yourself. I'll be back to see you in a day or two. I'll leave instructions with Margretta on what to feed you. After today I expect you to eat plenty of red meat to build your strength." He turned back to face her. "You don't still believe Noble shot you, do you?"

Already the medicine was taking effect and she was feeling drowsy. "No."

"Noble believes whoever shot you was aiming at him and hit you by mistake."

"Most likely," she said, yawning and drifting off to sleep.

Noble was waiting in the hallway when Dr. Stanhope emerged from the bedroom. His face was etched with worry. "How is she?"

"She'll be all right. It would have been a different story, though, if you'd waited to remove the bullet until I got here. Gangrene could have set in."

"I was scared as hell, Doctor. I never want to go through that again. I don't know how you do that day after day."

Dr. Stanhope chuckled. "So are you saying you have a little more respect for my profession?"

"I've always respected you. But more now that I had to . . . well, it wasn't easy to stick a knife in Rachel."

"I can imagine. Sometimes she's downright formidable. She's a rule unto herself here in Madragon County. Her pa raised her like a son, and she carries responsibilities many grown men would shirk. And yet everyone respects her. Hell, she could've been married a dozen times if she'd so chosen, and it isn't because she owns the Broken Spur. She's grown into the real beauty of the family."

Noble could have told the doctor just how beautiful Rachel was, but he only nodded grimly in agreement, wondering why Rachel had never married. His gaze met Dr. Stanhope's. "She must not be moved too soon or she could break open the wound."

"I already told her that," said Dr. Stanhope, gripping his bag and moving away.

Noble leaned against the wall and crossed his arms. "She's afraid of me. She thinks I shot her."

The doctor paused. "She did at first, but not now."

"Will you remain here until she's well enough to leave?"

"Can't. But I'll be back tomorrow or the next day. I'll just slip down to the kitchen and have some of Margretta's coffee and delicious tortillas. I'll need to instruct her on how to take care of our patient."

Noble walked down the stairs, out the front door into the morning air. He raised his head upward, his gaze tracing the high, thin clouds. Rachel was going to be all right. But somewhere out there was an unknown assailant who'd shot her.

The prayer he'd tried to say at his father's grave,

but couldn't, slipped from between his lips now. "Thank you, God, for letting her live."

Rachel awoke only once more that day. She witnessed a golden sunset, and heard the mournful sound of the wind whispering through the trees outside the double doors.

Margretta entered with a happy smile and a bowl of thin beef broth. After Rachel had pushed the bowl away, the housekeeper gave her a spoonful of the foul-tasting medicine, and Rachel fell asleep.

Later that night, Noble threw a blanket on the floor of the empty bedroom across the hallway from Rachel. Although Margretta was sleeping in the room with her, he wanted to be nearby so he would hear if Rachel should need him during the night. And he wanted to make certain that whoever shot her would not get that close again.

He lay down on his back and clasped his hands behind his head. The big house didn't seem quite so empty now. There was life here—there was Rachel.

He rolled to his side, trying to find a comfortable position. He couldn't shake the guilt that weighed heavily upon him; Rachel had been shot because of him. No one would want to harm her. The bullet had most certainly been meant for him.

He closed his eyes, but they crept open again and he stared into the darkness, watching the moon play tag with floating clouds. Unable to sleep, he got up and wandered to the window. Absently he gazed down into the courtyard, listening to the wind whispering through the trees and the rustle of dead leaves swirling about in the fountain courtyard. He made a mental note to have one of Alejandro's sons clean the courtyard tomorrow.

His mind turned again to Rachel. Who would want him dead badly enough to endanger her life to get at him?

Hell, it could have been any one of a dozen people. He was certainly not without enemies.

Whoever it was, he'd find them eventually.

Chapter Nine

Austin, Texas

The butler walked with practiced dignity across the ornate, red-and-gold Chinese carpet on his way to the dining room.

In the background, there were sounds of the house coming to life—a servant waxing the dark oak banisters, another shining the brass door handles downstairs, while still another washed the windows. Somewhere in the distance, faint kitchen sounds filtered into the front part of the house—the banging of pots and pans, the sound of a chopping knife, the murmured voice of the head cook giving instructions for the day.

The Chandler residence exuded wealth—

although if asked, few people could have said how Whit Chandler came by his fortune. He was popular with almost everyone—Texans, as well as Yankees. He walked the difficult path of courting both camps without offending either—a talent he was proud of. Such was Whit's personality that most people liked him, although, again, none could have said why. His easy charm, perhaps. His ability to listen to whoever spoke to him as if that person had his whole attention. He was likable, charming, and he did have a beautiful wife, which didn't hurt.

Delia sat across the table from her husband, observing him as he read the daily newspaper. Whit's face was angular, handsome in a boyish sort of way, and he looked much younger than his thirty-five years. His hair was blond and curly. He had a slightly crooked nose that had been broken in his youth, the result of his quick temper—a temper he'd long since learned to control. His eyes were deep-set and a nondescript color, somewhere between gray and blue. He was a complex man. Delia wasn't sure she understood him at all, nor did she really care to.

Her role was to play the dutiful wife when the world was watching, and she did that well. It was easy to fool everyone by pretending to adore her husband and hang on to his every word as if they were pearls of wisdom. But within their own home, they were little more than strangers. Whit came often enough to her bed, because lovemaking was the one good thing they shared. But there was no love between them, at least not on Delia's part. And Whit had never said he loved her, so she assumed he didn't—not that it mattered.

The butler entered the room, cleared his throat and held out a silver tray to Whit.

"Good morning, Hamish." Whit smiled as he took the note, then looked puzzled. "It's from Harvey Briscal."

"That little weasel. I didn't even know he could write," Delia said with disgust. She leaned closer to her husband, trying to read the letter, but it was badly written and most of the words were misspelled. "He's Ira Crenshaw's deputy. I only met him once, and he impressed me as being a fool. I didn't like him in the least."

Whit scanned the note and raised his gaze to Delia. "Dammit," he exploded, glaring at his wife. "That sister of yours has gone too far this time!"

Delia nodded for Hamish to leave, and waited until he departed to speak. "What are you talking about? What's Rachel done now?"

He slid the note across the smooth surface of the table, and Delia scanned it hastily. "If I read this correctly, it says she's been wounded"—her face drained of color—"but it doesn't say how bad she is or who shot her!" Delia rose quickly to her feet. "I must go to her at once!"

Whit gripped her arm and jerked her back into her chair. "Read on."

Her gaze went back to the letter and she sucked

in her breath. "It says she is recovering at Casa del Sol." She looked at Whit with a puzzled expression. "Whatever does it mean? Why would she be with Noble? She despises him."

"That's exactly what I intend to find out." Whit threw his napkin forcefully across the table. "Although I have someone watching her, she still finds a way to get in trouble. It's time I paid your sister a visit. You surely haven't gotten anywhere with her. This time you'll remain here and I'll go to see her. Your sister will ruin us all."

Delia glared at him. "You are too cold-blooded. My sister's been shot. We don't know how badly, and all you can think about is how it will affect you. Well, know this: Rachel's my sister, and not you or anyone will keep me from going to her when she needs me. And as for her ruining us, what about your own family? You never see your mother or your brother. You never invite them here. They're the only family you have left, and you act as if you are ashamed of them."

Whit's forehead furrowed with a frown, and his blond eyebrows almost met across the bridge of his nose. "I admit my family will never be a part of my life." He smiled, not with humor but with cruelty. "Do you think I don't know that my brother, Frank, always lusted after you? He wanted you, but I got you, God help me."

Delia dropped her gaze. "I have to pack if I'm going to leave this morning."

Whit's eyes narrowed. "I don't want you to go

near Noble, do you understand me? He's probably still in love with you."

Delia continued to keep her eyes averted so he wouldn't read her thoughts—he was good at reading people's thoughts, and especially hers. She had allowed Whit to think that Noble had once loved her, but it wasn't true; it never had been.

Wanting to change the subject, she pushed Harvey Briscal's note back toward whit and said, "Have you set this man to watching Rachel? If you have, I don't like it. Is your spy the deputy?"

"That's none of your concern. But if Rachel isn't watched, who can say what she'll do next? She has no regard for what I'm trying to do for this state."

"What *are* you trying to do for Texas?" Delia asked, avoiding his hand when he reached out for her. "I thought you were doing it all to line your own pockets. And you've done quite well there, haven't you?"

He pretended not to hear her. "Your sister could ruin everything if she's playing the harlot with Noble. The Rutledge sisters seem to have a thing for Spanish blood, do you not—hmm?"

Anger started in the pit of Delia's stomach and burned a path upward, until her face was flushed. "How dare you say such a thing to me? Rachel is not like that. And you know she despises Noble."

Whit walked across the room, leaned nonchalantly against the doorjamb and stared at her. "What upsets you most about this, Delia? Your sister's reputation or the fact that Noble might be in bed with her right now?"

"Don't go on with this, Whit."

He was silent for a moment as if he were pondering his next words carefully. Whit never said or did anything without thinking about it first. A mask slid across his face, and he glanced at Delia with a dreadful intentness that made her shudder. "Go get your sister and take her back to the Broken Spur, but stay away from Noble—is that understood?"

Delia walked over to him. "I'll take her home. And remain with her until I know she's all right."

"And you won't see Noble alone?"

"Why pretend you're so upset, Whit? You don't care what I do as long as I do it quietly and secretly, and don't upset your election plans."

He grabbed her arm, twisted it behind her and brought her face close to his. "You know nothing about my feelings. As long as I keep you in jewels and expensive gowns, you're happy. You have no notion just how much it costs me to keep you happy, my dear." He flung her away. "Don't you ever question where the money comes from, or what I have to do to get it?"

"Go to hell!" She rubbed her bruised wrist. "I don't want to know your dirty little secrets."

His smile was humorless and somehow frightening. "I undoubtedly shall, but I'll take you with me." His gaze took on a faraway look. "I'm sure your precious Noble is already in hell. He's no longer the studhorse for simpering young girls to dream about. He's touched the ground like the rest of us—without his father's money, he's just another mortal."

Delia looked at him with new understanding. "You are jealous of Noble. I knew you hated him, but I never realized that you were envious of him."

"Why should I be?" He took out his pocket watch and gauged the time, trying to act casual, but she saw that his hand shook. "Think what I have and look at what he doesn't have, and then tell me I envy him."

"What do you have?"

He made a wide sweep with his hand. "Why, my dear, I have all this and you. Noble has lost everything. He's hated and despised by his neighbors, and most probably he'll soon lose Casa del Sol. If I get my hands on the Broken Spur, it's just a matter of time before I take over Casa del Sol as well."

He started to move away and she fell in step beside him. "You are crazed, Whit. Do you hate him so much?"

"Hating someone takes too much time. I'm merely happy to see Noble finally get what he deserves."

"His father was good to you. Don't forget he paid for you to go to that fancy Eastern law school. If it hadn't been for the Vincente money, you wouldn't be where you are today."

"Yes, Noble's father paid for me to go to school. It seemed that the Vincentes liked to do charity work—I was Don Reinaldo Vincente's good deed. I admit that I owe my law degree to him, but I have never been grateful to him. I got where I am because of my brain, Delia." He tapped his head. "My brain!"

"You hated living on Vincente charity, didn't you? Even now it sticks in your throat like bile. So you aren't so brilliant after all."

"I can still feel the humiliation of writing all those glowing letters of my progress to Don Reinaldo Vincente, so the old man would continue to pay my expenses. When I earned my degree, I was glad that I no longer had to live on Vincente money."

"Just think where you'd be today but for their money. You'd probably be living in a sod hut with your family."

His eyes narrowed. "I don't think so."

"I understand why you hate Noble. But his father was good to you."

Bitterness laced Whit's words. "I was never once invited to their ranch. When they had dealings with me, it came through a paid sycophant. Well, I used them to suit my purpose—that's all."

"Just as you've used me?"

He smiled, lowering his voice so the servants wouldn't overhear. "We use each other, don't we, my dear?"

Delia lowered her gaze, no longer wanting to look at him. "I'll be leaving today for the Broken Spur."

He appeared beside her, taking her chin and holding it in a viselike grip. "Don't linger too long or I might be forced to come after you." He shoved her away. "In any case, I'm sending Daniels with you—to keep an eye on you."

"Another of your spies?"

"Yes, he spies for me, among others."

"Who are the others?"

"Wouldn't you like to know? Just remember that you'll be watched. And stay away from Noble."

"You don't scare me, Whit. And you can't order me about. I'm not one of your sycophants."

Whit's next words were spoken crisply, with just the hint of a threat. "Just remember that those who work for me are loyal to me. My enemies are their enemies."

With her husband's threat ringing in her ears, Delia turned away and hurried toward the stairs, shaken. She had just seen that other side of her husband—the side she'd rarely witnessed, and it always frightened her. His voice echoed in her head. *My enemies are their enemies.* Noble was his enemy.

Whit must suspect that part of her would always be in love with Noble—the part that had not been corrupted by ambition, the part that was still young and innocent.

When Delia reached her bedroom, she went to the liquor tray, poured herself a snifter of brandy and downed it in one swallow. Then she felt better. The warmth was spreading throughout her body. Now she could cope with Whit.

Then she thought of Noble and fought back bitter tears. She hadn't cried in a very long time. But she cried now. She took another drink, dried her eyes and yanked on the bellpull, summoning a servant. She had to get to Rachel as quickly as possible.

Whit entered the room, shut and locked the door, then dropped the key in his vest pocket. He went to the liquor tray, poured a liberal amount for Delia and less for himself. "I will miss you while you're gone. I thought we might have a drink together, and then make love."

She opened the wardrobe and removed several pairs of stockings and tossed them on the bed. "Not now. I have to pack."

He handed her the glass. "Surely you won't deny me this time together."

She gulped down the drink and he took the glass from her. She watched as he removed his tie, his shirt, and then his trousers. "I don't want to do it now, Whit." It was a weak protest; already she had untied the ribbon of her dressing gown.

He lowered his head, kissed her breasts, then pressed her down onto the floor, lowering himself on top of her. His hands were everywhere, caressing, stroking, firing her passion.

"I just want to show you what you'll be missing," he said thickly, spreading her legs and thrusting into her.

Delia threw back her head, gasping from his powerful thrusts. Somehow, in her brandy-drugged, passion-laced state, she felt used and soiled. Something wasn't right but she didn't know what it was. Her nails clawed at his back as he made love to her not just once, but twice.

Afterward she expected him to leave, but he gave her another drink. She tried to refuse, but he insisted. She was unaware that he carried her to bed, where she curled up to sleep.

When she awoke the next morning, Whit was beside her. He was charming and attentive. He'd brought her a tray of food, and fed her every bite. Afterward he gave her another drink and they made love again.

Somewhere in the back of Delia's mind, there was something nagging at her—something she needed to do, but she couldn't remember what it was.

Rachel awoke and lay still for a long moment, afraid to move because of the pain. Slowly the fragments of her memory fell into place. She was still at Casa del Sol. She tried to sit up, but weakness kept her pinned to the bed as if she'd been tied there. After struggling with the weakness, she finally gave in to it.

Jumbled thoughts swirled through her mind, climbing over each other, and she had to sort them out one by one. Every thought eventually led her back to the scene at the river with Noble, and she was overcome with shame. Noble wouldn't know that such brazen actions were not in her nature, or that she had never behaved that way with another man. At the time it had seemed the right thing to do, but now she saw it as pure folly.

Her eyes moved around the room. It was sparsely furnished, the furniture old and very valuable. She looked at the massive wardrobe, where the door was slightly open to reveal several pairs of black leather boots. Warmth flowed through her. This was Noble's room. She swallowed hard and closed her eyes. She was lying in his bed, her head resting on his pillow, her body where his body rested. She could almost feel him beside her. She turned her face and buried it in the pillow, beginning to tremble. Her body was weak, but her thoughts were strong. She remembered the feel of his hard male body against hers. His hands touching, stroking her. His lips plundering hers.

She made a fist, and her nails dug painfully into her palm. "I won't think about him like that," she told herself firmly. "I won't!"

Moments later the door swung open and Margretta entered. When she saw that Rachel was awake, she smiled cheerfully and her dark eyes brightened.

"What time is it, Margretta?"

The woman spoke rapidly in Spanish, while Rachel fumbled with the few Spanish words she knew.

"No . . . hablo español. I do not speak Spanish very well, señora."

Margretta smiled and nodded, rubbing her stomach and pointing at Rachel.

"Yes. I am hungry," Rachel said, feeling frustrated because she couldn't communicate with Margretta. She wanted to ask her for her clothing. She wanted someone from the Broken Spur to come for her, but how could she make Margretta understand? With resigned helplessness she said, *"Sí,* I am very er . . . *hambriento."* She pointed at her mouth. "Hungry—I am hungry."

Margretta nodded brightly. *"Sí, sí,* señorita." She hurried from the room, closing the door behind her.

Rachel sank into Noble's bed, feeling his strong presence beside her once more. If he had wanted her dead, he'd certainly had ample opportunity to get rid of her. Instead he'd saved her life. It did not sit well with her that she owed him her life.

A light knock fell on the door and Rachel turned in that direction. "Come in," she said, thinking Margretta had returned with her breakfast.

Noble entered the room, his eyes on her face. "Do you feel up to talking? I promise I will only stay a moment."

She had dreaded the moment she would have to face him after her performance at the river. She was acutely aware of him as a man since she'd felt his naked body against hers. A blush tinted her cheeks and her gaze wavered. She couldn't meet his brilliant brown eyes, fearing he would read her thoughts.

"I don't feel well," she said, wishing he'd just go away.

He ventured farther into the room and she looked up at him as he stood there, so handsome with the light from the window creating a halo around him. He wore tight-fitting black leather chaps and a stark white shirt. His ebony hair was slightly windblown, as if he'd been riding. She had the strongest urge to run her fingers through his hair and—

Dear God, what was she thinking?

Rachel closed her eyes because he seemed taller, more intimidating with her lying down and him standing over her.

"Are you in pain?" he asked with concern.

"Only when I breathe," she answered, trying to sound humorous while still avoiding his eyes.

Drawing the wooden chair close to her, he sat down. "Dr. Stanhope said you will be fine. There's no infection." His gaze dropped to the bandage wrapped across her shoulder. "You were fortunate the bullet wasn't lower."

Her intake of breath was painful, and she swallowed past her parched throat. "You saved my life." Now she did meet his eyes. "I feel obligated to thank you for that, and for your hospitality, which I'm forced to accept."

"Don't speak of it." He looked as if he hadn't slept, and there was stubble on his face—he hadn't shaved. "We both know whoever shot you was really aiming at me, Rachel. We must also consider that he saw us together in the river."

She lowered her gaze, feeling her shame like a knife in her heart. "Yes, I've thought about that."

"I'll find out who did it." He'd spoken softly, but there was tempered steel in his tone. "You can depend on that."

"If he doesn't find you first. As you said, whoever shot me was probably aiming at you. Since he missed his original target, he will probably try again."

Noble was silent for so long she glanced up to see him staring at her. He dropped his eyes.

"I wanted you to know you may remain here as long as necessary. I have sent word to your housekeeper and she will be here shortly. Perhaps you'd like her to remain with you until you are well enough to go home."

Rachel considered how comforting it would be to have the formidable Winna Mae with her. "Thank you. I would like Winna Mae here with me."

He crossed his long legs and laid a hand on his boot. Still feeling shy in his company, she concentrated on his hands. There was strength in those hands, but she had felt the gentleness in them as well. She blushed when she thought about him touching her in the most intimate way.

"Don't think about it, Rachel," he said, reading her thoughts. "It will never happen again."

She plucked at the sheet. "You must think that I'm—"

"I think you were an innocent, playing with fire. Thank God you didn't get burned."

"Only shot," she said with irony.

"I must not tire you. I just wanted you to know that I intend to do everything in my power to find out who shot you."

She watched the pulse beating at his throat. He was such an intense man and she had felt the passion that burned within him. She must not forget that he was her enemy. "This is your bedroom?" she asked, changing the subject.

"Yes." He smiled slightly. "It's the only room with a bed."

"Where do you sleep?"

"The room across the hall."

"I'll try not to put you out of your bed longer than necessary."

He stood, the smile still playing on his sensuous lips. "I like you in my bed."

Against her will, pleasure pulsed through her, and she could almost feel the touch of his hands on her body.

Without another word, he moved to the door and was gone, leaving her pondering his words.

Rachel realized that her life and Noble's seemed unendingly linked together. No matter how hard she tried, she would never forget that for a short time, their bodies had touched. And she had a feeling that Noble would never forget either.

She felt suddenly cold, and a shudder raced down her spine. Someone had seen her and Noble in the river. Who was it?

She closed her eyes. Whoever had shot her would still be gunning for Noble.

Chapter Ten

Winna Mae had been residing at Casa del Sol for a week. On arriving, she had made her presence felt right away. She had immediately taken over, issuing orders and expecting them to be obeyed. Fortunately, she spoke enough Spanish to convey those wishes to Margretta, who gladly relinquished Rachel's care to her and eagerly did Winna Mae's bidding.

Winna Mae had just finished braiding Rachel's hair, and now fanned her with a brightly colored folding fan. "You will be well enough to go home next week," she announced in her usual abrupt way.

"I've been here for twelve days," Rachel said ruefully. "I can't get back to the Broken Spur fast enough to suit me." She could have added that during the time she'd been there, Noble had visited her only twice. She didn't know why that should matter to her, but it did. She could imagine all sorts of reasons that kept him away, but only one seemed likely. He didn't trust her not to repeat her little performance at the river.

Would she ever be able to live down the humiliation?

Winna Mae was smoothing out the covers and she glanced up at Rachel, speaking with her usual directness. "You have been shown every kindness." There was reproach in her voice. "You are alive because of Noble Vincente's quick action. You should remember that."

"Yes, I know," Rachel concurred. "I have so much to think about. I have never been so confused."

"If you are worried about your health, the doctor said there would be no lasting effects and only a small scar. He praised Noble's steady hand as the reason the scar was not larger."

"It doesn't sit well with me that I must accept the hospitality of the man who murdered my father."

"There would be a strange contradiction in a man who kills the father but saves the life of the daughter. Don't you agree?"

"I admit that I have recently begun to have doubts about Noble's guilt," Rachel admitted grudgingly. "Do you think he did it?"

Winna Mae straightened and fluffed Rachel's pillows. "No. I never thought he killed your father, and I know he didn't shoot you either."

"No. He couldn't have shot me. But I am still not wholly convinced that he didn't kill my father."

"His gun beside your father's body was damning, I'll admit, but I'd stake my life on the fact that other hands put the gun there to make it appear as if Noble Vincente did the deed."

"Is that the only reason you believe in his innocence? If so, your reasoning isn't sound."

"I use my eyes and ears and not my voice," Winna Mae stated calmly. "That way I see and hear things."

"Such as?"

"All I'll say at the moment is that there are those who envied the Vincente family. Noble is the kind of man many want to be but never can be. There are those who were too eager to put a noose around his neck. I am glad for people like Sheriff Crenshaw, who is a wise and sensible man."

Rachel lay back against the pillow while doubts played in her mind. "I wish I were as certain as you are."

"Do you think Noble is a half-wit?" Winna Mae asked, her eyes boring into Rachel's.

"Hardly that."

"Then why would he commit a murder and leave his gun to be found?"

Delia had given Rachel the same argument and

Rachel had dismissed it. But coming from sensible, reliable Winna Mae, it sounded believable. "Perhaps Noble had not planned to kill my father, and when it happened, he panicked and ran away."

"Noble is a coward, then?"

Rachel pressed her fingers against her throbbing temples. "No. Of course not. But why didn't you say any of this to me before now?"

"You never asked me. It's not my habit to offer my opinion unless invited to do so."

"If he's innocent, why did he run away? Where has he been all these years? He fathered a child by Delia and then left her to face the shame alone. He had no way of knowing that Whit would save Delia from disgrace by marrying her."

Winna Mae picked up the water pitcher and moved to the door. "Why don't you ask Noble what happened?" She paused in the doorway. "And while you're at it, why not ask your sister some questions?"

Noble walked through the stable, looking into the stalls, unconsciously counting the six horses that made up his entire herd. He had no aversion to hard work. Already this morning he'd cleaned the stalls and tossed fresh hay to the horses. Without money and men, how would he keep up with all the repairs? Without rain, how long could he hope to keep Casa del Sol?

His jaw settled into a formidable line. He would

never turn away from the heritage his father had entrusted to him. A Vincente did not surrender when life got hard. A Vincente fought to win.

He blotted sweat from his face with his sleeve. The weather had grown even hotter, and it was stifling inside the brick structure. He rolled up his sleeves and walked out of the stable to stand beneath the spreading branches of a tall oak tree. One thing that could be said about West Texas: if you stood beneath a tree, and the wind was blowing—which it always was—you could cool down. His gaze went to the cloudless sky. If only it would rain to break the heat and end the drought, he thought wearily.

Noble narrowed his eyes against the glare of the sun, gazing at a dust cloud that indicated several riders were approaching. His hand automatically went to his holster, and he realized he'd left his gun at the hacienda. With grim determination he waited for the horsemen. When they were near enough for him to make out their number, he counted fifteen, sixteen, twenty-three men.

Alejandro had gone into town that morning, and his sons had ridden to the river to check its depth. Noble would have to face the trespassers alone and unarmed. He stood his ground and waited for them to approach.

He was puzzled when he heard shouting in Spanish and saw the riders waving. When they were near enough for him to make out their faces, he smiled.

Alejandro rode at the head of the vaqueros who had made their home at Casa del Sol; evidently they were returning, as the *gran vaquero* had predicted they would. Noble felt a lump in his throat and couldn't speak.

"Patrón!" Alejandro yelled. "Nothing could keep them away when they heard that you had returned. They have come ready to work. Their families will come later."

The vaqueros bounded off their horses, grinning at their *patrón*. Each man stepped forward and vigorously shook his hand, while Noble inquired about their wives and children.

At last they stood silent, waiting for the *patrón* to instruct them, each face with an expectant expression.

Noble spoke to them in Spanish. *"Muchas gracias, amigos.* But I must tell you that I have no money to pay you. I will think no less of any man who rides away, for I know most of you have families to feed."

Noble waited for a response but none came, so he continued. "If you agree to stay, we are in for a difficult time. To my way of thinking, you are the greatest vaqueros in Texas, and any rancher who hires you will be most fortunate. Please consider this before you make a commitment to me out of loyalty. While loyalty is a fine thing, it will not put food in your children's bellies."

Silently they watched him as if they were waiting for him to say the right words to them.

He nodded in understanding. "Very well, Casa del Sol is your home. Bring your families here and I promise none shall go hungry."

Many wide-brimmed sombreros were tossed into the air, and the men shouted in unison, *"Viva patrón! Viva Casa del Sol!"*

Alejandro smiled. "You have only to tell them what to do and it will be done."

"Welcome home," he said, with pride swelling in his chest. "We shall begin by rebuilding corrals, patching the roof of the barn and setting the house in good order. Carlos, Miguel, the two of you ride to the eastern butte. Find what strays you can and drive them to the west pasture where the grazing is better along the Brazos."

"Will we drive them to Kansas City, *Patrón?*" leathery-faced Carlos inquired hopefully. "I have heard it is a good market."

"Not this year, *amigo*. The few head we have will go on your tables to feed your children." Noble's gaze traveled over each familiar face. "Should the day come when we prosper again, I can promise each man here a sizable bonus. But there is no guarantee that this will happen."

"It will happen," Alejandro said with confidence.

Noble looked doubtful. "I feel I should give you another chance to consider. Who is to go and who stays?"

Alejandro spoke for them. "They will not go, *Patrón*."

Noble's throat tightened with emotion and it took him a moment to speak. "*Gracias, amigos*. I will never forget this day." He turned to the *gran vaquero*. "Alejandro, see that each man has a place to sleep. Make arrangements for them to bring their families home as soon as possible. Casa del Sol will soon know the sound of children's laughter again."

Noble turned and walked toward the house. He no longer stood alone. For the first time since returning to Texas, hope began to grow within his heart.

Rachel had too much time to think while she was convalescing. She relived the scene at the river many times in her head, and she became more convinced than ever that the shot had been meant for Noble. She had no enemies that she was aware of, and Noble had many.

She resented the nameless, faceless person who'd shot her, not because of her wound but because she had prior claim on Noble. *She* must be the one to bring him down, not some coward who'd hidden behind trees to ambush him. She knew Noble was alone and friendless, and she tried to find satisfaction in his misery. But strangely enough she pitied him, and that was her torment.

She closed her eyes, sinking into the pillow. Even the smallest exertion seemed to weary her. Moments later, her eyes flew open when she heard the sounds of hammering and banging from downstairs. What was Noble doing, tearing the house apart? She didn't care; her eyes drifted shut and she floated in the arms of oblivion.

A flurry of activity swirled through Casa del Sol. Under the *gran vaquero*'s direction the younger vaqueros had been sent into the hills to round up stray longhorns, while the older men had been set to' work repairing the hacienda. Missing stones were replaced, the roof tiles put back into place. The courtyards were swept clean. The fountains were scrubbed until they sparkled, although they remained without water. In the house Margretta directed the women in scrubbing and cleaning each room. Neglected fireplaces became spotless, banisters were waxed. The stone floors in the kitchen were scrubbed until they shone. Copper pots and pans were polished until the fastidious Margretta could see her own reflection in them. The furniture and rugs had been retrieved from their different hiding places and arranged as they had been before.

Casa del Sol was being reborn, but Noble knew the change was only outward. The day might well come when he could no longer keep the ranch going. But his footsteps were lighter, and the sadness he carried within his heart had lessened. He had a purpose now, a reason for living. And he had a debt to repay to the vaqueros and their families, who had stood by him when most people turned their backs on him. He would not forget their loyalty.

It was early evening and the western sky was still bloodred from a magnificent sunset. Rachel had convinced Winna Mae that she was well enough to go outside into the beautiful enclosed fountain patio she could see from the bedroom window. She was becoming restless and irritable, a sure sign that she was recovering.

Rachel reclined on a woven rope lounge in the inner courtyard, listening to a Spanish guitar somewhere in the distance, a nightly ritual she was beginning to look forward to with relish. Time passed peacefully, and she realized that it had grown dark. The moon was glorious, big and golden, looking as if it were magically suspended among the stars with the single purpose of bathing the garden with its magnificence.

She turned her head and stared at the huge fountain of a goddess riding a chariot pulled by four rearing steeds. Another statue, a young god of myth, stood atop an ornate pedestal, muscled and fierce-looking, with his bow drawn as if ready to fire at some unknown enemy. Rachel thought it was a pity that there was no water flowing through the fountains. She would have liked to have seen them as they were when Don Reinaldo was alive.

She leaned back to enjoy the beautiful plaintive song that wove its way through the courtyard.

"It's good to see you up and about, Rachel."

She turned to meet Noble's level gaze.

"I will be going home tomorrow," she said, voicing the first thought that came to her mind.

He pulled a chair up beside her. "So I've been told."

Her chest grew tight and she had trouble taking a deep breath. She felt almost shy in his presence, and she didn't like that feeling. "I was trying to imagine what this courtyard would look like if there were water for the fountains."

His gaze swept past her as if he were remembering. "There are three courtyards. This one is called Courtyard of the Gods. Did you know that, Rachel?"

"No, I didn't, but it is a fitting name. It must have been a glorious sight with water rushing through it and emptying into the pond."

He glanced back to her. "You have not seen the fountains before?"

"No. I was never in this courtyard until now."

"It was once very peaceful here." He inhaled deeply and turned his gaze on the marble steeds. "But that was in another lifetime."

The conversation lagged as they both searched for something to say. Rachel knew her feelings were too deep and confused to put into words.

Noble leaned back and glanced upward, his mind returning to the past. "Beyond this courtyard was once my mother's garden. The flowers are all dead now." His looked at her. "Nothing stays the same."

She sensed such a sadness in him. She had the strangest urge to reach out and take his head to her breast to comfort him. The urge passed quickly when she realized what his reaction would be to such an overture on her part.

"House of the Sun, Casa del Sol. It is a tragedy that it's fallen to ruin."

"Yes," he said, gazing upward to the stars. "Few families in West Texas have escaped the aftermath of the war."

"These are sad times for Texas," Rachel agreed, caught by a strange melancholy. "So many people I loved are dead."

"We cannot go back, Green Eyes. If we could, every man, woman and child would mend their mistakes, and this would be an ideal world."

His voice sounded wooden to her. "Surely the great Noble Vincente would have nothing to mend. Would you ever admit to a mistake?"

"Ah, Rachel, stack my mistakes one atop the other and you would have an archway to the stars. I am as flawed as the next man, maybe even more than most."

She could feel his gaze upon her, and she dipped her head to study her hands, quickly changing the subject. "I had heard that your sister, Saber, is staying with relatives in Georgia. Will you bring her home now that you have returned?"

"I have sent for her. She should be home before winter sets in."

"Although she was several years younger than I, I liked her very much."

"I believe she was fond of you as well." He studied her closely. "But then, all of the Vincentes were fond of you."

Noble turned his head from Rachel and she stared at his wonderful profile, thinking he could have been the model for the statue of the young warrior atop the fountain pedestal.

"When Saber returns, this will be a real home again." Noble's gaze caught and held Rachel's for a long moment. "A man needs his family around him. I have come to know this."

"My father is dead."

"So is mine. We have both known the hardship that comes with loss, Rachel."

She felt a pang of pity for him and she gripped her hands until her fingernails cut into her skin. She must not think of him with pity, and she must not think of him as a fountain god. "What do you know of hardship, Noble? When did you ever suffer? Have you ever known hunger? Did you ever have to boil parched wheat as an unsuitable substitute for coffee? Where were you when our men were fighting and dying on Northern battlefields?"

Noble's eyes suddenly flamed with anger, and they pierced Rachel. "What was I doing while *our* men were dying on Northern battlefields? I was at Antietam, holding the head of Jess McVee's seventeen-year-old son on my lap. My hands were pressed on both sides of his shattered skull to hold his brains in."

She heard the catch in his voice and choked back her tears.

"I stayed with him until he died, thinking he was too young to be fighting a war we couldn't win. I wanted to die in his place, but fate was not so merciful."

"Oh, Noble, how horrible. Have you told Jess and Mary?"

There was a coldness in Noble's eyes. "No." He shook his head. "I was in their store and I wanted to tell them about—" He shrugged. "It doesn't matter. Pity, though. Their son was a good soldier, and died bravely. I think they should know."

"You could have written them."

"It wasn't the kind of thing I wanted to put into a letter."

"Where else did you fight, Noble?" There was a heaviness in her heart. Here was a man of deep commitments, a proud man who didn't like to share his feelings with anyone. She could only imagine what it was costing him to tell her.

"I was at Gettysburg firing at a faceless enemy and watching my fellow soldiers die all around me. I watched the South lose the battle, and finally the war." His voice sounded devoid of feeling now. "You asked if I'd ever been hungry? I lived for three weeks on a diet of oats that I shared with my horse. Of course, I gave the lion's share to the horse, because as we know, the Confederate Calvary was nothing if it couldn't ride horseback."

She felt a sob building up inside her and she attempted to suppress it. She had never considered that Noble might have gone to war. *Please*, she told herself, *don't cry now—not in front of Noble*. She felt so ashamed of accusing him of never going hungry. He'd known hardships she could never imagine.

Noble stood, bowed and clicked his heels together. "Captain Noble Vincente of the Texas Light Horse Brigade—at your service, ma'am."

"I thought you'd run away after my father was killed."

He drew in a breath and walked to the fountain, where he placed a hand on one of the rearing horses. "Rachel, I got my orders to report to Galveston the week before your father died. I didn't run away. I went to war for Texas." He gazed not at her, but just above her head, as if he were looking inward. "Every time I fired my gun in battle, I was aware that I was killing fellow countrymen, not enemies." His gaze caught her. "Rachel, if we'd won that war, we'd have lost our souls. It was wrong from the beginning."

"You sound like Sam Houston."

"God, I hope so."

"And yet, feeling the way you did, you still fought for the South." She was trying to understand his reasoning.

"I fought for Texas—not for the South or any of the Confederacy's misguided beliefs."

He was quiet for a moment, as if he were grasping for words. When he turned to her, his eyes were transfixed. "Did you go hungry, Green Eyes?"

"No, I didn't, but I knew those who did. I hated the war, and I hate what it's done to Texas. It would have been far better if we had remained a country apart, like Sam Houston wanted us to do."

"I felt much the same way you do, Rachel. I didn't believe in the war, but I believed in Texas. And if she was going to war, I was going to be there to represent her as a native son."

It took her a moment to speak. "So you were courageous for the land, if not for the cause."

"No. Not courageous. Misguided like many others, but nonetheless a Texan. I make no apologies to anyone for what I did."

Her heart was beating violently. She tried to imagine him in a uniform. The gray and yellow of an officer's uniform would only have enhanced his handsomeness. Then a startling thought came to her. Noble could have been killed by a Yankee bullet! She drew in her breath and let it out slowly. "If I had been a man, I would have gone to war."

He grinned. "I'm surprised that you would allow a small thing like being a female to stop you. You should have gone to war; then the Yankees wouldn't have stood a chance of winning."

She looked indignant. "You would not have—"

He held up his hand to silence her. "Forgive my poor attempt at humor. Since you will be going home tomorrow, I just wanted to tell you good-bye, since I won't be here when you leave." He reached out to her but let his hand fall to his side. "If you need anything, you have only to ask. Now or in the future."

"Noble, I . . ." She twisted her hands in her lap, wishing she could say what was in her heart. He'd given her so much to think about tonight. "I don't . . . don't hate you anymore."

Sadness like an encroaching mask moved across his face. "*El amor vence al odio.*"

She watched him walk away, her mind whirling and sorrow eating at her. Dammit, why hadn't she learned Spanish? She repeated his words over to herself so she wouldn't forget them.

Closing her eyes, she listened to the night sounds around her. It was so beautiful here in Noble's garden. It was a home. There should be children laughing and playing, children with their father's dark, fiery eyes. She shook her head. No, she didn't want to think about Noble fathering a child, because that made her think of Delia and the baby Noble had fathered.

For a long moment she made her mind a blank, but Noble's likeness returned unbidden. He had fought in the war—she hadn't known that. If their neighbors knew he'd gone to war, they would be more tolerant of him. She knew why he hadn't told anyone about serving with the Confederacy;

his pride wouldn't let him. Moments ago she'd felt his loneliness and wondered what torment he carried within his heart. And why should she care?

But she did.

Rachel was beginning to believe in Noble's innocence. But she reminded herself that he was a master at manipulating people and making them believe in him. Why did she have this strong urge to lay her head against his shoulder and cry out her misery? Why did she feel as if she were breaking apart inside, piece by piece?

Standing on shaky legs, she stumbled through the door and across the room. Breathlessly, she grasped the banister and slowly made her way upstairs. When she reached the bedroom, she threw herself onto the bed, exhausted physically and mentally.

She buried her head in her hands, wishing she didn't have to think about anything at the moment. There was trouble ahead for Noble—she knew it, and so did he.

"I want to go home," she whispered as Winna Mae entered the room carrying a tray of food.

"Tomorrow," Winna Mae stated firmly. "Tonight you eat and rest. Every day you rest makes you that much stronger."

Rachel rose up on her elbow. "Winna Mae, what does *el amor vence al odio* mean?"

Winna Mae's brow creased and she placed the

tray on the bed beside Rachel. "It translates to something like, love conquers hate."

Warmth spread throughout Rachel's body. *Love conquers hate.* Could it be true?

Chapter Eleven

Noble stood in the gloom, staring through the doorway of his mother's music room. Her piano had been returned to its former position, the broken windows had been replaced and the wooden floors were clean and waxed to a fine shine. But it was just a room like any other because it would no longer reflect the essence of happier days; the echoes of laughter had long since disappeared with the ghosts of the past.

Like a man caught in a dream, Noble moved from room to room, finding the same emptiness. He wondered if Casa del Sol would ever feel like home to him again. It felt emptier than it had the day he'd come home and found the furniture gone and everything in ruin.

Now that Rachel had left, she'd taken her warmth with her, and his loneliness had become more crushing. Like the house, he was cold and empty inside.

His footsteps halted short of the door that led to the fountain garden. He feared that in his melancholy state of mind, he might conjure up visions of Rachel there. He was beginning to question his sanity. He took several steps backward, and with a resigned set of his jaw, walked toward the front door. He had things to do, and Rachel had no place in his life. After what had happened between them at the river he must avoid her in the future. His life was still in a tangle and he didn't need her to further complicate matters.

His most immediate problem was the vaqueros and their families, who were returning daily in great numbers. They were like his children, and they looked to him for guidance. At the moment he couldn't even guide his own life; how would he help them?

"*Patrón,*" Alejandro said, breaking into his musings. "My son, Tomas, has returned from New Orleans, and he has brought with him a man who wishes to see you."

"Who is it?" Noble asked irritably. He was in no mood to entertain guests.

"He is a very fine gentleman, and he came all the way from New Orleans to see you, *Patrón.*"

Noble brushed aside his annoyance. If the man had come so far, the least he could do was talk to him. "Show him into my study, Alejandro."

"*Si*." The *gran vaquero* rushed away. "I'll send him to you at once."

Every time Noble entered the study he expected to see his father sitting behind the massive oak desk, issuing orders that would set the day in motion at Casa del Sol. His gaze ran the length of the east wall, over the floor-to-ceiling bookshelves filled with leather-bound books. He felt sure his father had read all the books, some of them many times. He removed a thick volume on animal husbandry and quickly leafed through the pages. Some of the pages were dog-eared, and he felt his father's presence as he never had before.

Hearing footsteps, Noble placed the book back on the shelf and turned to greet his visitor.

The portly stranger had the look of a prosperous gentleman. His hair was gray at the temples and thinning a bit. His heavy, black frock coat and matching waistcoat were not suitable for the heat of West Texas, but would be more at home in some fancy New Orleans drawing room.

"Don Noble Vincente, allow me introduce myself. I'm George Nunn. I was your mother's attorney, and later your father engaged my firm to handle his legal work. I'm glad to meet you at last."

"I do not use my father's title," Noble said in a placid voice. "I am Señor, or Mr. Noble Vincente, whichever you prefer."

"Yes, er, Mr. Vincente."

"You are my mother's attorney?"

"Yes. I represented her family for many years. It was agreed long before your good mother died that the money held in trust for you and your sister would be under the guardianship of my firm."

Noble indicated a chair. "Please be seated and feel free to remove your coat. We are not so formal here at Casa del Sol. It is much too hot."

George Nunn looked grateful. Draping his coat over the back of the chair, he unbuttoned his waistcoat and loosened his tie. "Thank you. I was a bit warm," he said.

Noble went to the door and spoke hurriedly to Margretta, then moved to the desk and sat down. "My housekeeper will bring you something cool to drink. Unless, of course, you prefer something stronger."

"It's a bit early in the day for spirits, but something cool would be nice, sir. My throat's so parched it feels like I swallowed half the dust between here and town."

Noble folded his hands on the desk, hiding his impatience. "You spoke of trusts for my sister and myself. I was not aware that such trusts existed."

"Oh, yes—yes, indeed they do exist. Your sister's trust is quite substantial, and yours is a very sizable fortune, Mr. Vincente."

Noble was too stunned to respond. He was glad that Margretta had entered with refreshments, giving him time to gather his thoughts.

Mr. Nunn took several deep swallows of lemonade and nodded with satisfaction. Setting the glass back on the tray, he turned his attention back to Noble, assuming a businesslike pose. "As you know, your mother's parents, your grandparents, are both dead. They left everything to their only child, your mother."

"I'm beginning to understand."

"Your mother's trust states that you are to inherit the money on your twenty-fifth birthday. Of course with the war, we were unable to locate you. Imagine our joy when we learned you had survived and had returned to Casa del Sol."

"I was never told about any of this, Mr. Nunn. You will understand if I need a moment to grasp what you're telling me."

Mr. Nunn nodded, leaned back and folded his hands across his ample stomach. "I can well imagine this must be a shock for you."

"You spoke of my father."

"The only contact I had with Don Reinaldo Vincente was a bank draft of considerable size along with his last will and testament. His instructions for the trusts were explicit in every detail. Under no circumstances was the money to be changed into Confederate currency." Mr. Nunn smiled. "If only we had had your father's insight." He shrugged. "Ah, well, at least you and your sister will reap the benefit of his wisdom."

Noble placed his hands on the desk, lacing his fingers together. "Just how much money are we talking about here, Mr. Nunn?"

The attorney rummaged through his leather case, withdrew several papers and smiled. "I could read the will to you, if you like, or I can tell you what it contains and leave you to read it at your leisure."

"Just tell me what it says."

"Your share amounts to"—he cleared his throat—"three million, five hundred thousand dollars and some-odd cents. And, of course, you inherit Casa del Sol and all holdings, buildings and dwellings thereon. Your sister inherits her grandparents' plantation near Atlanta, Georgia, and ten thousand dollars per annum. I'm sorry to say I don't know what condition the plantation is in. I understand that most of the plantations around Atlanta were laid to ruin."

Noble stared at Mr. Nunn in stunned silence. A vision of a great manor with white columns and rolling green hills crossed his mind. He swallowed hard and swallowed again. He hadn't thought about the grand old plantation house being destroyed. He had to know that Saber was all right.

"Have you been in contact with my sister?"

"Ah, yes, sir. She is staying with"—he thumbed through several sheets of papers—"Here it is! Miss Vincente now resides with her great-aunt in Savannah, Georgia." He raised his head. "Your father wanted us to know where to locate your sister in the event that—that—"

"In the event I died in the war?"

Mr. Nunn nodded grimly. "You're a wealthy

man, Mr. Vincente. You and your sister should have no worries about finances. I might add that your father left your sister in your guardianship until she is of age, or is married."

Noble felt the warmth and comfort of his parents reaching out to him and his sister from beyond the grave. Moments ago he had felt alone and in the depths of despair. Now he could take care of his vaqueros and their families. He could buy cattle and horses. Casa del Sol would come back to life.

He realized that Mr. Nunn had spoken and he had not heard him. "I beg your pardon, what did you say, Mr. Nunn?"

"I asked if you would like me to deposit a bank draft for you in a local bank?"

"No. I'll want you to transfer some of the funds to a Fort Worth bank. But the greater amount will remain in New Orleans. If my mother and father trusted you, then I shall do likewise."

Mr. Nunn looked pleased. "I took the liberty of bringing five thousand in cash, knowing you might need it."

Noble smiled. "It seems that you thought of everything."

"We try, Mr. Vincente. If you allow us to continue to handle your affairs, we will serve you as faithfully as we did your parents."

Noble stood and walked to George Nunn and held out his hand. "I will use your firm and no other."

George Nunn stood quickly, shaking Noble's hand vigorously. "I'll have the proper papers drawn up for you to sign before I leave. It has been a pleasure doing business with your family. And I look forward to our further association."

"My sister and I are in your debt," Noble said. "Thank you for coming all the way to Texas, Mr. Nunn. I hope you weren't inconvenienced."

The older man smiled. "Not at all. Not at all. You and your sister are my firm's most important clients, and I wanted to meet you in person." He dabbed at the beads of sweat on his forehead. "I always wanted to see Texas, but no one warned me it was so hot."

"It's the drought. You must visit us when nature isn't so selfish with its bounty." Noble liked George Nunn. He seemed to be a man of great loyalty, and Noble trusted him. "Has Texas met with your expectations?"

"Oh, yes, and much more. Would you mind if I just look around a bit?"

"Please go where you will. You are my guest, and you are welcome to remain at Casa del Sol with us as long as you wish."

Regret showed in the attorney's eyes. "I will take advantage of your hospitality for the night, if you don't mind. But unfortunately, I must return to New Orleans tomorrow." He looked around the library. "Magnificent."

"It once was," Noble told him.

"It will be again, my boy." Mr. Nunn's eyes

rounded in horror at his error in etiquette. "You will accomplish it, Mr. Vincente."

Noble gazed out the window, where he could see one of the vaqueros hammering a loose board to the barn door. There would be no more trying to hold rotten wood together with rusted nails. Not after today.

Like the legendary phoenix of myth that rose out of the ashes, Casa del Sol would rise out of the ashes to reclaim its place.

Chapter Twelve

Although it was early morning, the grueling heat had already tightened its grip on the land. Noble pushed the stable doors open to circulate the stagnant air. The horses didn't seem to suffer from the heat as did humans, he thought. He gripped the curry brush and with wide, even sweeps ran it across the haunches of his mahogany gelding.

Since Mr. Nunn's visit last week, Casa del Sol had become a beehive of reconstruction. His men no longer had to act as laborers, because carpenters and stonemasons had been hired to make repairs. A new coat of paint gleamed on the barn. The corrals no longer sagged, and Noble had personally hung the new sign over the entrance to the ranch.

He moved past his gelding to the next stall to groom a three-year-old mare that would be perfect for Saber when she returned. The brush ran the length of the horse's back. Noble was so absorbed in his task that he didn't realize he was no longer alone.

"Hello, Noble."

He knew that voice well, and he knew it meant trouble for him. Laying the curry brush aside, he turned slowly to face his visitor. She hadn't changed much. Perhaps she was a little more polished in her appearance and manner, but the face was the same. She was still slender and beautiful. He caught a whiff of her perfume and it was almost overpowering, like a garden full of roses on a hot day. Rachel had smelled fresh and clean, like a spring morning. He wondered how two sisters could be so different.

"Hello, Delia, or should I say Mrs. Chandler?"

"You can still call me Delia," she said, tightly clutching the blue parasol that matched her gown. "We never stood on formalities, did we, Noble?"

His dark eyes probed hers. "I somehow never thought I'd see you at Casa del Sol." He went back to grooming the mare. "You will forgive me if I work while we talk."

"You haven't changed much," she said, moving closer to him.

He glanced up. "You have."

"A gentleman would never point out a lady's flaws."

"The change is for the better," he said woodenly. "You shook off the dust of the ranch and took on the refinement of a town dweller."

Her vivid blue eyes wavered and she concentrated on the brush strokes he applied to the horse, wishing he were touching her. "I'd heard that my sister was here, but Alejandro tells me she was well enough to go home."

"Yes. I expected you to come earlier, when your sister needed you."

She blinked her eyes and watched his hands as they glided over the mare. "I would have, but I was detained."

There was anger in his voice. "I see."

"No, you don't," she said wistfully. "But it doesn't matter."

Noble tossed the brush into a wooden bucket and turned his full attention to her. "Your sister left yesterday, Delia."

She stepped closer, her eyes devouring him. He was still the most beautiful man she'd ever seen. His features were perfect, his body hard and lean, his legs long, his shoulders wide—he was perfect. Danger emanated from him, and that was more intriguing than anything else about him. When he gazed into her eyes, as he was doing now, she wanted to melt against him.

"What can I do for you, Delia?" he asked coldly.

"Is that all the greeting I'm to expect, Noble?"

His eyes darkened intensely. "What do you want from me?"

"I want nothing from you. I . . . just wanted to say that I'm . . . sorry."

"You've said it before." His voice was devoid of feeling. All pretense of politeness had been stripped away. "Now you may leave."

Delia reached out to him and then let her hand fall away. "Will you ever forgive me, Noble?"

His gaze swept over her as if he didn't really see her. "I forgave you a long time ago, Delia. I wonder if you will ever forgive yourself?"

She was overwhelmed by shame, yet she could not look away from his searching gaze. "I don't know if I can, Noble. So much has happened between our two families. Will anything ever be good again?"

"Don't look back, Delia." He breathed deeply and his voice grew a little kinder. "You are married now, and I understand you could one day be the first lady of Texas. That's something to anticipate."

She touched his hand; he did not pull away but waited for her to speak.

"How is Rachel, really?"

"She will still need more time to heal, I think. But she's strong in will and resolve. It'll take more than a mere bullet to discourage Green Eyes."

"You . . . admire her, don't you?"

"Yes."

Delia opened her parasol and spun it around to give her something to do with her hands. "Do you know who shot her or why?"

"I believe whoever shot Rachel was aiming at me and shot her by mistake."

Delia frowned. "You were with her when she was shot. I didn't know that. What happened?"

"Why don't you ask her yourself? Now, if you'll excuse me, I have work to do."

He stepped around her and walked away, leaving her to stare after him. She ached deep inside from wanting him, but she knew in her heart that if he were not a gentleman he'd have thrown her off his ranch. She had felt his coldness and it had chilled her to the bone.

On arriving at the Broken Spur, Delia immediately directed one of the cowhands to take her trunk upstairs. Then she removed her bonnet and patted her flattened curls into place. She didn't hear Winna Mae when the woman came up behind her.

"So you are here."

Delia jumped and turned to the housekeeper, trembling. "The Indian in you allows you to sneak up behind people when they don't expect it. I would appreciate it if you would announce yourself before scaring me out of my wits." Her gaze went to the scarred, work-worn hands of the housekeeper, and she recoiled. "I don't appreciate your skulking around corners."

Winna Mae's expression remained calm. "Will you be staying long this time?"

Delia and the housekeeper had been adversaries

from the beginning, at least as far as Delia was concerned. To her way of thinking Winna Mae had ingratiated herself into the family, and ran the household as if it belonged to her. "It depends on how long my sister needs me," Delia said haughtily. "I was afraid of what I would find when I got here."

"She's mending well." Winna Mae nodded toward the stairs. "She's resting."

Delia moved to the banister and Winna Mae stepped in front of her, blocking the way. "Let her rest for now. She's tired after the trip home from Casa del Sol."

Delia pushed past her. "You see to your duties and I'll tend to my sister."

"If you care about her health, you will let her rest a bit."

Delia sighed, knowing the woman was probably right. "I'll just go to my room and put on something cooler—unless, of course, you object."

Winna Mae stepped aside, and without a word disappeared through the door as quietly as she'd appeared.

Delia ground her teeth. She couldn't understand why Rachel permitted that woman to stay on at the ranch. If it had been up to her, Winna Mae would have been dismissed long ago.

Once in her own room, Delia removed her dusty clothing and dressed in a cool, flowered chintz gown. She tied her hair away from her face and lay down upon the bed, thinking about her meeting with Noble. Whit had told her that Noble had lost everything except Casa del Sol. The hacienda hadn't appeared run-down to her. If Whit had his way, he'd own Casa del Sol and the Broken Spur. Then he would control the whole western tributary of the Brazos River.

The thought of Noble losing Casa del Sol made her terribly sad. She didn't want to take anything more away from Noble; she'd already taken too much.

At that moment Delia heard Rachel's voice. She moved off the bed and left the room. The minute Delia saw her sister, she realized there was something different about her. Rachel reclined against her pillow, her red-gold hair falling in ringlets about her face. Her skin, usually tanned from being in the sun, was now pale, and there was a wistfulness reflected in her eyes. Delia thought her stunningly beautiful.

Rachel smiled with genuine fondness. "Delia, how wonderful of you to come."

Pleasure filled Delia. It occurred to her for the first time that Rachel really did love her.

"I came as soon as I could." She touched Rachel's face and was satisfied that she had no fever. "How are you?"

A small smile tilted Rachel's mouth and she shrugged, then grimaced in pain. "I'm better now that you're here. I detest being confined to this room, but the doctor says I can't get up for another week. You can entertain me."

"Poker?"

Rachel nodded. "Make it five-card stud." She took Delia's hand. "It'll be just like old times. You being the bossy big sister, me the meek little sister."

They both laughed at that. Neither of them would ever consider Rachel meek.

"Rachel, you were born knowing what you wanted and reaching out for it with both hands, while I stumbled around and still never found what I wanted."

Rachel's eyes seemed to cloud. "I don't know what I want anymore, Delia."

"I went to Casa del Sol before I came here."

"Did you speak to Noble?"

Delia nodded. "I understand he was with you when you were shot."

"Did he tell you what happened?"

"No. He said to ask you."

Rachel was quiet for a moment as she decided how to answer her sister. "There are only three people who know what happened that day. Me, of course, Noble, and whoever shot me. Noble is too much of a gentleman to speak of it, and I won't talk about it. The man who shot me can't come forward because he'd give himself away."

"Have you told the sheriff?"

"No."

"You should so he can be looking for the man," Delia exclaimed. "The man who shot you ought to be brought to justice."

"I know. But we may never know who did it."

Delia looked into Rachel's eyes and saw more than her sister imagined. "Noble thinks you were shot by mistake. He believes the bullet was meant for him."

"Do you remember, Papa always said that those who stood too near a Vincente got swept away in a storm? It was very perceptive of him, don't you think?"

Delia saw a flush rise to Rachel's cheeks and she knew her sister had been captured by the Vincente charm. She could only imagine the battle that raged inside Rachel at that moment. "Just how near were you to Noble when you were shot?"

Rachel turned her face to the pillow, and Delia could hardly hear her murmured reply. "Too close. I was standing too close."

Chapter Thirteen

"Delia, will you stop fussing over me!" Rachel said with impassioned annoyance, feeling smothered by her sister's constant care. She much preferred Delia when she was trying to wrestle the Broken Spur from her, than with this new motherly demeanor that was driving Rachel to distraction. Her nerves were raw and she had a lot of thinking to do—most of it involved Noble, and she couldn't do it with her sister's continuous coddling.

Rachel hurried upstairs with Delia right behind her. She spun at her bedroom door. "Go home and pester Whit! I'm healed. The wound doesn't even hurt anymore." To demonstrate her point, Rachel flexed her arm and made a wide circle with her shoulder, swinging her arm back and forth. "Go back to Austin. Winna Mae will look after me."

Delia seemed undaunted by Rachel's outburst. "I have no intention of leaving you until Dr. Stanhope tells me that you are completely well." Delia moved about the room, straightening a picture, shaking the curtain until it fell in even folds, arranging Rachel's dressing table for the second time that day.

"Please, Delia, leave me to myself. I'm well enough to ride a horse. I even roped a maverick without difficulty or pain yesterday. I don't need your mothering."

Delia tightened the covers on Rachel's bed and was in the process of fluffing the pillows when Rachel gave her a warning glance.

"I just never knew how much you meant to me until I thought I might lose you," she said with some affront. "We only have each other."

Rachel's heart softened. Her arms flew around her sister and they hugged each other for a long moment, their closeness conveying more than words ever could.

At last Rachel laughed and stepped away. "I really do appreciate your taking care of me. But I really am well now. You can go home. Whit must miss you terribly."

Delia twisted her wedding band around her finger in a nervous gesture. "I haven't told you." She shrugged as if she didn't understand it herself. "I got a letter from Whit this morning. He'll be here tomorrow."

Rachel rolled her eyes upward, not at all happy that Whit was coming to Broken Spur. "Lord, just think about it—our loving little family united under one roof."

"You don't like Whit, do you?" Delia asked in a strained voice. "You never ask about him or invite him to come here."

Rachel fell silent as she pondered her sister's words. She'd never thought of Whit one way or the other. He'd been poor as a boy and had managed to better himself. His friends were now the most elite of Texas society. She had always felt uneasy in his company, although if asked, she could not have said why. She supposed he was good to her sister, and that was what really mattered. "I don't dislike Whit," she said at last, sidestepping Delia's question. "But you said yourself that you don't love him, Delia."

"You think he should have fought in the war, don't you?" Delia looked as if she might cry, and Delia never cried. "You believe he's a coward, don't you?"

In that moment, Rachel knew that her sister was stating her own feelings about Whit. "Every man had to do what was right for him, Delia."

"But most of the men we knew fought in the war."

"And most of them didn't come home," Rachel reminded her.

Something wasn't right about Delia, but Rachel didn't know what it might be. She decided to skip to another topic. "If Whit's coming here because he thinks he can talk me into selling the ranch, he might as well save himself the bother. I haven't changed my mind, and I never will."

"He said in his letter that he wants to attend the Harvest Dance and mingle with the people." Delia appeared diverted for the moment as she moved purposefully to Rachel's wardrobe and looked over her sister's few gowns. She wrinkled her nose in distaste. "You'll need a stunning creation for the dance. None of these will do. When is the last time you bought a new wardrobe? For that matter, when's the last time you had a new gown?"

"Forget that," Rachel said, bringing the conversation back to her brother-in-law. "Why is Whit attending the dance? He never cared about our little get-togethers before."

"Silly little sister. Whit is coming as a future candidate courting votes." Delia ran her hand down the skirt of one of Rachel's faded calico gowns. "No, none of these will do for the future governor's sister-in-law."

Rachel closed the wardrobe and walked toward the door. "It might interest you to know that I ordered material for my gown months ago. I'm going into town today to visit the dressmaker. I can assure you that neither you nor Whit will be ashamed of my appearance on the night of the dance."

"I'll go into town with you." Delia moved to the door. "You shouldn't go alone."

"No need. Zeb will drive me in the wagon."

To Rachel's surprise, Delia didn't insist on going to Tascosa Springs with her. Her sister probably realized she had nothing in common with the people there.

"Choose a flattering pattern, Rachel. You do have such a dreary notion about fashion."

Rachel picked up her hat and set it squarely on her red-gold head. "Wait until you see my gown."

She hurried down the stairs and out the front door, fearing Delia would change her mind and decide to come with her.

She was free!

Tascosa Springs

Two sullen-faced men stood outside the Crystal Palace Saloon, watching Noble ride into town. The half doors of the saloon swung open, and a third man joined them.

"Look there. It's Noble Vincente," Deputy Harvey Briscal said, crossing the street to stand beside the others. "The bastard comes riding in here big as daylight, thinking we're just dirt beneath his polished boots."

One of the men who'd been drinking all morning raised his voice so it carried to Noble. "He oughta be run out of town. Killing's too good for him."

Noble gave no indication he'd heard the man, but rode toward the bank and halted his mount.

"Someone needs to tell Noble Vincente he ain't welcome in this town," Harvey said, stirring insurrection among his companions. He'd never take Noble Vincente on by himself.

"You could arrest him," Bob Foster suggested. "Just walk up to him and take him in."

"Nope. The sheriff won't let me," the deputy stated, his lips twisting into a snarl. "Noble Vincente's too powerful to touch. He just goes about like he never killed nobody."

Red Berner, a drifter who'd been hanging around town for a few weeks, downed his whiskey and turned blurry eyes on Noble. His hand rested on the handle of his gun. "Are you sure that's Noble Vincente?"

" 'Course I'm sure," Harvey replied sourly.

Red Berner was a huge man, barrel-chested, with a rough-hewn face. His gray eyes were close-set and bloodshot. His broad shoulders rolled with muscles, making it apparent that he could handle himself in any situation. He looked mean as hell.

Harvey decided this just might be the man to best Noble in a fight. "You act like you've been waiting for Noble Vincente. Do you know him, stranger?"

"I don't know him, but I heard of him," Red stated, hitching up his gun belt. "Nothing good, though." Red's small eyes narrowed. "If'n anyone was of a mind to stand me a round of drinks," he offered with a sneer, "I might rid you of Señor Vincente."

Harvey glanced across the street to see if Sheriff Crenshaw was watching. The sheriff had ridden out to one of the ranches that morning and apparently hadn't yet returned. Harvey's gaze dropped to Red's hairy hands, which looked as though they could crush the life out of a man with very little effort. He noticed the man's six-gun and counted six notches on the scuffed handle.

"What's your name?" Harvey asked.

"Are you asking as a lawman, or friendly-like?"

"Hell, don't let my badge bother you. I can see that you don't like Noble any more than I do. That makes us on the same side."

"Name's Red."

"Red what?"

"Just Red."

"Well, Red, I reckon I could buy you a whole bottle if you was to rough Mr. Vincente up a bit."

With an ominous laugh, Red Berner swooped down the steps, paused at a horse and removed a rope from the saddle horn. "Set the bottle on the bar, Deputy. I'll be back to collect it."

Noble was in the process of dismounting and still had his boot hooked in the stirrup when a rope loop fell over his head with deadly accuracy. Giving him no time to react, Red yanked on the rope, tightening the noose about Noble's neck. With a hefty yank he pulled Noble to the ground.

"Who in the hell do you think you are?" Noble said through clenched teeth, scrambling to his feet with lithe quickness. He swung around and landed a fist in his assailant's stomach and watched the man double over in pain.

In a tight voice Red called out, "He's stronger than I thought! Help me with him—or are you all yellow-livered cowards? He can't take us all."

Harvey Briscal and Bob Foster needed no further encouragement. The two men circled Noble, and Bob pulled his gun while Harvey grabbed for a shovel that was leaning against a wall, and sneaked up behind Noble.

By now, a crowd had gathered, providing the attackers with a false sense of courage. The three men worked as a team now, each circling so two of them were always behind Noble. Harvey drew the shovel back and struck Noble hard across the back, and Noble crumpled to his knees. Bob hit him with the handle of his gun, while Red yanked tighter on the rope.

Noble tried to shake off the pain, but he saw the ground come up to meet him. He fought against the blackness that threatened to overtake him.

Red grinned and moved in quickly. He was swinging his end of the rope and wielding it as if it were a whip. He struck Noble's cheek, carving a deep gash. He struck again and again, cutting into Noble's white shirt until it was red with blood.

Noble tried to rise, but the corded rope tightened around his neck and he fell to his knees gasping for breath. Harvey kicked Noble in the ribs while Bob kicked him in the stomach. Smelling the fresh blood of a kill, Red slashed at Noble's back over and over. Then, with a wolfish look, Harvey retrieved the shovel and slammed it hard across Noble's shoulders.

Suddenly Bob and Harvey backed off, their eyes fearful, when Noble rolled to his feet and wound the rope about his hand, jerking the redheaded man forward.

Red's gaze shifted to Noble Vincente, and he cringed inside—he saw a vision of his own death in the Spaniard's cold, brown eyes. His bravery shattered, he looked at Bob and the deputy for help. Their frightened expressions attested to the fact that they were having similar visions.

Red leaped quickly on his horse, wrapped his end of the rope around the saddle horn and nudged the animal forward—first at a walk, then at a gallop, jerking Noble forward and dragging him through the dusty street.

Noble grabbed the rope, clawing at it, trying to keep from being choked to death.

The crowd was strangely quiet now. Even Bob had backed away, trying to distance himself from Harvey and Red. No one had ever dared treat a Vincente in such a way. Mothers shielded their children's eyes from the cruel spectacle, and some of the men watched the cowardly act with disgust.

But no one came to Noble's defense. Noble tried

to work his fingers between the rope and his neck, but Red urged the horse onward. "You aren't such a big man now, Mr. Vincente, are you?" Red taunted.

Noble felt blackness closing in on him and pain shot through his body like knife wounds. He didn't know who the hell this man was, but he suspected he might be a hired gun. In his pain-dazed state he wondered if this might be the man who'd shot Rachel.

Red whipped his horse into a full run, tightening the rope so it cut into Noble's flesh and he couldn't breathe. Still, no one stepped forward to help him.

Chapter Fourteen

Suddenly a gunshot rang out and a woman stepped into the street, courageously placing herself in front of the charging horse. The animal reared on its hind legs and she aimed her rifle at the rider.

"Rein in your horse, mister, if you want to see another sunset."

Red gawked at the woman and made a quick decision. Her rifle was aimed right at his heart. Even a woman couldn't miss at this close range. He controlled his horse as he spoke to her. "Lady, if you'll just step aside and let me get on with this, I'll buy you a drink afterward and we can get to know each other, kinda friendly-like."

"Get off the horse and release Mr. Vincente—

now!" Rachel said quietly, drawing on the rage buried deep inside her. "I don't waste my time on cowards like you."

"Out of my way, little gal," he ordered. "Or I'll swat you aside like a pesky fly."

Rachel cocked her rifle and said in a soft voice, "Mister, I don't know who you are, and you don't know me, but you can take this for the gospel truth—I never aim at anything I can't hit, and you're too big a target to miss."

Red threw back his head and laughed. "Tell me, should I be afraid of a little lady wearing a man's britches and carrying a man's gun?"

"You tell me, mister—did you know when you got up this morning that you were going to die today?"

At that moment fear crept up Red's spine, and he lost some of his swagger when he looked into those determined green eyes. "What do you care if this man gets what's coming to him?"

Rachel followed the stranger's gaze as he looked at his two cohorts for assistance. "Let's just say," Rachel told him coldly, "that I don't like the odds." Her gaze fastened on the deputy, who'd struck Noble from behind with the shovel, and then she turned her attention to Bob. "Tell this man that I'll not hesitate to shoot if he doesn't do what I say. I don't think he believes me—maybe he'll believe you."

"You'd better do as she says, Red," Bob Foster

warned him. "Let Vincente go or she'll shoot you deader than dirt."

With a surly expression, Red dismounted and retrieved the rope from around Noble's neck with a savage yank. "This man'll not soon forget that he tangled with me."

In a protective gesture, Rachel stepped across Noble so she straddled his body. "You'd better hope he does forget. I'd sleep with one eye open from now on if I were you. Noble will come after you. Perhaps not today or even tomorrow, but he'll come, you can be sure of that."

Red took several stumbling steps backward. "I ain't afraid of him or no other man."

Rachel bent down to Noble, her rifle aimed all the while at the stranger. "If you're smart—which I doubt you are—you won't let the sun set on you in Tascosa Springs. If you hang around, you'll be a dead man."

Red dropped the rope and took a few more steps backward. "Let him come. I'll not run from the likes of him."

Rachel looked into the stranger's eyes and saw fear. She knew he'd be gone from Tascosa Springs long before sundown. "Someone go for the doctor," she called out, sitting down and placing Noble's head on her lap. He was a bloody mess. She couldn't tell how badly he was hurt, but he must be bad, or he wouldn't still be lying on the ground.

Noble opened his eyes and managed a smile that turned to a grimace of pain. "Forgive me if

I don't get up." He bit his lower lip when she dabbed at his bloody face with her neckerchief. "But then . . . I like it just fine where I am."

"Your face is dirty," she said, brushing dust from his cheek.

He tried to rise and she pushed him down. "Lie still," she commanded. "Or must I use my gun on you?"

"You no doubt enjoyed my humiliation today, Rachel." He groaned when he tried to shift his position. "Did you?"

"I don't like rogue animals that run in packs to find their courage. And I take no pleasure in anyone's humiliation, not even yours." She glanced around her, raising her voice so the gathering crowd could hear. "Not one of you cowards would have taken Noble Vincente if he'd been facing you. You had to catch him from behind."

Noble tried again to rise but Rachel held him down. He smiled wanly and said, "I didn't know you held me in such high regard."

Rachel glared down at him. "I don't. Let's just say we're even now. After today I owe you nothing."

"No." He gritted his teeth when pain stabbed through his ribs, and it took him a moment to catch his breath. "I still owe you, Green Eyes."

She forced him back down. "What can you owe me?"

"To find out who killed your father."

"You killed him."

"You know I didn't." His expression softened. "You just can't admit you were wrong about me." He managed a smile. "You can't admit you like me."

He had come too close to the truth. Her voice was almost gentle as she touched his cheek. "Let's just say I'll miss hating you. You made such a worthy adversary."

He burrowed deeper into her lap with a devilish grin on his bloody face. "How long do I get to stay like this?"

She took a deep, aggravated breath, upset by her growing concern for Noble. "Just lie still and be quiet until help comes."

Dr. Stanhope appeared at that moment. He bent down to Noble and tested him for broken bones. When he determined there were none, he called on several men to help him get Noble to his office.

Noble insisted that he could walk, but his first step convinced him otherwise, and he leaned heavily on the doctor for support.

Rachel watched three men assist Noble; then she walked away without a backward glance. She suddenly heard the sound of a galloping horse and dodged out of the way just in time to keep from being run down by Red Berner's horse. The stranger was riding out of town as if the devil himself were pursuing him.

Sheriff Crenshaw had just returned to Tascosa Springs. When he heard what had happened, he grabbed Harvey and spun him around. "I'll take your badge and your gun."

"Why? If it'd been anyone but that Spanish bastard, you wouldn't have cared."

"Your badge."

Harvey dropped the badge in the dirt and ground it beneath his heel. "To hell with you and to hell with this town."

"So long, Harvey."

"You'll all hear from me again, Sheriff." His gaze went to Noble, who was being assisted up the stairs to the doctor's office. "It's his fault. Him with his arrogant ways, thinks he can walk on the rest of us like we was nothing."

The sheriff squinted at the afternoon sunlight, and without looking down said, "You are nothing, Harvey. I don't squander my time on cur dogs, cowards or fools, and you're all three."

Harvey stalked away, hatred burning strong within his heart. He glanced at Rachel, who was just entering the mercantile. That woman was the cause of his public humiliation—the root of his trouble—and she'd pay. Sooner or later, she'd pay.

Dr. Stanhope's office was small but efficient. Bottles, jars, bandages and scissors cluttered the shelves that lined the walls. Noble was aided onto a table.

Dr. Stanhope examined Noble's head. "You've got quite a bump here. It'll pain you for a few days."

Sheriff Crenshaw ambled in and glanced at the wound on Noble's head. "Someone said you were hit with a shovel. Bet it hurts like hell."

"Where have you been?" Noble asked in an ir-ritated voice. "I've tried to see you several times, but you're always out of town." Noble leaned back against the wall, suddenly feeling weak. His whole body ached and throbbed.

Ira Crenshaw shrugged. "Since the Yankees took over the running of Texas, they're been teach-ing us their brand of law."

Noble winced when the doctor applied liniment to the wound on his cheek. When he could find his voice he said, "I can well imagine. I experi-enced some of their laws at Gettysburg."

Crenshaw smiled. "I'm glad your pa didn't live to see the day three men could take his son down. Imagine, one of them armed with a shovel, one with a rope and the other—what did Bob use?" He laughed heartily while Noble scowled. "You're getting soft, Noble. Must be too much easy living."

Noble's voice was defensive. "They took me by surprise."

"Your pa wouldn't like that either. I'm told that redheaded fellow charged like a bull. Can't believe you didn't hear him coming."

"Yeah." Noble gritted his teeth against the pain. "I'm feeling embarrassed enough about that."

"Why did you want to see me?" Ira Crenshaw asked.

"I want to know what's been done about finding

Sam Rutledge's killer. Surely you've had time to find out who had a grudge against him."

Ira hooked his fingers through his gun belt, and rocked back and forth on his boots. "There are those who say you did it."

"We both know I didn't."

The sheriff became serious. "I doubt the crime will ever be solved. Too much time's gone by. And we haven't had any leads."

Dr. Stanhope turned to Ira Crenshaw. "You can have him when I'm finished. But for now, he's my patient and his wounds need attention."

"Come by the office when you've finished here, Noble. But I don't have anything to add to what I already told you." He smiled widely. "I am glad you came home. Some of us have missed you."

Without another word, the sheriff left.

Dr. Stanhope ripped Noble's shirt and examined the rope burns around his neck and across his back. "Maybe next time you ride into town you'll watch behind you."

"Next time I will."

"You should have a care, Noble. You have too many enemies."

"Are you one of them, Doctor?"

"I'm just a healer, Noble. My doctoring is for the worthy as well as the unworthy."

"Which means?"

This time Dr. Stanhope applied the stinging ointment to the cuts on Noble's back, making him grit his teeth and groan.

"You are worthy," he said, capping the ointment bottle. "Your father was my friend for many years. I consider his son my friend as well."

Dr. Stanhope probed Noble's ribs, and Noble gritted his teeth again as agonizing pain ripped across his back and through his gut. "If this is the way you treat your friends, I'd not like to be your enemy."

The older man stood back and surveyed his patient. "You've got cuts and bruises but no broken bones. You're going to hurt like hell for a few days, especially when you first get up in the morning. I could give you something for the pain."

"No, thank you. I have a bottle of good brandy at home; that's all the medicine I'll need."

Dr. Stanhope took Noble's chin and turned it toward him, smiling. "The cuts on your face aren't deep. I don't think the girls need to cry that your pretty face will be permanently scarred."

Noble took the rumpled plaid shirt the doctor offered him, since his own was in bloody shreds. "You know what really hurts most, Doc? The fact that none of my attackers needs your services."

Dr. Stanhope smiled, and then he became serious. "Today wasn't just a random occurrence. Someone wants you dead real bad. He's tried twice; he'll probably try again."

Rachel stalked up to Jess McVee, her anger still raging. "Tell me, Jess, why didn't you try to help Noble today?" She glanced over at Mrs. McVee, who was thin and birdlike, with a tight little mouth and round black eyes. "Or you, Mrs. McVee, why didn't you intervene?"

"We think Noble had it coming to him," Jess answered with feeling, although he did not meet Rachel's eyes.

"I think what you did was disgraceful, Rachel," Mary McVee said. "Imagine, getting involved in a street brawl. I declare, you are a disgrace. What would your pa have said if he could have seen you today?"

Rachel turned away from the woman and concentrated on Jess McVee. "Tell me what you know about your son's death, Mr. McVee."

"I—What?" He looked puzzled. "Why would you want to know about young Jessie?"

"Tell me what you know about how Jessie died," Rachel persisted.

Mrs. McVee chimed in. "Why would you want to bring up a subject that is still so painful to—"

Rachel held up her hand to silence the woman, while taking several quick breaths to calm herself. "Tell me, Jess, about your son's death."

His eyes clouded with sorrow and he seemed to age before her eyes. "I don't mind telling you, Rachel." His voice trembled with emotion. "We got a letter from our son's commanding officer explaining about his last hours. He told us that our son didn't die alone, that one of the officers from Madragon County stayed with him all night talking to him, and never left his side. Just kinda bringing him comfort in his last hours."

"Do you know who the man was who stayed with your son?"

"No, we never learned his name. Sure would like to meet him, though. I'd like to tell him how grateful we are for what he did for our son. I guess he probably got himself killed too. If he did, I hope he found someone to sit with him in his final hours."

"If the man who aided your son that night was in trouble and needed your help, would you help him?"

Tears streamed down Mrs. McVee's pale cheeks. "How can you ask such a thing? Of course we'd help him! We'd love him like a son. We'd like to talk to him and know our son's last thoughts."

Rachel walked to the door and turned back to Mary and Jess McVee. She wondered why she felt so little pity for them. Perhaps she was becoming too hard, or perhaps she was sickened by pious people who preached one thing but practiced another.

"Today," Rachel said, surprised by her steady voice, "you had your chance to help the man who stayed with your son in his last hours. But you stood by with everyone else and watched those cowardly dogs do their worst to him. I wonder what your son would have thought of you, Mr. McVee, Mrs. McVee, if he could speak to you. Noble Vincente was the officer who took care of your son the night he died."

Mrs. McVee's lips trembled before she clamped her hand over her mouth, little animal sounds escaping her throat. Mr. McVee's face reddened; he placed his hand over his heart and sank into a chair.

For several moments, no one spoke. The only sound was the soft gasps coming from Mrs. McVee.

Rachel was still enraged. She shoved the door open with such force that the tinkling bell could still be heard when she was halfway to the blacksmith shop.

Zeb was loading the wagon. He took one look at Rachel and grinned. "You got yourself all riled, didn't you?"

"Let's go home," she said flatly.

The old man's leathery face crinkled with worry and he scratched his white head. "I heard there was a mite of a ruckus in town this afternoon."

She swung around and glared at Zeb. "Where were you when this was happening?"

He let out a stream of tobacco juice and patted the rifle at his side. "I had me a good aim on that redheaded man. I knew you didn't need my help, but just in case . . ."

Rachel suddenly started laughing, and Zeb looked at her as if she'd lost her senses.

"God help us all," she said in a choked voice. "Papa was right. When you stand too close to a Vincente, you get swept away in the storm."

Chapter Fifteen

Sunflowers bent their heads and danced in the wind beneath the somber blue sky. The air that brushed across Rachel's face felt hot and dry. A slight stirring of the water caught her attention, and she watched a catfish bob its head up momentarily and then disappear into the shadowy depths.

She was leaning against the cottonwood tree on the bank of the Brazos, where she'd swum naked with Noble. She tried to gather her scattered thoughts. Why had she come back to this spot? What need had drawn her here?

She removed her boots, pushed her trouser legs up and dipped her feet into the river, wiggling her toes, much as she'd done as a young girl. Now she was a woman, trying to find solace for her troubled mind and her battered heart. Why couldn't she be like other women her age? Most of her friends were married with several children, while all she had was the Broken Spur. She'd worked hard since her father's death, and there had been little time for socializing. Several men had come calling on her, but she had brushed them aside with one excuse or another. The truth was, none of them had interested her.

She had always felt as if she were waiting for something or someone. Now she knew that someone was Noble, and it wasn't to put a bullet into him either. No matter what had passed between them, he had always occupied her heart. She could admit that now. But she would get over him—she had to.

Suddenly she choked back a sob, trying not to cry, but her throat burned from the effort. Noble had been so terribly alone yesterday in town. And no one had wanted to help him. She had wanted to tear the hearts out of the men who'd hurt him. Tears sprang to her eyes and ran down her cheeks. Burying her face in her hands, she cried and cried until she had no tears left.

She wiped her cheek with the back of her hand, remembering Noble's words. *You don't believe I killed your father.* All doubts had been purged from her heart. Noble had not killed her father. How could she ever have thought he had?

185

Who, then, could have killed her father, and why?

Rachel was so lost in her own wretchedness that she didn't hear a rider approach.

Noble dismounted and walked toward her. "Hello, Rachel. This is becoming my favorite place."

Then she turned in his direction and his heart contracted. She had been crying. In all the years he'd known her, he'd never seen her cry.

His voice caught in his throat and it took him a moment to speak. He knelt down beside her and looked at her with concern. "Are you hurt? Ill?"

"No. Just go away."

He stood up, knowing she was embarrassed because he had seen her weeping. He gazed across the river. "Sure is hot."

Her gaze went upward to all beautiful six feet of him. Black leather chaps fit tightly about his long legs. She saw the gauze dressing on his cheek. "How are your wounds?"

"Not so bad."

"I'm glad."

"I didn't get a chance to thank you for what you did for me yesterday, Rachel."

Her voice was strained as she tried to sound indifferent. "I'd do the same for anyone."

"Be that as it may, I'm still grateful to you."

"As I told you, that makes us even. I don't owe you anything now."

He laughed.

She didn't find anything funny.

He suddenly became solemn and glanced down at her, knowing she was troubled. So was he, if she but knew it. He couldn't get her out of his mind; the sweet, intoxicating smell of her lingered with him long after she was gone, and came to him unbidden at night when he lay awake, unable to sleep.

"We still have unfinished business between us, Rachel."

"I suppose you want me to tell you the name of the men who attacked you yesterday."

"No. I already know their names. Let's just say that I had a talk with Bob Foster. The deputy and that redheaded man had both left town."

"Cowards. That doesn't surprise me."

He said almost too casually, "I'll find them eventually."

She stood up and pushed her trouser legs down. "If I were a betting woman, I'd say you did more than talk to Bob Foster. I know all about the Vincente pride. And those men stepped on your pride, didn't they, Noble?"

He reached out and cupped her chin, turning her fully toward him. He gently touched her damp cheek and she allowed it, not knowing what else to do. "Pride is something I can ill afford these days, Rachel. This isn't the same Texas I left. I wonder if it ever will be."

"As you told me that night in your garden, nothing stays the same."

His gaze fell on her upturned face. "You remain the same. If you loved a man, I believe that you would fight for him to the very end. Would you do that, Rachel?"

She realized she'd been holding a sunflower in her hand and she'd shredded all the petals. "First I would have to find a man worthy of loyalty."

"Rachel, Rachel." Her name sounded like a caress on his lips. "Yesterday your eyes burned like green fire because you saw what you thought was an injustice and did something about it. That was your pride at work, wasn't it?" He looked at her closely. "Or was it something more?"

"It was pride. Mine. I told you yesterday that I didn't like the odds."

His gaze went across the river, and it seemed that he was a long way off. "Pride can sometimes be a good thing, Rachel. It separates the men from the animals."

"Winna Mae always says 'Pride goes before a fall.'"

"Perhaps." His strong fingers moved across her face and lingered there while his expression softened. "But you know something has happened between us, Green Eyes. You may not want to admit it, but you know it's true."

Pain stabbed through her. She silently struggled against her own heart and finally won the battle, at least for the moment. She jerked away from him and stared down at her bare feet. "Nothing happened between us."

He smothered a smile, thinking how like a little girl she seemed at the moment. Yesterday she had been a flame-haired Amazon ready to fight the whole town. "And who takes care of you, Green Eyes? Are you as alone as I am?"

His mesmerizing gaze flowed through her like a warm stream, and left her with the same giddiness that she'd felt when her father had allowed her a glass of champagne one Christmas Eve. "I can take care of myself." She looked up at him, frowning reprovingly. "I don't need anyone."

"You could let me take care of you," he said, laughing at some private jest. Then he went on to explain. "Perhaps you are right and it's the other way around. After all, it was I on the ground yesterday, and all that stood between me and hell was you and that damned rifle of yours. Maybe I need you to take care of me, even if my pride takes a beating for it."

"As far as you are concerned, Noble, it would take the whole Yankee army to take care of you. As far as I'm concerned, you still have much to answer for. What good is pride if it comes at the price of honor?"

"My honor or yours?"

"Yours."

"You are speaking of your sister." His voice sounded stilted. "Are we back to that again?"

"So it would seem," she answered in a sharp voice. "You wronged her, Noble. Don't you care that she suffered so after you went away?"

"Have you discussed this with Delia?"

"I . . . we always end up in an argument when we talk about you."

"And so, it would seem, do we. I told you before, Rachel, ask Delia about what happened between the two of us. I can tell you nothing."

She wondered if it was his damned pride again. His pride kept him from talking to the McVees about their son. His pride kept him from asking for help of any kind. Was it his pride that kept him silent about Delia? She had to know.

She wearily arched her back. "Why don't you tell me about you and my sister."

"The story isn't mine to tell—it's Delia's."

She wondered what he could mean. What was it that he wanted Delia to tell her?

Noble reached down and plucked a sunflower and pushed it gently into her hair. "Let's talk about something else, shall we?"

She removed the flower and tossed it aside, then dropped down on the grass and began to tug on her boots. "I don't have anything to say to you. I must get home."

He plucked a blade of grass, gnawed on the end, watching her closely, his mind envisioning her beautiful body as it had been that day she'd stripped off her clothing and joined him in the river. He felt his body burn with desire and pushed the feeling aside—with difficulty. Now was not the time to think about that. He smiled to himself. She'd probably shoot him if he even suggested they go for a swim.

"What were you doing in town yesterday?" he asked, trying to keep her from leaving.

"If you must know, I was picking up some material I'd ordered from the East."

"Ah, a new frock."

"Yes. It's for the fall dance."

He sat up straight. "Do they still have the Harvest Dance?"

"Of course. But why would you care about that? A Vincente would never attend a town dance. Of course, you are always invited should you choose to come. Perhaps our local dances are too common for you?" She pulled on her other boot. "Very few people of Madragon County ever received an invitation to a Vincente fiesta."

He stood and offered her his hand. She considered refusing, but decided that would make her appear childish.

"My father was from the old way of thinking, Rachel. He believed that a man should not marry or entertain out of his class. I don't even know what my class is."

"The lofty class," she said archly.

Noble drew her up beside him and gazed at the light sprinkle of freckles across the bridge of her pert little nose. He didn't know why most women cherished white skin. Rachel was enchanting with freckles. He wanted to crush her in his arms and kiss every one of them.

"So," he said at last. "You'll go to the dance and break every man's heart." His grip tightened on her hand. "I never asked. Is there any special man in your life?"

She twisted her hand away from his grip. "That is none of your affair," she answered shakily.

He laughed and walked to his horse. Thrusting his boot into the stirrup, he mounted. "By the way, you wouldn't happen to know why Mr. and Mrs. McVee showed up at my house today, oozing human kindness? Mrs. McVee brought pies and cakes and enough jams and jellies for me to open my own store."

"Why should I know anything about that?"

"I seem to recall spilling my guts to you about their son's death."

She fastened her gaze on the tip of his black boot. "If they decided to like you, Noble, then they are probably misguided in their judgment and will come to their senses sooner or later."

"Rachel, you are the most baffling female I've ever come up against. When taking your measure, I've had to ignore the rules I use to understand other women. You're like quicksilver that can't be held or contained. You are totally unpredictable."

"And I'm sure there have been many women tramping through your life."

With a quick smile he touched the brim of his hat and nudged his horse in the flanks. "Until next time, Green Eyes."

As soon as he was out of sight, she retrieved the

Thrill to the most sensual, adventure-filled Historical Romances on the market today...

FROM  LEISURE BOOKS

As a home subscriber to the Leisure Historical Romance Book Club, you'll enjoy the best in today's BRAND-NEW Historical Romance fiction. For over twenty-five years, Leisure Books has brought you the award-winning, high-quality authors you know and love to read. Each Leisure Historical Romance will sweep you away to a world of high adventure...and intimate romance. Discover for yourself all the passion and excitement millions of readers thrill to each and every month.

SAVE AT LEAST $5.00 EACH TIME YOU BUY!

Each month, the Leisure Historical Romance Book Club brings you four brand-new titles from Leisure Books, America's foremost publisher of Historical Romances. EACH PACKAGE WILL SAVE YOU AT LEAST $5.00 FROM THE BOOKSTORE PRICE! And you'll never miss a new title with our convenient home delivery service.

Here's how we do it. Each package will carry a 10-DAY EXAMINATION privilege. At the end of that time, if you decide to keep your books, simply pay the low invoice price of $16.96 ($19.98 CANADA), no shipping or handling charges added.* HOME DELIVERY IS ALWAYS FREE.* With today's top Historical Romance novels selling for $5.99 and higher, our price SAVES YOU AT LEAST $5.00 with each shipment.

AND YOUR FIRST FOUR-BOOK SHIPMENT IS TOTALLY FREE!*

IT'S A BARGAIN YOU CAN'T BEAT! A Super $21.96 Value!

LEISURE BOOKS A Division of Dorchester Publishing Co., Inc.

GET YOUR 4 FREE* BOOKS NOW—
A $21.96 VALUE!

Mail the Free* Books
Certificate
Today!

Get Four Books Totally
F R E E* —
A $21.96 Value!

(Tear Here and Mail Your FREE* Book Card Today!)

PLEASE RUSH
MY FOUR FREE*
BOOKS TO ME
RIGHT AWAY!

Leisure Historical Romance Book Club
P.O. Box 6613
Edison, NJ 08818-6613

sunflower he'd put in her hair and held it to her heart. Why had he come back to Texas? If only he'd stayed away, she could have spent the rest of her life hating him.

No, she had never hated him; she knew that now.

Chapter Sixteen

The leather saddle creaked when Rachel shifted her weight. She nodded her head as she counted each maverick that was driven into the corral to be branded. Stray cattle had no brand and belonged to the ranch that put its brand on them. In years past there had been many head roaming the open range; now there were so few.

Zeb was beside Rachel, absently helping her count. His expression told her what she already knew. "Not many, Miss Rachel."

"Zeb, with Texas under the confining boot of military law, and taxes being high, cattle are the one thing that can save or ruin a ranch. In the East, the price of beef is at a premium."

"Yep. The trick, Miss Rachel, is to get the cattle

to a railhead to ship them to the East. We don't have enough cattle to make it worth our while."

"I know."

"Maybe next year," he said encouragingly.

She fit her booted feet snugly into the stirrups. "I counted twenty-two, Zeb." She nodded for him to close the gate. "Not a bad roundup for this time of year."

The old cowboy removed his hat and scratched his head. "I 'spect we found these 'cause it's so dry and they keep coming to the river to water."

Rachel leaned forward in the saddle and watched her foreman, Tanner Gibbons, throw a rope over one of the mavericks while another man wrestled it to the ground and a third applied a red-hot branding iron in the shape of a spur. The familiar smell of burning hide assaulted Rachel's nostrils. With the Broken Spur brand on their rumps, the cattle belonged to her.

Tanner was tall and slender with light brown hair and honest gray eyes. He was born to the saddle and was a damned good foreman. He'd lived his life on the Broken Spur and had risen from cowhand to foreman. He climbed the fence and watched with his lady boss.

"I thought I'd move them to the north pasture. There's some grass there, and it's near enough to the river." He raised his head and looked at the cloudless sky. "If it doesn't rain soon, we'll probably lose most of the herd."

Rachel shaded her eyes with a gloved hand. "I

know. We've got the Yankees, the drought and the weather to contend with. I don't know which is worse." She smiled down at Tanner. "Probably the Yankees. I expect to hear any day now that they're building a fort at Tascosa Springs."

Tanner could hardly speak when Rachel looked at him with those beautiful green eyes. Everyone on the ranch, except her, knew that he was in love with her. He wanted to tell her how he felt, but he knew he wasn't good enough for someone like her. She was quality, and he saw himself as just a broken-down old cowboy. He had never admired a woman as much as he did his lady boss. She could ride neck and neck with any man, rope with the best of them, and never complain when she had to ride for hours in the rain. She was from prime Texas stock. Her pa had brought her up as he would have a son, and that was all right with Tanner, because underneath that toughness was a surefire woman, so beautiful it almost hurt his eyes to look at her.

He settled deeper into his saddle. Rachel could have any man she wanted. And he could never tell her about his feelings for her. He took his courage in hand and asked, "You going to the dance, Miss Rachel?" He nervously rotated his hat in his hands. He wished his voice wouldn't always tremble when he spoke to her about personal matters.

"Of course. Isn't everyone?" She nodded toward the house. "Even my brother-in-law arrived today from Austin to attend the event." She arched an eyebrow. "Let's hope he doesn't go into one of his speeches at the dance."

Tanner nodded. "He's probably going to be the governor one day. That is if the damned Yankees—" His face reddened and he sought her eyes. "Sorry, ma'am, if I spoke out of turn. What I meant to say was, if the Yankees in Washington ever give us back the vote."

She looked upward and watched buzzards circling toward the east. Probably another calf down, she thought. They had lost so many. She turned her attention back to her foreman. "If we are allowed the vote again, you can be sure my brother-in-law will get his share of votes—he'll see to that."

"Miss Rachel—ma'am." He tried to smile but his lips quivered and his face reddened.

"Yes, Tanner?"

When he could breathe, he asked, "Would you . . . er . . . could I . . . ?"

She smiled. "I'll be sure and save a dance for you, Tanner."

"You will, ma'am?" he asked incredulously, pleasure spreading across every angle of his face.

Whit looked out the window at the scenes of a working ranch. He could hear the lowing of cattle and the cowboys' voices as they went about their day-to-day chores. The Broken Spur was not a big ranch, but it was important because it backed up to the Brazos River. That made it important to Whit because it bordered Casa del Sol, the king of

197

all Texas ranches. In the past, that great ranch had been responsible for bringing prosperity to Tascosa Springs. The stores had thrived selling supplies to the ranch. The bank had handled all Casa del Sol's transactions, and the Vincentes had hired hundreds of men to work the spread. He longed to stand in Noble Vincente's boots, rather than standing in his shadow. Every time he looked at Delia, he was reminded that Noble had been with her before him, and he hated him for it.

"Whit." Delia twined a golden strand of hair about her head and secured it with a jeweled comb. "What are you staring at?"

"A ranch that is run by a woman and thrives where others have failed. She can't win, though. She'll be in trouble before next spring."

"What do you mean?"

"The taxes." His eyes narrowed and he turned back to the window to watch Rachel walk toward the house. He could clearly see the way her shirt stretched tight across her breasts and the way the leather chaps didn't quite hide her soft curves. "Even with her frantic effort to round up stray longhorns and mavericks, Rachel will never raise enough money to pay the taxes on the Broken Spur."

Delia looked perplexed. "For heaven's sake, Whit, don't bring up the subject of selling the ranch to Rachel tonight. She'll be mad all evening if you do."

Whit moved away from the window and stood

behind his wife. His voice was laced with sarcasm as he watched her artfully apply the merest bit of rouge to her cheeks. "The time-honored Harvest Dance. What a fine evening we'll have, conferring with old friends. What witty conversations we'll have with them. How will I endure it?"

Delia grew annoyed. "Sometimes I think you forget where you come from, Whit. You grew up in West Texas, your father worked as line foreman at the Bar C, where you were born. These are your people. You just forget it when you are in Austin trying to impress your la-di-da friends there."

Whit had pulled himself out of the mire he'd been born into. He had a fine house in Austin, a beautiful wife, and friends of influence. No, he did not like to be reminded that his father had been a lowly cowhand. Of course, it sometimes worked to his advantage when he was garnering votes from ranchers to remind them that he had once been part of their world. He had the happy ability to slip in and out of character to fit the situation or the people he was with at the time.

His voice was silky smooth and layered with contempt. "My people are *all* the citizens of Texas," he said, settling his hands on her shoulders and looking at her in the mirror. "They love me, don't you know?"

She held his gaze. "Do you love anyone or anything?"

His hands slipped down to cup her full breasts. "I desire you, and that's much more powerful than love." He bent to kiss her neck, then pulled her up to fit her petticoat-clad body against his. "I chose well when I took you for my wife, Delia." A cruel light came into his eyes. "Yet your little sister is turning out to be the real beauty of the family."

Delia pushed him away. "You'll muss my hair."

His voice became taunting when he said, "You don't like it when I talk about your sister, do you?" Then his voice became hostile. "You don't like it at all, do you, hmm?"

Delia turned on him, her eyes blazing with animosity. "I'm aware of your indiscretions, Whit, and I don't care about your women as long as you don't flaunt them in my face. But if you go near my sister, I'll kill you."

He pulled her back into his arms. "I wonder if your anger comes from wanting to protect Rachel, or from jealousy. Little Rachel has grown into a tasty morsel."

"If you ever touch my sister, you'll die." Her eyes held his. "I mean it, Whit. Leave her alone. She's not like you and me. She's . . . special."

His eyes shone with humor. He lifted a bottle of brandy and poured some into a glass. "What if I told you I wanted you to be jealous of me? Would you believe me if I told you I'd never look at another woman if you loved me?"

He handed the glass to Delia and she drank it down without taking a breath. Then she held the glass out for more.

"No more, my pretty one. You're forming a bad habit."

"You introduced me to it." She tossed her golden mane and laughed with amusement. "I have come to depend on brandy to get me through the day."

"Would you believe me if I told you I wanted you to stop drinking?"

"No, I wouldn't believe you. You like me drunk. I don't know why."

He ran his finger along her delicate jawline and then traced her lips. "Why did you marry me?"

Again she laughed. "Because you asked me. You never saw me as a woman, but a possession to flaunt before your friends."

He pressed his cheek against hers, inhaling her soft perfume. "You are probably right." His teeth nibbled at the lobe of her ear. "But you stir my blood as no other woman ever can, and you desire me, too, don't deny it."

His lips smothered hers so she couldn't breathe.

Delia's arms slid around Whit's shoulders and he led her to the bed. As he undressed her, another face flashed through her mind. Dark eyes—Spanish eyes—Noble's eyes, which pulled and tore at her heart, even after all this time. She kept repeating to herself while her husband made love to her, *Noble is touching me. Noble's lips are on mine. Noble. Noble. Noble.*

"We should be getting ready for the dance," she

whispered, pretending it was Noble's hands caressing her, and not Whit's.

"There's time," he whispered thickly in her ear. "It's been too long, Delia. I've missed you."

She blinked in astonishment, and looked into his eyes, seeing what appeared to be sincerity reflected there. Did Whit really love her? She would never know, because it was a game they played. In public they were the loving couple that everyone envied, but in their bedroom they were two bodies seeking and finding only pleasure and fulfillment.

Delia gave in to the passion that he stirred within her. Slowly the image of Noble faded and she saw only her husband.

He gripped her hips and rammed into her with such force it almost sent her off the bed.

Whit had such anger in him, such passion, that it made him a good lover. The heat of him reached deep inside her, and she answered each of his animal thrusts with her own.

At one point he slipped off the bed and pulled her on top of him. Positioning her just right, he eased her upward, and she wanted to scream with pleasure when he opened her up and slid inside of her, pounding and thrusting against her.

"This isn't love," she whispered as her body climaxed with his.

"No," he agreed in a breathless tone. "More than love—animal lust—much better than love."

"How long before we burn out, Whit?" she asked as his tongue swirled around a nipple.

"When we are both in hell, and maybe not then," he answered.

Chapter Seventeen

The gleeful sounds of music and laughter blended to welcome the people of Madragon County to the Harvest Dance, the social event of the year. The dance was a tradition that had sprung forth the first year the town had been established in 1844. Of course, there had been no dance during the war years because it had been considered unpatriotic to celebrate while young men were dying in a confrontation so far away from home.

The dance was held in the old town hall, and the joyous sounds drifted down the empty streets of Tascosa Springs. There was hardly a man, woman or child in the whole county who was not attending the festivities tonight.

Many of the women had saved all year to buy a

new frock for the occasion. Young, unmarried females waited with anticipation for this night so
they could flirt and dance with the gentlemen of
their choice. Gentlemen in suits mingled easily
with cowboys wearing boots and Western finery.

Rachel arrived with her sister and brother-in-
law in their town carriage. The minute Whit's feet
touched the ground his mouth thinned into a
smile and he merged with the crowd, shaking
hands, slapping backs, inquiring about family
members—campaigning.

Delia dutifully followed, looking bored and unhappy. She'd always hated this affair and she still
did, much preferring the elegant balls and soirees
of Austin society.

Whit's hand clamped on Delia's arm, steering
her forward, while his eyes were riveted on Rachel. He made Rachel feel uneasy. Why did he
keep staring at her? she wondered, hanging back,
hugging the shadows. She was suddenly overwhelmed by melancholy and was reluctant to enter the hall. She thought about all the men who
had been killed in the war. Those absent had faces
and names—they had been her friends and neighbors. She prayed there would be no Yankees present, no blue uniforms, no enemies.

Glancing in the window at her sister, she could
read boredom etched on Delia's face. Rachel
threw off her sadness, knowing that her sister
needed her. Rachel noticed that the hall had been

skillfully decorated with streamers, colorful lanterns and lace hangings. The ladies' quilting circle had done themselves proud. She'd probably belong to the quilting circle when she was an old spinster, she thought whimsically.

For a moment, as Rachel's gaze swept over the crowd, she paused at the top of the three short steps that would take her into the room. She had no way of knowing that her entrance had drawn every eye in her direction and that she had eclipsed every other female in the building. Her off-the-shoulder blue velvet gown flared over a wide hoop, accenting her tiny waist. Her red-gold hair spilled down her back, making her skin appear creamy and smooth. She moved down the steps and walked toward her sister, still unaware that every eye followed her.

Greeting friends as she passed, Rachel went directly to Delia. "Smile," she whispered. "You are always preaching to me about helping Whit's image. Shouldn't you take your own advice?"

Delia looked at her archly. "These events have always been tedious, and I doubt they have changed." But she managed a tight, sparing smile.

Rachel said with just a hint of humor, "Don't think of it as a dance, Delia—think of it as a room filled with potential voters."

Delia grinned at her sister's comment. "Look at my husband; he's certainly making himself popular tonight. See how he mingles with the locals, trying to make them believe that he's still one of them? Everything he does is carefully thought through and calculated beforehand. Tonight he wants to be perceived as a successful hometown boy who's come home to visit with his old friends." She continued, her tone now laced with disgust, "My husband is such a hypocrite."

"He's a prospective candidate," Rachel countered, throwing Delia's words back in her face.

The two sisters stood side by side, drawing everyone's attention. Each sister's beauty was a contrast to the other's. Delia looked poised and elegant in her apricot satin gown with yards and yards of expensive beaded lace at the hem. Rachel, with her flaming hair spiraling about her face, looked wild, unpredictable, breathtaking. She drew and held everyone's attention in her blue velvet gown, which had little adornment and needed none.

Whit looked less formally attired than usual because it suited him not to wear a tie and to leave his shirt unbuttoned. He came back to stand between Delia and Rachel, smiling and exchanging pleasantries with everyone and slipping his hand about the waists of both women.

Rachel didn't think any less of Whit for what he was doing. After all, she thought, suppressing an amused smile, one lived by different rules when one wanted to become governor of Texas.

Rachel's face lit up when she saw Sheriff Crenshaw striding toward her.

He nodded to Delia and Whit, then took Rachel's hand. "I declare you to be the prettiest woman here tonight, Miss Rachel. You surely are."

She liked the sheriff. He smelled of leather and spice and reminded her of her father. "Shall I tell Matty Sue you said that?" she asked in a teasing voice.

He chuckled. "My wife would agree with me." He gallantly extended his arm to her. "Let me fetch you a glass of punch so I can be the envy of all those young fools who stand there gawking at you, but are too afraid to ask you to dance."

She placed her gloved hand on his arm and accompanied him across the room. Rachel had the strangest premonition that something was about to happen. She didn't know what it might be; she didn't even know if it was good or bad. She'd had the same feeling when her father had been killed. She shook her head, trying to rid herself of the feeling. She was relieved when Sheriff Crenshaw handed her a glass of punch.

Rachel's gaze moved searchingly over the crowd, and her stomach tightened in knots. She realized what she was feeling—she was hoping Noble would come. Of course he wouldn't come, but still . . .

The evening progressed, and Rachel danced with so many different partners, she lost count. Finally she stepped back into the shadows, hoping to rest for a moment. Her feet hurt; she wasn't accustomed to wearing satin shoes. She met the eyes of her foreman, Tanner, who watched her from the edge of the dance floor, and she smiled at him.

Tanner hadn't torn his eyes away from Rachel all evening. He was sure that if an angel had come down to earth, she would not be as beautiful as Rachel. Her blue velvet gown billowed out about her, swaying gently with each movement. Her red hair glistened with golden highlights, and her skin was creamy and smooth. The foreman knew he'd never have the courage to ask her to dance—never.

Tanner stepped back as Rachel approached him. He swallowed, wishing he could find something witty to say. He shifted from one foot to the other and back again. Hell, he hoped he could speak past the lump in his throat.

The angel spoke to him. "Are you having a good time, Tanner?"

"Yes, ma'am." He silently cursed himself because his voice trembled—for that matter his whole body shook.

"Tanner," Rachel said, smiling gently at him. "Remember, you promised me a dance?"

"I, uh, I did. Yes, I did." He gulped in air. "Will you dance with me, Miss Rachel?"

She offered him her gloved hand. "It would be my pleasure."

He took her hand, praying that he wouldn't stumble over his own feet. He'd never been much of a dancer, and he hoped he could keep time with the music. He almost pulled away when his hand touched the soft velvet about her waist. Could she see that he was falling apart inside? Did she think he was a total lout?

Rachel gave Tanner an encouraging smile. He was such a capable foreman, and there was nothing he didn't know about ranching. But he was shy around women, and she wished he would find someone nice and marry her. She didn't want to lose him as a foreman, and if he was married he would be more likely to settle permanently on the Broken Spur.

"Tanner," Rachel said, hoping to encourage him in a courtship, "I've noticed Sally Crenshaw watching you. I believe she likes you. Have you asked her to dance this evening?"

He had been counting steps so he wouldn't make a mistake, but when Rachel spoke to him he stumbled over her satin slipper. "I'm so sorry, Miss Rachel," he stammered. "Did—are you hurt?"

She shook her head and offered him her hand. "I was speaking to you of Sally."

Tanner had thought it would be heaven to dance with Rachel, but it was hell. He couldn't think clearly when he was this close to her. She smelled of some sweet fragrance, and he wanted so badly to touch her hair and see if it was as soft as it looked. He gulped. "Sally, the sheriff's daughter?" he asked, wondering how any man would notice another woman with Rachel in the room.

"Why don't you ask her to dance?"

"I . . . ain't much of a dancer."

"Nonsense. You are doing very well."

Was he? He suddenly felt as if he were floating above the floor. "I'll ask her if you want me to."

Her laughter was musical. "I'm not your boss tonight, Tanner. You ask a pretty girl to dance because *you* want to."

He glanced over at Sally Crenshaw and met her soft gray eyes. He'd never thought of her as a woman. She was past her prime, probably in her thirties. But then, Tanner was forty. Sally was the schoolmarm, and she looked the part with a tight bun at the nape of her neck and a sensible gray gown, trimmed with black braid. He supposed she was pretty enough, but not to be compared with the angel in his arms.

"I'll dance with her," he said at last. "If she's of a mind to dance with me."

Rachel knew Noble was standing behind her before he spoke. A stir of excitement filled the air as everyone stared and pointed, whispering and speculating about what had brought mighty Noble Vincente to a dance with the local people. She wondered too. Might he have come for her?

"I believe this is my dance," Noble said softly, with the merest glint of mockery in his dark eyes.

Tanner hurriedly relinquished his partner, stepping back a few paces. He mumbled something about a glass of punch and moved off the dance floor. Rachel seemed to float into Noble's arms as if he willed her there, and she had no strength to refuse him. He seemed to will her to look at him, which she did. Neither spoke for a moment. His hand rested lightly against her waist, guiding her steps and drawing her firmly under his spellbinding power. His fingers felt strong and warm; she could feel the heat of them through her gloves. He was a good dancer, strong and commanding, as in life. His footsteps matched hers, and their bodies fell into tune with the music and with each other.

Every eye was drawn to Noble and Rachel. Noble was so dark, so handsome—Rachel was fair and beautiful. He wore tight-fitting black trousers with silver braid down the legs. His white shirt was ruffled and a startling contrast to his dark skin. His short bolero jacket had the same trim as his trousers. He looked every inch the Spanish don.

Green eyes stared into liquid brown eyes, and it seemed to Rachel that she and Noble were the only two people in the room.

Her mouth went dry and her voice came out in a breathy whisper. "I didn't expect you to come tonight."

Noble watched conflicting emotions play across her beautiful face—first stubbornness, then uncertainty, lastly pride. "Didn't you, Rachel?"

"No. I didn't."

"But Rachel, you issued me an invitation. It was

the least I could do since you honored *my* invitation."

"I don't know what you mean."

He laughed softly and dipped his dark head to whisper in her ear. "I invited you to swim; you invited me to the dance."

"I don't recall inviting you to the dance."

"Not in so many words, perhaps, but you did want me to come tonight, didn't you?"

She tensed. "If you were a gentleman, you would forget about that day I . . . I—"

He drew her so close that she was aware of every breath he took. She trembled from being so close to him.

"If it is your wish, I shall never mention our swim again." He smiled. "But my thoughts will be my own."

"Why did you come?"

"To dance with you."

A rush of pleasure surged through her. When he whirled her around, Rachel caught the yearning expressions on several of the other ladies' faces. "There are many women who would like to change places with me tonight. Although they are probably in awe of you."

"Are you?"

"Am I what?"

"In awe of me?"

"No. Why should I be?"

He laughed down at her. "Why indeed? I see

many men who would like to be holding you in their arms."

"You flatter me."

His breath fanned her cheek. "No, Green Eyes. I speak only the truth with you." His grip tightened on her hand. "Will you be equally honest with me?"

"I must hear the question before I give my answer."

His eyes danced with humor. "It's really quite simple. Should I be jealous of one of the men in this room?"

"No." Her eyes were clear and honest. "There is no one."

He let out a tight breath. "Then the men in Madragon County are all fools."

Delia watched her sister dance with Noble while Whit watched Delia. "You wish it were you in his arms, don't you, my dear?"

"Don't be ridiculous. I'm just concerned about my sister," she replied chillingly.

Whit stared at the man he despised most in the world—the man who possessed everything he wanted but could never have. Noble had breeding, wealth and power. The wealth and power, Whit could obtain, but he would always be the son of a line foreman. He'd been born in a sod hut with dirt floors and no windows, while Noble had been born into an illustrious family and wore his name like a badge of honor. "Look at him, Delia. He's even managed to convince everyone that he didn't kill your father."

"He didn't kill him."

The evening had turned sour for Whit. "The town's so willing to welcome the prodigal son home. Look at their faces—see how they kowtow to him—the butcher, the baker, the candlestick maker, all anxious to bask in Noble's bounty. I've heard that Casa del Sol is undergoing extensive repairs, and everyone in Tascosa Springs wants a slice of the pie."

"It seems that you hear a lot of things for someone just arrived from Austin."

"I told you before that I have my sources."

"And I told you, Whit, that I don't want to know any of your sordid little secrets."

"Keep your voice down, my dear." Although he had spoken softly, the threat was real. "Do you want everyone to think that our marriage is less than ideal?"

She turned on him. "You are good at making people believe what you want them to believe. Just don't tell me how you do it."

His eyes were like burning coals. "That's right, Delia. As long as you don't know the truth, you don't have to feel a part of it, do you? But let's just suppose that I'm the one who brings about Noble's downfall." His gaze rested on Noble as he spoke. "What would I have gained by it?"

"Some sick satisfaction, I suppose. All I heard about tonight is how bravely Noble fought in the war. Where were you while Noble was fighting, Whit?"

He looked at her through half-closed eyelids. "I was at home pleasuring you, my dear."

"Insufferable fool," she whispered, feeling hysteria rising inside her. "I want to go home."

His grip tightened painfully on her fingers. "Get a hold of yourself, Delia. Say and do what you will when we leave here, but you will conduct yourself with dignity tonight."

"I detest you."

His eyes hardened. "Does it matter? You are my wife, and you will remain my wife until one or both of us are dead." His hand slid up her shoulder, and he urged her forward. "Now, suppose we pay homage to Noble. Don't you think it's time you renewed an old acquaintance?"

Noble saw Whit and Delia moving in their direction. "Rachel," he said, turning her toward the door. "Will you walk outside with me?"

She was afraid to accompany him. He was the forbidden fruit, and that only made him more exciting. Wordlessly, she placed her hand on his arm, and people moved aside to make a path for them.

Neither of them saw the anger on Whit's face because Noble had publicly slighted him, nor did they see Delia's confusion. She thought Rachel hated Noble, but her sister wasn't acting like it tonight.

"Delia, my dear," Mrs. McVee said, watching Rachel and Noble leave. "I wouldn't be at all surprised if we have a wedding before long."

Delia felt stunned. "You can't mean my sister and Noble."

The storekeeper's wife nodded. "They are perfect for each other. And there would be nothing better than to have Broken Spur and Casa del Sol united."

"I didn't know you held Noble in such high regard," Whit said, his brow furrowed into a frown.

"I wronged Noble terribly and I want the world to know it." Mary McVee dabbed at her eyes with a linen handkerchief. "Did you know that Noble took care of our dying son?"

The smile Whit gave Mrs. McVee was hard, and his eyes were harder. "Imagine that," he said smoothly. "Noble Vincente, a hero."

Not a breath of air stirred. The night was studded with stars that twinkled like thousands of diamonds against the ebony backdrop. Other people walked about the deserted streets—young couples mostly, but Noble and Rachel paid the others no heed. He assisted her up the plank walkway, and they both glanced up at the moon.

"I shouldn't have come out here with you," Rachel said. "Everyone will talk."

"Yet you came anyway. I don't think you really care what anyone says."

She glanced up at him. "Yes, I came anyway,"

she echoed. "But you're wrong about me. I do care what people think of my behavior."

His gaze brushed over her from head to toe. "It was worth coming tonight to dance with you, to hold you." He touched her velvet sleeve. "You are beautiful in this gown."

"If that's a compliment, I'll accept it."

He smiled. "I like you in trousers too. But I don't like other men to see you wearing them."

"Why? What I wear is none of your affair."

He allowed his hand to move down her sleeve to her hand. "You are right. It's not my affair—not yet."

She glanced at his face and saw the faint scar. "I see you have recovered from your ordeal."

"So it would seem."

The closeness of his body to hers made her feel giddy and weak. "I should return to the dance."

His hand clamped onto hers. "Is that really what you want to do, Rachel? I have a feeling that if you would give yourself over to love, you would find what you are searching for."

She stared at him in confusion. "Love. Surely you aren't suggesting that there can be any love between us?"

"Perhaps love is a bit premature."

She took a hasty step back. "You are confusing me."

"No, Rachel. You are confusing yourself. Will you meet me by the river tonight?" His hand went to her bare shoulder. "I want to be alone with you. We could talk uninterrupted."

"No," Rachel replied almost too quickly. She wanted to be alone with him more than she'd ever wanted anything. "You know I would never do such a thing. I fear that my outlandish behavior that day at the river gave you the wrong opinion of me."

He raised her hand and placed it against his chest. "Can you feel how my heart beats when I am with you?"

She jerked her hand back. "Don't say these things to me," she said adamantly, shaking her head. "I don't want to hear them."

But, oh, her heart was gladdened by his confession.

He held his hand out to her and she stepped away.

"Don't, Noble."

"You feel it too, Rachel. You know that when we are together something magic happens."

Suddenly she thought of Delia, and she was rescued by her anger—it helped her regain her composure. "Did you feel that same magic with my sister?" The moment the words left her mouth, she wished she could call them back.

Noble fell quiet for a moment. "Come to me tonight at the river and we'll talk about it."

"I think not. Terrible things happen to me when I'm with you at the river. Besides, what can you say to me there that you can't say here?"

He pulled her into the shadows, and before she knew what was happening, his warm mouth covered hers, cutting off her speech and making her heart thunder in her ears. She felt as if she were drowning and there was no escape.

He raised his head and she heard the gruffness in his tone. "Come to me tonight." It sounded like a plea, and she could feel his tension. "I'll be waiting for you."

She swallowed hard so she could speak past the tightening in her throat. The need to say yes jolted through her—instead she said in a whisper, "Never."

He pulled her to him once more, his lips sliding across her cheek to her mouth. She was startled when he plunged his tongue into her mouth—it made her tingle all the way to her toes, and she clung to him, knowing she could not have pulled away at that moment if she'd wanted to, and she didn't want to.

He raised his head and stared at her for a breathless moment. "I want to kiss you and keep on kissing you," he said gruffly.

"Please don't kiss me anymore," she pleaded, backing away from him, afraid that if he kissed her again, she would do anything he asked of her.

With a sad smile, Noble turned and walked away from her.

Rachel watched him mount his horse. She heard the leather saddle creak beneath him, and she watched as he rode away, soon to be swallowed up by night shadows that spread across the deserted street. Within moments the sound of his galloping horse faded into silence, and she felt so alone.

She clasped her hands tightly together as if trying to hold on to her willpower. She wanted to go to him tonight, but she must not. She felt as if he had been testing her in some strange way, although she did not know why.

"No, I will not meet him tonight," she whispered. Then she said more forcefully, "I will not!"

Noble rode straight to the river and dismounted. Walking along the bank, he could still smell the sweetness of Rachel's silken hair; in fact, the scent of her was all over him. He closed his eyes as a breeze cooled his face.

He knew she wouldn't come to him tonight. But the time would come when she could no longer deny the magic between them. One day she would come to him.

The old loneliness returned to haunt him, and he felt the tightening in his chest. He had an ache and a need that only Rachel could ease. He wanted her—no, dammit, he needed her. She belonged to him; didn't she know that?

He leaned against the tree trunk, waiting, hoping she'd come, but knowing in his heart that she would not.

Delia stood between them. Perhaps she always would.

Rachel tossed and turned upon her bed. She pounded her pillow with her fist. Another sleepless night, for which she blamed Noble. She felt some power, some deep need pulling her and calling her to the river.

She shook her head and moaned. "No, no, I must resist. I will not go to him." After the dance, she realized she was too susceptible to his touch to chance a match of wits with him.

In the quiet predawn hour, sleep still eluded Rachel. She balled her fists and pounded her pillow as if she were hitting Noble. "Help me understand," she whispered plaintively. "I don't want to love him."

But it was too late. She hadn't known that love could be so consuming or hurt so badly. It was a fragile thing, love. Perhaps she could starve it to death by ignoring it.

She set her chin firmly. "I will overcome this. I will."

Her head sank into her pillow. She squeezed her eyes tightly shut. "Starve it to death. If I don't see Noble again, my love for him will soon shrivel and die."

She didn't believe it, even as she said it.

Chapter Eighteen

The smell of strong coffee wafted through the air as Rachel neared the bunkhouse. She smiled and stopped to speak to Zeb, who was sitting on the steps whittling something resembling the figure of a horse.

"Want some coffee, Miss Rachel?" he asked, glancing at her from under bushy eyebrows.

"Did you make the coffee again, Zeb?" She sat down beside him and watched his deft hands whittle away at the wood. While the other cowhands liked their coffee strong, they complained that Zeb's coffee was more like witches' brew and so bitter it was undrinkable. Rachel also knew that they had an agreement between them that Zeb was not to be allowed to make the coffee.

The old man's eyes lit with pleasure as they always did when his lady boss stopped to talk to him. "Yep. I made it, Miss Rachel. Charley and Bud complain they have to pick the grounds out of their teeth for a week when I make it." He chuckled. "But they drink it all the same, and they're glad to get it. Want some?"

She grinned. "No, thank you."

He shrugged, and continued whittling while the two of them basked in companionable silence.

Rachel glanced up and watched the smoke curl from the chimney to disappear against the slate-colored sky. She was reluctant to return to the house because Delia and Whit were there. She had purposely avoided their company today, knowing that Delia would want to question her about Noble's appearance at the dance last night. For the time being, she didn't want to talk about Noble with anyone, and especially not her sister.

"Winter's coming early this year, Miss Rachel. Gonna be a bad'n. Worse than in fifty-three," Zeb mused aloud while his gnarled but creative hands worked their magic on the horse he was carving. He'd presented Rachel with many of his carvings over the years, and he was proud that she displayed them on a shelf in her office for all to see.

It never occurred to Rachel to doubt Zeb's weather predictions. He was seldom wrong. "I can stand some cold weather after the heat of the summer," she remarked, her eyes going wistfully to the cloudless sky.

Zeb kept at his whittling. "Heard the dance went right nicely last night."

"Yes, I suppose it did."

He watched her carefully. He'd known Rachel all her life, and he took liberties none of the other ranch hands would dare. "Heard Noble Vincente was there."

She looked at him and then lowered her eyes. "If you know that, then you also know that I danced with him and then went outside with him."

He chuckled. "I heard that too. Some say Noble's right taken with you, Miss Rachel."

She drew in a tight breath. "Well, I'm not taken with him."

The wily old eyes fastened on her face. "But you don't think he killed your pa anymore do you?"

"No. I'm sure he didn't." She regarded his steady gaze. "Do you think he did it?"

"Never did. There was nary a reason for Noble to kill your pa. I liked Noble when he was a boy; I like him now."

"You've seen him since he came back?"

"Sure. He ain't high on himself like folks that don't know him might think." Then the old man said with pride shining in his eyes, "We call each other by our Christian names—he calls me Zeb and I call him Noble."

"When did you see him?"

Zeb ran his hand along the stubble on his chin in contemplation. "Now, let's see. It was the day I took myself off catfishing down ta' the river. Noble came upon me and we kinda talked for a spell."

"About me?"

He started to whittle faster. "No, not about you, at least not directly. He's a gentleman and would never talk 'bout no lady—not personal-like, anyway. But he did ask if we needed anything here at the ranch. Wanted to know if he could do anything to help, and he said I was to let him know if you ever needed anything."

Rachel stared at Zeb in disbelief. "I consider that very personal. Noble assumes too much. Does he think I need help from him, or that I'd accept it if I did?" Her eyes were blazing with anger. "What did you tell him?"

Zeb's busy hands did not falter. "I told him nope." He grinned at her. "I said you'd get riled if I did that."

"What right does Noble have to interfere in my life?" Her words vibrated with raw emotion. "Noble Vincente . . . is . . . he's—"

"Neighborly and kindly," Zeb said, sober faced.

At that moment Bud Cadey ambled by and tipped his hat. "Ma'am, we rounded up twelve more strays today."

Rachel tried to push all thoughts of Noble to the back of her mind to deal with later when she was alone. She looked up into Bud's angular face. He, like the other cowhands on Broken Spur, was protective of her, although they tried not to show it since she was the boss.

"Are they all branded?" she asked.

Bud nodded. "Yes, ma'am. Branded and bedded for the night."

Bud went inside the bunkhouse, soon to reappear to join Rachel and Zeb on the steps. He balanced a mug of coffee in his hand. "It's a right pretty evening, ain't it, Miss Rachel?"

A sudden breeze touched her cheek and stirred her hair. "I love this time of year," she said softly. "It was Papa's favorite, too—fall roundup."

"Not me." Zeb carefully watched Bud as he raised the coffee mug to his mouth. "My bones ache in cold weather. 'Course, this year's been dry so I ain't ached as much."

Bud took a sip of coffee and shuddered, grimaced and closed his eyes. "Zeb, did you make the coffee again?"

Zeb's amused howls and triumphant whoops could be heard all the way to the big house. "I made it and you can drink it, Bud, if'n you're man enough to."

Rachel had to smile. What would she do without Zeb? He was as kind as he was full of mischief. And the one person with whom she could be herself. Sometimes, though, she thought that he knew her too well.

Several other cowhands ambled up from the corrals, respectfully removed their hats and nodded at Rachel.

"Coffee's on the stove." Zeb gave them a furtive glance; then he howled with laughter when they disappeared into the bunkhouse to get a cup.

"You're hopeless, Zeb," Rachel said softly.

"Ain't I though?" He gave her his brightest toothless grin. "Ain't I just?"

By the time Rachel returned to the house, night had fallen. She stepped into her office, where a single lamp burned, adding a ring of light to the darkened room. She glanced toward the stairs, hoping Delia and Whit were tucked in for the night. She had managed to avoid them all day by leaving the house early, staying busy, and returning late. If Delia and Whit left in the morning as they'd planned, she'd have to spend only a few moments more in their company.

Rachel stood over her father's scarred desk, feeling lonely and lost. For a time after he'd been killed, she had felt his presence in this room, where he'd spent so much time going over the books. But now she didn't feel him with her, and the loneliness was almost more than she could endure.

Her hand swept across the desk as she tried to recapture the essence of her father, but his memory was fading. It had occurred to her today that she had kept his memory alive by blaming Noble for his death—by dreaming of revenge. Now that she knew Noble was innocent, she had to let the bitterness go.

She closed her eyes, willing herself not to think of Noble. Had he waited long for her by the river last night? Had he known how much she wanted to go to him?

"Rachel, I left you a plate warming on the back of the stove." Winna Mae stepped out of the shadows and into the light. "You look all done in. You should eat and go to bed."

"I'm not hungry."

"Eat anyway—at least a little."

Rachel nodded wearily. It did good to argue with Winna Mae, because she'd only lose. She cast a cautious gaze toward the stairs.

"Your sister and her husband went to bed about an hour ago," Winna Mae said with her uncanny perception.

As Rachel walked to the kitchen Winna Mae followed her, and when Rachel sat down at the table the housekeeper put a plate in front of her.

"Does my sister still plan to leave tomorrow?"

"She says she is."

Rachel felt so exhausted she wanted to drop her head on the table and sleep. She saw Winna Mae watching her as if she could read her thoughts.

"Just take a bite of my stew and drink your milk. You can't go to bed on an empty stomach. If I know you, you didn't eat lunch."

More to satisfy Winna Mae rather than from hunger, she took two bites of stew and drained the glass of milk. Then she smiled and stood up, walking to the door and calling back laughingly over her shoulder, "Was I a good girl, Winna Mae?"

"You're too good for that unwholesome pair up-stairs," Winna Mae mouthed to herself.

Moonlight flooded Rachel's bedroom, so she didn't bother to light the lamp. She removed her boots and stripped off her trousers and shirt, folding them neatly and placing them across a chair. She might wear men's garb on the outside, but the feminine side of her chose frilly undergarments. She was unlacing her camisole when she heard a noise.

"Delia, is that you?"

A dark shadow detached itself from the corner and walked toward her. It was a man, but she couldn't see his face. It flashed through her mind that a man would not come into a woman's bedroom uninvited unless he had something sinister on his mind.

"Who are you?"

A strong hand reached out and clasped her arm. She smelled the strong fermented scent of whiskey and she knew who it was. "Whit, what are you doing in my bedroom?"

"Don't you know?"

"Is my sister ill—does she need me?"

"I need you," Whit said in a slurred reply. "I've needed you for a long time. Don't tell me you didn't notice that I've been burning for you."

She jerked free of him, her heart thundering against her chest. "Get out of my room," she threatened, "or I'll call out to my sister."

"Delia wouldn't hear you," he said with a sneer, and stepped closer to her. "Your sister drank too much of your father's fine stock of whiskey." He grinned ominously. "I had my share too."

Rachel recoiled from his touch. "Delia doesn't drink enough to get drunk." Even as she said the words, she realized what she'd known all along but hadn't admitted even to herself—Delia did drink too much.

He laughed, tightened his hold on her, and she could sense the unleashed malice in him. "You don't know the things your sister does. But I don't want to talk about her." His mouth fastened on her neck. "Don't you know you have half the men in the county panting after you? You sashay around in tight-fitting britches, daring a man to take what he wants."

"I'm not like that," she said disbelievingly. "Get out of here! You're crazed."

"Yes, crazy to have you."

Rage tore through Rachel like a whiplash, and she managed to wedge her elbow between herself and Whit while she shivered with revulsion. "Get out."

Whit staggered backward, almost losing his balance, and Rachel took the opportunity to move toward the door. "Get out of here now and my sister won't ever have to know you were here." Her voice sounded unsteady, and she could feel fear tighten her stomach. "You are drunk and need to sleep it off."

Whit lunged at Rachel, whirling her around with a strength that took her by surprise. His arms enfolded her and he brought her body against him. "Do you think Delia gives a damn what I do? She only wants me for pleasuring her in bed." His hand swept up to tangle in Rachel's hair, and he jerked her face toward his. "I want to bury myself deep in you. I want to pump you so hard that you'll cry my name, begging for more."

Rachel thought she was going to be sick. Faint moonlight illuminated the room, and she caught his expression. His eyes were menacing and his expression colder than a West Texas norther.

"Get your filthy hands off me!" She shoved him away and backed up several steps, wondering if she could make it to the door before he caught her again. "If you ever touch me again, I'll kill you."

He was like a mad bull charging at her. He hit her with the full force of his body and drove her backward onto the floor.

Rachel struggled and fought, but he was too strong for her—she was losing the battle. She could scream, but who would hear her?

"I thought a lot about you as I waited for you to come to bed tonight. I watched you undress, wanting to tear off your clothing. But I was patient, and now I'm going to have you, Rachel. We both know nothing can keep me from taking you."

She twisted and kicked, but his grip only tightened on her wrists, and he slammed them above her head. "I'll have you just the way Noble Vincente did."

Her eyes had become more accustomed to the

dark, and she saw the chilling smile on his lips. "You don't know what you're talking about."

"Noble bedded you and he bedded my wife. It's only right that we should share our women, don't you think?"

He was disgusting, malignant, evil. Why hadn't she seen these traits in him before now? "You are loathsome," she said bravely, while shaking inside. "I haven't been with Noble in the way you imply."

"Don't take me for a fool," Whit said coldly. "I know much more than you think I do about you and Noble."

She tried again to throw him off her, but his hands grasped the thin material of her chemise, and when it ripped, he kneaded her breasts while his sickening, whiskey-scented breath choked her. His mouth was hot and slippery, and she gagged when he covered her lips with his. She could sense the urgency in him, and fought even harder.

He was going to take her right here, in her own house, with her sister sleeping next door, and there was no one to help her. Paralyzed with dread, she knew what was going to happen to her.

"Please, no," she said, turning her head away from him. Her chest felt tight with terror, and her shallow breathing was painful. Still, she managed to say with feeling, "Leave me alone, Whit!"

He fumbled with his pants, and she struggled with all her might. She did not see it coming, but he struck her hard across the face, and she tasted her own blood.

"Be still! I'm going to drive into you like I dream of doing every time I see you. You'll like me better than that bastard, Noble."

At that moment the door opened and light spilled into the room. Rachel threw her head back and cried out to Winna Mae, whose figure was outlined by the lamp she held. "Help me. Dear God, help me!"

Whit froze with his trousers halfway down. "What the hell?"

"Miss Rachel," Winna Mae said as easily as if she'd been discussing the weather, "I put the milk on the back of the stove to clabber. Will you be wanting me any more tonight?"

Whit scrambled to his feet, jerking up his trousers. "Rachel wanted me here," he said to Winna Mae. "She's been asking for it." When he drew even with the housekeeper, he hissed at her. "If you are thinking of telling my wife, I wouldn't if I were you. Delia doesn't need to know that her sister's a whore."

Winna Mae's free hand was crammed deeply in her apron pocket to hide her balled fist. Her voice was soft, but it cut through Whit's drunken stupor. "If you ever come near Rachel again, I'll kill you, you bastard. We Indians have ways of dealing with your kind, and it involves cutting off private parts."

Whit turned quickly away and stumbled down

the hallway, the echo of his weaving footsteps finally fading behind Delia's bedroom door.

Rachel was still dazed from Whit's blow. She stood and stumbled to the bed, collapsing across the multicolored quilt. She was shaking violently and couldn't stop.

Winna Mae put the lamp on the table and rushed to her. She bent down and brushed Rachel's hair out of her face, and frowned when she saw that her lip was bleeding, and a purple bruise was visible on her cheek. The housekeeper pulled the quilt over Rachel and said soothingly, "Rachel, child, did he get to you?"

Rachel sobbed and threw her arms around Winna Mae. "No, but he would have if you hadn't come in when you did. I hate him! I hate him more than I ever hated anyone. My poor sister. She's married to a monster. No wonder she drinks too much."

Winna Mae held Rachel in her arms and rocked her back and forth, much as she would have a child. "Hush now. He can't hurt you anymore. I'll stay with you. Hush, go to sleep."

Rachel threw the covers aside and slid off the bed. "I can't sleep. I keep feeling his hands on me." She shook so badly she wrapped her arms around her shoulders, hoping to stop.

Winna Mae took her hand and led her back to bed. "You've had a shock. You need sleep."

"How can I sleep under the same roof with that man?" Panic rose in Rachel's voice. "I want him to leave the Broken Spur right now, and never come back."

"No, what you want is to sleep." Winna Mae folded aside the covers and helped Rachel into bed; then she covered her. "I'll be right here if you need me."

"You won't leave me?"

"I won't leave you."

Rachel finally fell asleep, but she dozed fitfully, waking several times, frightened that Whit might be in the room with her.

But Winna Mae was always there, and Rachel went back to sleep feeling safe.

Chapter Nineteen

Rachel awoke to find sunlight streaming through the window. When she remembered what had happened the previous night, she paled and looked fearfully about her. She had expended all of her energy fighting Whit, and she felt as limp as a rag doll.

She'd never been frightened of anyone, not until last night. She had never realized that there were men and situations that she couldn't control. Whit was dangerous. A haunting thought swept through her mind—he wasn't through with her, not yet. But the next time he tried anything with her, she would be ready for him. She'd blow his damned head off!

The door opened and Winna Mae entered, carrying a tray with Rachel's breakfast.

"I thought you might like to eat in bed, and then sleep for another hour or so."

Rachel shook her head.

"He's gone. They left at first light. Delia said to tell you she'd write."

"What about Whit?"

"I never saw a man in such a hurry to leave. Delia wanted to wake you and say good-bye, but he ushered her straight downstairs to his waiting coach." A slight smile curved Winna Mae's lips. "I guess an important person like Whit Chandler has much to do elsewhere." She placed the tray on Rachel's lap. "Eat."

"I'm not hungry."

"You didn't eat much yesterday, so you need breakfast."

Rachel sighed and obliged her.

"You must put last night out of your mind." Winna Mae sat down in the big rocker that had belonged to Rachel's mother. "He won't come near you again if I can help it. If any one of your cowhands knew what happened here last night, they'd give him Indian justice and castrate him."

Rachel's eyes widened. "You won't tell them. You won't tell anyone what happened, will you?"

"No. Of course not."

Rachel lifted a fork full of fluffy scrambled egg, and took a bite. "I've been thinking about Delia. She's married to such a monster, and I feel pity for her."

"Your sister wouldn't want your pity," Winna Mae said with her usual directness. "She knew exactly what she was getting when she married Whit."

Rachel remembered Delia telling her much the same thing. She shoved the tray aside and sank back onto her pillow. "I always thought the act of love would be beautiful. Whit made me see that there is no beauty in the act." An involuntary shiver ran down her spine. "It was so ugly—so ugly."

"That wasn't love." Winna Mae's eyes took on a glow as if she were remembering. "Love—real, deep love—can be beautiful."

Rachel thought of Noble and closed her eyes. "I want to believe you." She threw off the covers and with strong strides walked to the window, staring at the far horizon. Numbness spread over her like a blanket, stifling her beneath its heaviness. She inhaled a long, shaky breath, wishing she could forget the sickening feel of Whit touching her, his disgusting kiss, his hateful words.

She wondered what torment her sister must endure with that man. A tight knot formed in her stomach and squeezed her like a physical pain. She took another deep breath. "Winna Mae, I just have to believe there is beauty in love—beauty that feeds the soul as well as the heart."

"I have known such a love," Winna Mae said softly.

Rachel went to her bed and sat down, trying to

think of Winna Mae with a man. "You loved someone?"

The older woman closed her black eyes as if she were remembering. "I had a love so pure and sweet that it is still with me, even now after all these years."

"Tell me," Rachel said gently.

"I have never spoken of this to another living soul, and it won't be easy."

For a long moment it seemed as if Winna Mae was lost in her own memories. At last she said, "My father was a white man, a buffalo hunter. My mother was of the Kiowa tribe." She paused as if gathering her thoughts. "I was named after my father's mother. He left when I was a baby and didn't come back into my life until the spring I turned sixteen. My mother had died, and to be fair to my father, he did what he thought was right. He put me into one of those boarding schools. I was miserable there. The other girls were all white, and either made fun of me or ignored me completely. I threw myself into my schoolwork, studying hard and trying to ignore the others. I did get a good education, so something good came of those years."

Rachel touched Winna Mae's hand, wanting to comfort her. "What did you do?"

"After two years I could not stand another day, so I ran away and found my way back to my mother's people. That's when I met Lone Wolf. He was so brave, so daring, and I loved him immediately."

"And he loved you?"

"I didn't think so at first. I was a woman alone, and unless someone claimed me for his wife, I would have no respect and no man to hunt for me. In the harsh Indian world such a woman cannot survive for very long." She smiled, and it softened her eyes. "I was so happy when Lone Wolf asked me to be his woman. He was considered a mighty warrior, and yet he was so gentle with me. He found no shame in the fact that I was half white. The three years I spent with him were the happiest of my life."

Rachel sensed a change in Winna Mae's mood, and she felt her sadness as if it were her own. "Don't tell me more if you don't want to."

"I want you to know." Winna Mae looked at her for a long moment before continuing. "When I lay in my husband's arms and our bodies became one, it was a precious and beautiful gift. It is because of his love that I was able to go on living when life got hard."

Rachel took Winna Mae's scarred hands in hers, hoping to give her comfort. "What happened to Lone Wolf?"

"We had a son," she said, smiling sadly. "He was dark skinned like his father, and Lone Wolf was so proud of him. He would ride through the village with our son propped in front of him, just so everyone would comment upon what a remarkable son he had. We called our son Silent One, because he never cried. Of course when he was older, he would have earned his own name."

Rachel lowered her eyes, dreading what was to come and feeling it like a chill in her bones.

Winna Mae drew in a trembling breath. "On this one day, I rose early, leaving my husband and baby sleeping while I went into the mountains to pick chokeberries. I did not know when I left that it would be the last time I would ever see them."

Rachel glanced to the window, willing herself not to cry, but tears still gathered in her eyes and slid down her cheeks.

"I returned to the village around midday to find nothing but smoldering ashes and dead bodies. I saw enough to know that the bluecoats had raided the village. Those they didn't kill, they had taken as prisoners." Her shoulders slumped and she was quiet for a moment, as if she couldn't find the words to express her grief.

At last she said, "Our lodge was burned, and I searched frantically among the ashes, trying to find my husband and son."

Rachel's eyes dropped to Winna Mae's scarred hands. So that was how she'd been burned. "You didn't find them, did you?"

She shook her head. "There were so many burned bodies, and it was difficult to identify anyone. Hoping that they had been taken away as prisoners, I decided to follow the tracks. I walked many days and nights without food, following the trail left by the white soldiers. Finally I came to a fort. I inquired about my husband and son there, but the soldiers drove me away. A kind man, a sergeant I believe, came to me and told me that those of my people who had not been killed had been taken to a reservation. He explained where it was, so I walked for many more days until I came to the place he'd told me about. None of my tribe were there. It was as if they all died that day, or the earth opened up and swallowed them."

"Winna Mae, I am so very sorry," Rachel said, trying not to cry. "Did you never find them?"

"I looked through the long summer and into the fall. Years passed, I don't know how many, but I was compelled to keep looking. My aim was always to find my husband and son, but each lead proved as false as the last one. One winter, several men came upon me—they were buffalo hunters. I will not speak of what they did to me, but afterward I wanted to die, and I would have if your father had not found me and brought me here. I cry no more tears, because I have none left."

Winna Mae took Rachel's hands and gripped them tightly. "I only told you about myself so you would know that love can be beautiful. There are different kinds of love. There is the love I had for my husband and son"—she raised her eyes to Rachel—"and there is the love I had for a young girl who was the age of my son. You became the daughter I never had, Rachel. My comfort has been in looking after you. Whit is a fortunate man that I did not cut out his heart last night."

Rachel laid her head against Winna Mae's shoulder and sobbed while Winna Mae tightened her arms around her. "Do not cry for me, Rachel. I have known a love so beautiful that I still carry it within my heart."

Rachel could only guess what it had cost Winna Mae to tell her story. "Surely there is something we can do to find out about your husband and son."

Winna Mae shook her head. "I found out early in my search that the army doesn't keep informative records on Indian captives. Their ledgers would simply say Indian male or Indian female." Her face showed no emotion as she said, "I accepted long ago that they are both dead."

"There must be some way to find out for sure. If only we knew someone with enough influence to ask questions. Noble might be able to help." Rachel shook her head. "No, he would not have much influence with the Yankee army."

"They are dead." This pronouncement was delivered in an even voice, but Winna Mae's eyes held such profound sorrow that it ripped at Rachel's heart.

"I am glad Papa brought you to us. The Broken Spur will always be your home, Winna Mae."

"I know." She took her apron and dabbed at Rachel's tears. "I also know that you are special, Rachel. One day you will find a love worthy of you.

When you find this love, treasure it, whether it lasts a day, a year or a lifetime."

"But what if the man I love doesn't love me?"

"That too can happen. Life carries no promise, and nothing is certain."

"How will I know if it's real?"

Winna Mae stood and picked up the tray. "You will know."

Autumn spread across the land and still no rain came to break the terrible drought that gripped West Texas. Because of the intense heat, deep cracks scarred the land. The persistent winds blew constantly, whipping the dry dust into a frenzy of destructive, choking sandstorms. These storms sometimes lasted for days, blackening the skies, bringing misery to animal and human alike.

The life-giving Brazos River was getting dangerously low, and in places it had dried up all together. Cattle were dying from thirst; each day buzzards circled in the sky, keeping their death watch, waiting to devour some hapless beast who had fallen prey to the harsh elements.

Rachel and Bud had been scouring the countryside since sunup, looking for a missing bull, Samson, who was the pride of her herd. Samson came from hardy Mexican stock, and she hoped to use him to breed a sturdier herd that would adapt to the harsh West Texas climate.

Now it was early afternoon. Rachel shaded her

eyes and gazed at the shadows in the canyon, where it would be easy for Samson to hide. "Bud, you search the rim of the canyon and I'll ride along the river. If you find him, fire your gun twice—I'll do the same."

"Yes, ma'am." Bud touched his hat, spurred his mount into a lope and disappeared down the ravine.

Rachel rode down a steep incline to the river, her gaze on the ground, looking for tracks. After she'd been riding for an hour, she halted her mount, thinking she heard a noise. There it was again—the unmistakable bellow of a bull in distress. She spurred her mount along the riverbank until she spotted the animal.

It was Samson, all right, and he was definitely in trouble. He'd tried to cross the river and gotten caught in quicksand. The more the bull struggled, the more of his body became mired in the quicksand.

Rachel reached for her rope, looped it and tossed it expertly though the air to lock onto Samson's horns. Wrapping her end of the rope around the saddle horn, she urged her mount forward. The horse strained, pulled and slipped, unable to budge the fear-maddened bull. Samson fought too, thrashing and being drawn further into the quicksand.

Rachel jumped off her horse, yanking and pulling on the rope. She had no idea how long she and her faithful horse fought to save the bull, but the situation looked hopeless. Suddenly the end of the rope that was wrapped around the saddle horn snapped, and Rachel grabbed on to the frayed rope as it slipped through her gloved hands. She had no time to fire her gun to alert Bud and without the help of her horse she was being drawn closer and closer to the quicksand.

Stubbornly she fought, digging her heels into the dry riverbed, while Samson's thrashing drew her closer to danger. Her hair came loose from the bandanna and slid across her face, blinding her.

"You've got to help me, Samson." Rachel tossed her hair to get it out of her face. She gripped the rope tighter, gritted her teeth and yanked with all her strength.

She was so involved with trying to save the bull that it was too late when she realized she was in serious trouble herself. The rope was wound so tightly about her hands, and Samson had pulled it so taut, she couldn't get free. With fierce determination, she dug her heels in, wrestled and fought against the force that was pulling her closer to a horrible death. Inch by inch she was being drawn closer to the deadly mire.

She fell face forward into the mud, and she was too dazed to react. She knew that the more one struggled in quicksand, the faster one was sucked under. She tried to remain calm, but the rope that held her and Samson together would take her down with him.

Cold fear overcome her, and she struggled and fought with renewed strength.

Suddenly she felt another presence. A knife sliced through the tangled rope that held her captive.

"Be still, Rachel," Noble cautioned. "I'll have you free in a moment." He pulled the rope from her hands and lifted her into his arms.

She was free! Her head fell weakly against Noble's shoulder. Then she remembered her bull. "Samson," she sputtered. "You must help Samson!"

Noble set her down hard on the riverbank, and she could see by his expression that he was angry. Even so, he threw a rope over Samson's horns, then threw a second rope. He quickly wrapped the first rope around his own saddle horn and the second rope around Rachel's. With the combined strength of both horses, the troublesome Samson was soon free.

When Noble removed the ropes, the bull stumbled to his legs and plunged up the bank, into the thicket.

Then Noble turned to face Rachel, his expression dark and disapproving. "Rachel, why did you do such a fool thing? What would have happened to you if I hadn't come along?"

He made her feel like an errant child being scolded for some misdeed. "I . . . know it was foolish. I just didn't think about—"

"No," he said, winding his ropes. "That's the

trouble with you, Rachel—you just don't think. You go rushing headlong into danger and damn the consequences."

"Don't talk to me that way. I'm not like that."

"No?"

"No."

She raised her hand to her face and in horror realized it was caked with mud. "I . . . thank you for your help. I don't need you now."

He shook his head. "You need someone to look after you. It would take a lifetime commitment to keep you out of trouble, Rachel."

She stood up, brushing mud from her clothing. "I can take care of myself."

"*Sí*," he said with an indulgent twist to his mouth. "You proved that today."

When she took a step, her legs trembled. She was still frightened by what had almost happened, but she didn't want Noble to know it.

He took her hand and led her down the riverbed until he came to a place where water had pooled on a rock. "Wash yourself as best you can. You don't want to go home like that."

From past encounters she knew that his liquid brown eyes emitted power—the power to entice, draw, enslave. So she avoided his eyes, wishing he'd just go away. He'd witnessed her humiliation, and he was the last man to whom she wanted to be indebted. "You can just leave now."

He chuckled and led her horse forward. "All right, Green Eyes."

She bent to wash her face as best she could, but mud still clung to her eyebrows and lashes.

She heard Noble mount his horse and ride up the riverbank. "I wanted to meet you here again, Rachel, but this was not what I had in mind."

She turned around, glaring at him. "Go home, or I'll . . . I'll—"

He held up his hands in mock surrender. "I'm going, I'm going." His eyes sought hers and the smile left his face.

For a long moment they stared at each other.

His voice was deep with feeling as he said, "I'll be waiting for you tonight. You know the place."

She watched him ride away, wishing him in hell, then wishing he hadn't left her.

"Noble, I won't be there tonight," she cried out, but her protest was carried away by the wind, and he had already ridden out of sight.

Mud splattered and sore, she mounted her horse and galloped in the direction of the Broken Spur. Noble could wait all night, for all she cared—she wouldn't go to him. He'd chosen the wrong sister this time. She wasn't like Delia.

When she reached the house, she dismounted and handed the reins of her horse to a startled Zeb.

"Samson got stuck in quicksand. He's all right now," she said, hurrying away before he could ask her to explain.

Chapter Twenty

The sun had gone down hours ago, and everyone was in bed but Rachel. She sat at the desk, her head bent over a ledger, trying to concentrate on the blurred column of figures that danced before her eyes. At last she closed the book, extinguished the lamp and decided to go to bed. She walked to the stairs, turned back and looked at the front door.

She thought of Noble waiting for her at the river—there was no doubt in her mind that he'd be there again tonight. She'd tried to push thoughts of him to the back of her mind, but it was impossible. He pulled at her, enticing her to come to him as surely as if he were in the room with her.

And she wanted to go.

She shook her head, trying to hold on to her resolve. She felt adrift, removed from reality, yet she had never felt more alive. Her mind was attuned to the night sounds—the constant chirping of crickets, the occasional hooting of a barn owl somewhere in the distance. She listened to the lonesome howl of a wolf and, moments later, the answer of its mate. She closed her eyes and leaned against the stair post, digging her fingernails into the soft wood.

Noble was by the river, waiting for her, just as the wolf was waiting for its mate.

She hurried to the door, ripped it open and ran to the barn. Moments later she rode off into the night in the direction of the river. Her heart was beating so fast she could hardly breathe. She didn't know what force was driving her, but there was no turning back now.

Rachel rode beneath a crystalline sky, and the rising moon seemed as if it were suspended above her like a bright, polished ball, drawing her under its spell. The warmth of the night wind caressed her cheek. She was set on a path that would take her to Noble, and nothing was going to stop her.

A jackrabbit jumped in front of her horse, but she easily controlled the startled mare and continued onward. Fireflies blinked and flitted on the wind, but she paid no heed. She had only one purpose in mind. She needed Noble. She wanted to melt into his arms, to be a part of him.

When she reached the riverbank, she slid off her horse as a shadow detached itself from the darkness.

Noble appeared beside her. He did not touch her, but just looked down at her for a long moment. "I waited here tonight just as I did the night of the dance. You didn't come then, and I waited until dawn."

A sudden breeze rustled the leaves above them and riffled through his dark hair. Rachel's lower lip trembled and unwelcome tears gathered in her eyes. She said in an unsteady voice, "I'm here now."

He reached for her and she went willingly into his arms. His hungry lips slid across her face, nudging her ear, nipping at her lashes and at last covering her mouth. His arms held her gently at first and then tighter, more possessively.

Rachel melted into him, feeling the swell of him against her. It was as if she were a lightning rod and Noble was the lightning. His magnetism streaked through her with such intense energy that it left her weak with longing.

"Rachel, Rachel," Noble murmured against her lips. "I have dreamed of the moment when you would freely come to me." His strong arms closed even tighter about her. "Only you can take away this emptiness inside me."

Her fingers slid into his midnight hair and she brought his lips to hers. She was drowning and could not even save herself. Only this moment existed, this night, no tomorrow—just the touch of his body, the feel of his hands, the sensuous mouth that came nearer, touching her lips, featherlike. Then his lips were hot, devouring, glorious, dragging all resistance away from her.

Caught in a powerful deluge of desire like nothing she could have imagined, Rachel did not protest when Noble began to undress her. Slowly and expertly he unlaced, unfastened and removed her garments until she was naked. Strangely, she felt no shame as he stared at her, his eyes brightened by passion.

"You are so beautiful."

She felt pleased by his words, and a flame burned within her as his hot gaze drifted down her body.

Noble slowly guided her down onto the grass and lay down beside her. The stars arched across the sky like a sparkling umbrella, and their reflections glowed in the depths of his dark eyes. The hot wind blew softly, stirring the fragrant wildflowers and perfuming the air.

"Tell me to stop and I will, Rachel." His voice was insistent, and she knew he would let her go if she asked him to.

Her mouth was inches away from his throat. She turned her head the merest bit and touched her lips to the throbbing pulse, feeling life flowing through his body. Heat rose in her and her heart pounded, pounded to match his pulse. Did he hear it? She was playing with danger and she knew it.

Noble was like a swirling undertow, like the quicksand that had been drawing her under today. Noble was her peril tonight, perhaps more dangerous than the quicksand.

For her answer, she raised her arms to him.

Noble uttered a cry as his body sought hers. He kissed and caressed her, and she wanted to savor the moment. She thought she would die of longing when he moved his hand between her legs to stroke and caress her there. She bit her lip to keep from crying out at the delicious sensations that quaked through her body. Why was he torturing her? she wondered. She pressed forward so she could get closer to those wonderful hands that were robbing her strength and awaking her sleeping passion.

"Why do I feel this way with you?" she asked, needing to know.

"Because we were destined to be together," he answered simply, his eyes somehow sad. "I knew this would happen the day you came to my father's grave. You knew it too."

"Yes, I think I did know it then," she admitted. "Although not consciously." She touched his cheek, and her fingers drifted into his hair. "I fought you, Noble, but I lost tonight."

He pressed his rough cheek to hers and whispered, "Neither of us could escape this moment, Rachel. If ever a woman was created for a man, you were created for me."

He stood up, and her eyes followed him. She

watched him remove his shirt and drop it onto the ground. His skin was bathed in silver moonlight as he slipped out of his trousers and stood naked before her. She had once compared him to one of the gods of his fountains, but he was more beautiful than any myth. And he was flesh and blood—not cold stone.

Noble came down to her and she melted against him. Hard muscles met soft curves, as if they had been created to fit perfectly together. Warm, liquid sweetness crept through her body.

Yes, he was right; they did belong together. She had first felt it that day when she was only sixteen and he'd given her Faro. But at sixteen, it had been a young, budding love. Now it was explosive—deep and consuming, a woman's love. Her woman's heart must have known the instant she'd looked at him through her gun sights—the moment she knew she couldn't shoot him.

"I need you so, Rachel," he whispered into her ear, his breath stirring against her cheek. "You feel it too."

"Yes," she said at last. "But I didn't want this to happen."

"Green Eyes, sweet Green Eyes," he murmured softly, drawing her close to him. "It had to happen."

She was unable to do anything but moan with pleasure as he touched her in all the right places, kissing her into final submission.

Rachel had come to him tonight willingly. She

wanted to be so close to him that she could feel every breath he took as if it were her own. He awoke within her something wild and wonderful, and as frightening as it was consuming.

Noble pulled her forward, grasped her hips. His body shook with the effort to take her slowly. With hard-won restraint he slipped gently inside her. Her velvet softness closed around him, and he whispered her name in agony.

He heard her gasp from the stinging pain he caused her when he stabbed past her virginal barrier. He stopped, holding himself there, allowing her to become accustomed to the feel of him inside her. Then gently, slowly, he glided forward, then with the same gentleness he slid back.

Rachel had never imagined that the act of mating could be so wonderful. Her eyes were wide with wonder as she waited for each new motion. She felt him inside her as if he were a part of her. When he slid back, she felt wild excitement— when he lunged forward, it was all she could do to keep from crying out at the passion that ripped through her. Her heart furiously thumped against the wall of her chest. She closed her eyes and gasped, trying to hold on to reality, but this was her reality—he was the reason she existed.

When Noble slowly inched deeper inside her, he measured his thrusts with temperance, introducing her untested body to the pleasures of the flesh.

Rachel bit her trembling lip and groaned. Her

nails dug into his back when he moved faster inside her, setting a sensuous tempo.

When Noble was certain that he had not hurt her, he rested his hands on the small of her back, guiding and instructing her.

His movements escalated, and Rachel tossed her head back, arched her hips forward, meeting each of his powerful thrusts with one of her own.

Their bodies seemed to merge like the moon and the stars—like the wind in the trees—like the earth and the wide Texas sky. They moved together in silken harmony, blending flesh to flesh, fusing, heart against heart.

Rachel felt as though every step she had taken her whole life had been bringing her to this moment—this man.

She bit her lip and cried out as her body erupted, trembled and erupted again. Noble stroked her damp hair, kissed her cheek, holding her tightly in his arms. She felt so much a part of him that she had the sensation that he was breathing for both of them.

Long after their torrid lovemaking, they lay silent in each other's arms. There seemed to be no words to describe what had happened to them.

Noble brushed his lips against her cheek and then gave her a heart-melting smile. "Green Eyes, you . . ." He couldn't find the right words. "I have never felt this way before."

Rachel touched his face with the tips of her fingers, and her eyes misted because of the beauty of their coming together. She'd been purged of hate and left with only love, desire—need.

Winna Mae had been right; love could be beautiful.

Rachel looked at him quizzically. "What about the woman you are betrothed to in Spain?"

"That was finished years ago. I wrote her father and declined the honor of her hand. Since we had never met, I don't think the lady grieved much. Probably she was as relieved as I."

"If she had known you, she never would have let you go." Rachel didn't know what had possessed her to say such a thing to him. She slowly raised her gaze to his. Warmth emanated from his velvet-soft brown eyes.

"Say that you will always belong to me," he urged in a deep tone. And then he closed his eyes in growing frustration. He had expected to marry her after tonight, and he had desired her more than he'd ever desired any woman. But he hadn't expected to feel so deeply about her. "Say it," he demanded. "Say you belong to me."

Rachel felt her mind caving in upon her. Sudden awareness of what she'd done made her tremble with self-loathing. Had he made love to her sister in this same way, impregnated her and then left her? She turned away from him, wishing she could run and never stop. Visions of her sister stood between them like the slicing edge of a sword. She sat up and dropped her head in her hands. She was no different from her sister, after all.

Noble watched her with a bewildered expression. "What's wrong, Rachel?" His hand went to her stomach. "Did I hurt you, Green Eyes?"

Her voice came out like a gunshot. "Tell me about you and my sister."

His lips thinned and he took on the expression of a man marshaling his patience. His hand dropped away from her, and she could feel him stiffen and emotionally pull away from her.

Escalating frustration sharpened his tone. "You haven't spoken to Delia about me, have you?"

"I don't have to. I already know what happened between the two of you." She glanced into his eyes, feeling guilt settle on her like a swirling black fog. "If there was nothing between you and her, you would have said so long before now."

"Ask your sister," he said coldly.

She rested her folded arms on her knees and gazed at the river. "I don't know. I'm so confused."

"Are you blaming me for what happened between us tonight, Rachel?" He took in a deep breath. "I shouldn't have rushed you. I should have waited until—"

"No," she said, turning to him, her long hair swirling about her face. "I came to you of my own free will, and I'm not sorry." She hung her head. "Even the thought of you and Delia together didn't stop me. But now my sister is all I can think about."

"Only Delia can give you the answers you seek," he said, feeling somehow betrayed by her lack of trust.

"Delia wouldn't have lied to my father."

"And yet you believe that I'd get a woman with child and desert her? Don't do this to us, Rachel. I'm asking you to trust me."

She stood up, and silvery moonlight caressed her naked body. "Give me time, Noble."

He stood beside her, turning her toward his arms. "Have I done wrong in taking your innocence, Rachel?" He looked at her carefully when he said, "You could marry me."

In spite of her resolve not to let him touch her, she snuggled against his broad chest, and his arms surrounded her. He tilted her chin and kissed her tenderly, his hands running up and down her back and then settling her against him.

Suddenly she broke away from him and stepped back. "I can't be your wife, Noble." The words were ripped from her throat. "And you don't really want me. You only want to make amends through me for what you did to Delia."

His voice was soft with regret, his gaze so powerful that she had to dig in her heels to keep from going to him. "Is that what you really think of me?"

Convulsive sobs built in her throat. She had to get away before she broke down completely. "You have never denied that you fathered Delia's child."

"I asked you to trust me. I have asked you re-

261

peatedly to speak to your sister about what happened."

She shook her head. "I have to go now."

He pulled her to him again; his arms tightened about her and he rested his chin on the top of her head. "I will be waiting for you."

She looked up at him, his handsome face half in shadows, but she still saw the expression of pain and sadness. "We can never meet like this again, Noble."

He put her away from him and leaned back. He stared up at the stars, drawing a slow, deep breath. "Not even if I promise to keep my hands off you?" He turned to look at her. "If you will just let me talk to you sometimes, I promise not to touch you."

"No. I can't."

With a smothered oath, he glared at her. "Dammit, Rachel, how can I make you understand?" He paused, groping for words. "Tonight was a mistake; I admit that. I blame myself because I wanted you. I should have exercised more restraint."

Rachel felt as if someone had thrown a dash of cold water in her face. Pain pulsed right where her heart was located. "I understand more than you think I do, Noble."

"No, Green Eyes, you don't. As long as your sister stands between us, I have no right to . . ." His voice trailed off.

He had physically distanced himself from her,

and had turned off his emotions as one would snuff out a candle. Had Delia once felt this same coldness in him?

She fought against the tears that burned at the back of her eyelids. She wiped her cheek, hoping Noble hadn't noticed. "I must be going." She quickly dressed, knowing that he was doing the same.

At last he stood before her, close but not touching, anguish etched on his handsome features. "Rachel, if you ever need anything, promise that you'll come to me."

He was dismissing her, sending her away. But it was her fault. She was the one who kept seeing her sister in his arms. "Good-bye, Noble."

"There is no good-bye between us, Rachel. I will wait for you to come to me."

"Then you will wait a very long time."

"I know you will never come here again. I'll wait for the day you come to me at Casa del Sol."

She turned away, not understanding what he meant. She mounted her horse and rode across the river. The Brazos separated their two lands like the emotional gulf that stood between them.

Would she ever be able to cross it again?

That night Rachel was haunted by nightmares. She dreamed that she was running toward Noble and he scooped her into his arms. She was kissing him; he was touching her. But then her face turned into Delia's and she moaned in pain.

"No, no."

She sat up in bed, her body trembling, feeling empty inside. She pulled up her knees and rested her head on them, wishing her heart would stop pounding. Sudden realization hit her, ripped through her, leaving her stunned. She loved Noble much more than she'd ever hated him. But it was a one-sided love, all on her part. What did he want from her? she wondered. He certainly didn't want her love, or perhaps he did. For some reason known only to him, he probably needed her forgiveness.

Forgiveness was harder to give than love. A person could choose to forgive, but love was thrust upon one.

She was not sorry about what had happened between her and Noble. She would take the memory of this night with her into an uncertain future. She would never allow him to touch her again, but she would always have her memories.

Noble had asked her to trust him. But if she did, she would have to assume that her sister had lied to their father—a lie that had caused his death. That thought was too painful to contemplate.

One of them was not being truthful. No matter which one had deceived her, the truth would break her heart.

Rachel gazed up into the robin's-egg-blue sky, hoping to see rain clouds, but there were none looming on the horizon. She removed her leather gloves and tucked them into her belt. Then she undid the top button of her blouse and rolled up the sleeves. It was unusually hot for October.

She halted her cutting horse, pushed her hat to the back of her head and observed the cattle being run into the corral, branded, and herded out the other side. Today would be the final tally, and fear gripped her heart when she saw that there were so few.

Tanner rode up beside her, keeping a keen eye on his men. "We got one hundred forty head, Miss Rachel."

She felt his revelation like a crushing blow. "We lost too many to the drought. I'm going to have to sell off all the rest, Tanner." She unhooked her canteen and took a drink of water and then splashed some on her face. "There isn't enough grass to feed them all, and Zeb tells me he hasn't seen the river this low in thirty years."

"They won't bring more than three dollars a head." Tanner watched her face as he spoke. "Of course, the Yankee army's giving four dollars a head."

Rachel raised her head to a stubborn tilt. "I'd rather take a loss than sell to a Yankee." Her gaze was wistful as she glanced toward the men doing the branding. "If only we had a large enough herd to drive them to Kansas City. They're giving forty dollars a head there."

"It's too dry, Miss Rachel; the cattle would never

make it. And with such a small herd, it wouldn't be worth it."

"I know." She closed her eyes for a moment, trying to draw courage for what she must do. "All right, sell to the Yankees."

He nodded. "I know it goes against your beliefs, but there's nothing else to do, ma'am."

"How many cowhands do we have, Tanner?"

"Seventeen, if you don't count Zeb and me."

"I'm going to have to let at least ten of them go." There was pain in her eyes. "I don't like it, but I can't pay them, Tanner."

"You could ask them to take less money, ma'am."

"That wouldn't be fair to any of them. The thirty dollars a month they get now is little enough to live on."

"It's my job to tell them, Miss Rachel."

She nodded, knowing he was better able to judge which men they should keep. "Don't lay off the hands with families to support."

He nodded, knowing how difficult it was for her to lay off loyal cowhands. "I'll handle it. They understand that times are hard."

She watched the last longhorn being branded, her mind on the men she must let go. Of course two or three of them were the usual drifters who only worked during roundups and then moved on afterward—she wouldn't worry about them. But the loyal hands that had been at the Broken Spur in her father's time were another matter. It hurt like hell to send them away.

She pointed her horse in the direction of the river. When she reached the Brazos, she stared at the dry riverbed without seeing it. Her shoulders slumped and she laid her head against the neck of her horse, allowing the tears she'd been holding back to fall. Her body shook as she cried silently. She cried for the men who had to leave the Broken Spur, she cried for Delia, and she cried because she wanted so badly to see Noble.

The real fear at the back of her mind was that she would lose the Broken Spur. Her most immediate problem was her taxes. Many of her neighbors blamed the Yankees for inflated taxes, claiming it was the North's way of punishing Texas for its part in the war. Already two ranchers in Madragon County had lost their spreads.

Who would be next? Rachel wondered sadly. She could see her way of life disappearing. Her gaze swept across this land she loved.

Texans had withstood much worse: Santa Ana, Goliad, the battle of the Alamo, and the strife of civil war. This enslavement by the Yankees they would withstand as well.

Chapter Twenty-one

Thin, tattered clouds hung suspended between earth and sky—empty clouds that would soon disappear into nothingness without dropping moisture to heal the tortured land.

Zeb watched Rachel dismount and walk in the direction of the house, her face furrowed with worry. He handed the reins of her horse to Joe, a tow-headed, freckled ten-year-old who was one of the cowhands' youngest sons. Something was wrong with Rachel. He rushed to catch up with her before her first foot hit the bottom porch step.

"Weather's turned colder, Miss Rachel," he said, sidling up to her and jamming his hands in his pockets. "I think we're gonna have us a cold winter this year."

"You're always right about the weather, Zeb." Rachel paused, knowing he wanted to talk about a subject she wanted to avoid. She tensed visibly. "Did Tanner pay off the men who are leaving?"

"He did. While you were gone. At least kinda."

"What do you mean?"

"Not all of 'em left."

Rachel lowered her head. "I must seem like such a coward because I couldn't face them myself and tell them the bad news. Dammit, Zeb, I'd rather cut off my arm than let anyone go."

"They know that. 'Sides, it ain't your duty to hire and fire. That's why you have a foreman."

"I should have at least—"

Zeb must have guessed that she was eaten up with guilt, so he cut in, leading their conversation in a different direction. "Shorty and Deke said they was taking themselves off to Californey. But the others said they'll hang around here for a spell, seeing as how they ain't got no place to go anyway." He held up his hand when she started to interrupt him. "They know you can't pay right now. But they're staying anyway."

She stared at her interlocked fingers, afraid that she would cry if she looked at him. Tenuously she controlled her emotions. "I admire their loyalty, but I don't know if I'll ever be able to pay them."

"Did you go to the bank?"

She nodded. "Mr. Bradley can't loan me the money. Three more ranchers were forced off their land in the last two weeks because they couldn't pay their taxes: the Everests, Abe Fletcher and the Masterson family." Her throat grew tight with sadness. "They are my friends."

"Miss Rachel, something'll turn up. Why, the way my bones been aching, I'd say it'll rain any day now."

She smiled at him. "I trust your bones, Zeb, but I don't think rain will help us now. There are so many things in my life I can't control, so many friends who need help and I can't help them—I can't even help myself. If I had one wish, it would be that I could help Winna Mae find her family."

"They're most likely dead."

"You know about her family, Zeb?"

He gummed a plug of tobacco and studied her briefly. "Yep."

"When did she tell you?"

"The day after she told you. Said she wanted me to know."

Rachel was amazed—but why should she be? Winna Mae and Zeb shared a common bond: they both had no family. And Winna Mae had known she could trust Zeb. "I feel like I'm caught in an old dream that I had as a little girl. My legs were buried in molasses and something dangerous was chasing me. Although I tried to run, I could hardly move, and I couldn't get away."

"It fair breaks my heart to see you go through this alone." Zeb stepped closer to her. "I've put a right goodly sum of money in the bank, and I'd like to give it to you to pay the taxes." His eyes were as shiny as those of a child offering a piece of hard candy to a friend. "I ain't got no use for money."

She reached out and kissed his rough cheek, drawing a bright smile from him. "Thank you, Zeb. I never had a kinder offer, but I'm afraid you don't have that much money. The taxes on Broken Spur are twelve hundred dollars—Yankee dollars, at that."

He whistled through his two remaining front teeth. "That high?"

"I don't understand it. It's unreasonable. When I spoke to the tax assessor, he said the matter was out of his hands. The taxes have to be paid by the end of the month."

Zeb scratched behind his ear as he did some quick calculating. "Seventeen days."

Her shoulders drooped. "Exactly." She tried to concentrate on the lacy pattern cast against the house by the sun shining though the rose trellis. She drew in a steadying breath. "I don't know what I am going to do, Zeb. I'm going to lose the Broken Spur." She hung her head. "Who will tend Papa's and Mama's graves when I leave?"

The old cowhand watched Rachel enter the house, wishing he could do something to help her. She couldn't raise the taxes in seventeen days, or even seventeen months. It was more money than anyone had, except . . . except Noble Vincente. But Rachel would be mad as hell if he took her troubles to Noble. He ambled back to the barn, his mind worried and his steps slow.

Rachel removed her hat and hung it on the rack; her gloves she absently dropped on the settee. "Winna Mae, I'm home," she called.

The housekeeper appeared, her footsteps silent. "You didn't get the money, did you?"

Rachel shook her head.

"Are you hungry?"

Again Rachel shook her head.

"You had a caller today. It was the strangest thing."

"Who?" Rachel asked with little interest.

"Harvey Briscal. That man who was the deputy in Tascosa Springs."

Rachel looked dumbfounded. "I detest that man. Why would he come to see me?"

"He never said. I told him you were in town and he said he'd wait anyway, and that he needed to speak to you. I showed him into the parlor and left because I had to hang the laundry. When I came in the house later, he was gone."

Rachel rolled her eyes. "I guess it couldn't have been too important." She slowly climbed the stairs. "I'm going to wash some of the dust off. I'll be down directly."

When Rachel reached the top of the stairs, she noticed that her bedroom door was closed, and she thought that was strange. When the weather was hot, she always left the door open to circulate the air. Shrugging, she entered her room and removed her dusty clothing. After washing her face and hands, she changed into a print gown. She sat on the bed to slip into her shoes, wishing she could just lie back and close her eyes, and all her troubles would disappear.

She sank backward onto the bed, but she didn't close her eyes. The moment her head hit the pillow, she heard an ominous sound that could not possibly be mistaken for anything but what it was—a rattlesnake—and it was on her bed!

Cold dread rushed through her veins, and she slowly turned her head to stare into glasslike eyes that gave the illusion of glazed yellow porcelain. The unmistakable markings on the snake's scaly back were diamond shaped. It was a deadly diamondback rattler, coiled and in its strike pose, with fangs bared. With her knowledge of snakes, Rachel knew that the rattler could strike lightning quick—faster than a human could move—and its bite was almost always fatal.

Heart pounding, mouth dry, Rachel waited for death, knowing there was no escape.

She could hear the clock on the mantel ticking—from the open window she heard a horse whinny. Time passed slowly, and she waited as if frozen in time. But the rattler didn't strike.

She watched in horror as it performed a grotesque ritual. Its forked tongue slid out of the small slit of its mouth, gliding in and out, actually touching the back of her hand. Her father had once told her that rattlers smelled with their tongues. The horrible creature was actually smelling her hand! Her stomach heaved with revulsion and fear.

Rachel was never to know how she got from her bed to the window so quickly, or why the snake didn't strike her. On the verge of hysteria, she leaned out the window, calling over and over for someone to help her.

Moments later Zeb, Winna Mae and Tanner come bounding into her room. She clung to the windowsill, her gaze riveted on the loathsome reptile that was still coiled on her bed.

Rachel closed her eyes when Tanner stepped between her and the rattler. She heard his gun fire once, twice. She refused to look at her bed to see if he'd hit the target; he never missed his aim.

"Damned big one." Tanner lifted the disgusting thing and dangled it at arm's length. "Must be over six feet long."

"How'd a snake get up them stairs, and what's it doing on Miss Rachel's bed?" Zeb asked the question that was on all their minds.

"Ain't no snake going to climb no stairs," Tanner said. "Besides, they'd be looking for someplace to hole up this time of year. Somewhere away from people."

Winna Mae went to Rachel and took her trembling hands in hers. "Come on downstairs." She turned to Tanner. "Get that thing out of here. Zeb, bring Miss Rachel's bedding. I'll remake the bed later."

Rachel was still trembling when she sat at the kitchen table while Winna Mae shoved a cup of coffee at her. "Drink. The warmth will do you good."

Rachel shuddered. "Why didn't it strike me? I was on the bed with it and it actually touched my hand with its tongue."

"Smelling you."

"Yes."

"The Creator seems to look out for you, Rachel. By rights, you should be dead or dying right now."

Zeb came into the kitchen and dumped Rachel's bedding. He then sat down beside Rachel and poured himself a cup of coffee.

Rachel took a drink of the hot brew and then another, wishing she could stop trembling. "Someone had to have put the snake in my room. But who? Why?"

Zeb and Winna Mae exchanged glances.

"Could Harvey Briscal have done it?" Zeb asked.

"He would have had time while I was out back," Winna Mae answered. "I believe we should suspect him unless we learn otherwise. We shouldn't trust anyone," she added.

Rachel took another drink of coffee, wishing it were her father's whiskey. She couldn't stop shivering. She was hardly aware of the conversation between Zeb and Winna Mae. "This is the third time in as many months that I've faced death," she said in an amazed voice.

Again, Zeb and Winna Mae exchanged glances.

Winna Mae answered a knock at the door. She was surprised to see Noble Vincente standing there, hat in hand.

"I am sorry, Señor Vincente, but Miss Rachel is not at home. Two of the horses broke out of the corral and she's helping round them up."

"I know. It's you I came to see. May I come in and talk to you for a moment, Winna Mae?"

She nodded, wondering what Noble Vincente would have to say to her. "Can I get you anything, coffee or, if you like, something stronger?"

"No. Nothing, thank you."

She led him into the parlor and offered him the cushioned chair by the window. With his polished manners, he remained standing until she was seated.

Winna Mae's face was stoic. She was accustomed to hiding her feelings—that was the Indian in her. "How can I help you, Señor Vincente?" she asked politely.

"I have come to help you, if that's possible."

"What makes you think I need help?"

He smiled slightly, and Winna Mae thought he was the handsomest devil she'd ever seen. She wondered if any woman, regardless of her age, would be safe when Noble Vincente displayed his charm.

"Tell me about your husband and son."

"What? How can you know about them?"

"Zeb told me. I hope you won't scold him; he only wanted to help Rachel. It seems she won't be happy until you have news of your family."

"They are dead." This was said with conviction. "So you see, you can't help me."

"They may very well be dead, but I have a man who can look into the matter for us. I'm not saying he'll find your family, but if anyone is capable, it's he."

"And who might this man be?"

Knowing her story, Noble was amazed by the peacefulness that seemed to surround her. He answered her with directness. "A lawyer from New Orleans named George Nunn. I trust him completely."

"And you think he can help me?"

"I don't honestly know. But what have you got to lose?"

She nodded, seeing the sense of his words. "I will tell you what you need to know," she said, realizing he was helping her for Rachel's sake. She looked into his eyes and saw raw emotion there, although he was almost as good at masking his feelings as she.

Winna Mae knew in that moment that he was in love with Rachel. She wasn't sure if he knew it yet.

She told him her story and he listened patiently. He took no notes, but she could see that he was memorizing names and places. When she could tell him no more, he stood.

"I hope we can help you, Winna Mae. But I don't put too much faith in the endeavor. It's been such a long time. As you said, the army doesn't keep records on their Indian prisoners."

She walked him to the door, where he turned back to her. "I would appreciate it if you didn't say anything to Rachel about my visit today. You know how proud she is."

Winna Mae opened the screen door for him and stood back for him to pass. "I will say nothing to her."

Winna Mae watched Noble ride away on his mahogany horse, his back erect, his head at a proud tilt. Rachel would be happy with this man, she thought. But he had been right when he said that Rachel was very proud, and pride, when wrongly directed, could kill love. Or perhaps Rachel did not return his love. Winna Mae did not know.

Noble dismounted before the telegraph office and went inside. Moments later, after sending a telegram to George Nunn in New Orleans, he crossed the street and entered the sheriff's office.

Ira Crenshaw's head was bent over his book work. He glanced up with an amused glint in his eyes. "I guess you don't have enough to keep you occupied at Casa del Sol and have to come into town to ruin my day." His broad smile and the dancing light in his gaze bore witness to the fact that he was glad to see Noble.

"I thought you might get fat and lazy in your mundane job, and need a diversion."

Ira reared back in his chair, balancing it on the back legs, and shook his head. "I hear nothing but good things about you these days. I'm getting mighty sick of the sugary praise heaped on you by Jess McVee and his missus. They've got the whole town thinking you can sprout wings and fly, or even walk on water."

Noble sat down in the rickety wooden chair opposite the sheriff and folded his arms across his chest. "I know. They can't do enough for me. It always amazes me how quickly a person can change sides. When I first returned, they hated me so much they didn't want my money."

"Yep. I know what you mean." Ira shoved aside his paperwork. "What brings you to town?"

"I have been hearing some nasty rumors about high taxes and families being forced off their ranches. Is it true?"

The sheriff nodded, his expression suddenly somber. " 'Fraid so. The culprit is a company called Land and Trust out of Austin."

"Could they be land speculators? What do you know about them?"

"It's possible. I can't seem to find out much about them. I wrote to the state tax assessor last week and should hear something soon. I wager they slapped a high tax on Casa del Sol."

"You'd win your wager."

"But you can pay."

"Yes. But many others can't." Noble looked at his old friend. "I'd like to know if the high taxes are statewide, or if they're merely focused on Madragon County."

"If you can find out, you're a better man than me." Ira grinned broadly. " 'Course, I don't have the power you wield, with the Vincente name behind you."

Noble smiled. "Hell, you're much too modest." He rolled to his feet. "I'm going to speak to Thomas Bradley at the bank and find out what he knows about the sudden rise in taxes."

"He doesn't know anything. He's as sickened by this mess as the rest of us. His two brothers lost their spreads."

Austin, Texas

"You did what?" Whit looked at Harvey Briscal in anger and disbelief.

"I put a rattler in her bedroom—a big one. There were four bedrooms upstairs, but I didn't have no trouble finding hers. Thought a snake would be better than just shooting her outright."

"Fool! Do you think Winna Mae isn't clever enough to have figured out that you're the culprit who put the snake in the bedroom? Dammit, do I have to do everything myself?"

"You said to get rid of Rachel Rutledge, and to

do it in such a way that everyone would think it was an accident."

Whit paced the floor, his eyes revealing little of what was hidden behind them. "Oh, so they are supposed to think that you just happened by on the day a rattlesnake was found in her room? I believe we can safely assume that the snake has been found by now. If she's been bitten, God help you, because I won't."

Harvey wondered why Mr. Chandler was so riled. He'd had to hunt for five hours to find that snake. Then he had had to catch the damn critter and bag it. "Your sister-in-law might be dead," Harvey said hopefully.

Whit looked at Harvey as if he'd lost his mind. He'd hired him after failing to enlist Tanner or any of the other hands at the Broken Spur to keep him informed of Rachel's movements. He'd ended up with the biggest, most feebleminded bastard in the state of Texas.

Whit's anger was apparent from the thick veins that stood out on his forehead, and Harvey realized that this was a dangerous man to cross.

"I want you to do one more thing for me, Harvey. Then I want you to lay low for a while. This time I want you to follow my instructions exactly. And be careful. If any of that bunch from the Broken Spur gets hold of you, they're so protective of Rachel, they'd as soon shoot you as look at you." His eyes hardened. "Do I make myself clear?"

"Yes, sir, you do." Harvey's gaze darted to the

door, then nervously back to Whit. "After I do this one thing for you, I reckon I'll just take myself down to El Paso for a spell. Go across the border and have me a look-see."

"Now you're using your head." Whit bestowed an enigmatic glance on Harvey. "I'll have someone contact you in El Paso with money enough to keep you in style for a long time to come."

Harvey nodded vigorously. "Just tell me what you want me to do, and I'll do it."

"We have to act fast, Harvey. Now that Noble Vincente has started looking into—" Whit's voice broke off. He'd confided too much in Harvey already. If he was caught, the fool would probably spill his guts. "Time is running out, and if you fail me this time, Harvey, you'll regret it."

"I won't fail you this time, Mr. Chandler," he said, looking into the coldest eyes he'd ever seen. A chill started at the base of his skull and ran all the way to his spine. If he failed this time, he wouldn't live long afterward.

Whit glanced down at his desk and tapped his finger impatiently. Word had reached him that Noble Vincente was asking questions and poking his nose where it didn't belong. It wouldn't take long for a man with Noble's connections to discover that Land and Trust was owned by Whit and some of his business partners, or that some of those partners were getting scared and wanted to pull out of the deal.

Whit felt eaten up with hatred for Noble. Nothing and no one must stand in his way of buying Broken Spur for back taxes. Broken Spur was just a river crossing away from the real prize—Casa del Sol.

Whit could hardly wait to see himself as owner of that great hacienda.

Chapter Twenty-two

It had always been Rachel's habit to wake before sunup, but this particular morning she was up even earlier. The bunkhouse was still dark, so the hands weren't even stirring yet. Usually she ate a quick meal and then joined her men, ready for the day's work.

This morning she carried her cup of coffee out onto the front porch, absorbing the essence of the land she loved so well.

She listened with her heart to the night sounds that were just giving way to the whispers of day: the hooting of the barn owl was soon replaced by the cooing of the morning dove, and the howling of the wolf gave way to a mockingbird's trill. Two scissortails were perched on the corral fence, nervously watching one of the barn cats crouched nearby.

Rachel feared she would soon lose everything—that someone else would own the Broken Spur before spring. She watched as the lamps were lit in the bunkhouse, sending out a glow from the windows. The men were preparing for the day's chores. She took a sip of coffee and inhaled the sweetness of the earth, feeling anguish so sharp it stole her breath. If she lost the Broken Spur, she would have failed her father a second time—the first was in not discovering who had killed him.

How could she live with such failure? she wondered bleakly.

She watched the sunrise, at first just a faint, ghostly glow in the east, and then a splash of color, a radiance that washed the land in golden light.

She placed her coffee cup on the porch railing, her hand fisted at her side. She swallowed several times, overcome with heartsickness. She could sell the Broken Spur to Whit. That would at least keep the ranch in the family. Every fiber of her being cried out against such an outrage, while sickening turmoil churned inside her.

No. Whit would never own one grain of dirt from the Broken Spur. Not as long as she lived.

A chill wind blew out of the north, sweeping across her face like cold fingers and making her shiver from some unknown fear. At least the weather had cooled down, she thought, a blessing since the summer had been so unbearably hot.

She tried to think about all the wonderful years she had lived with her family in this house, then braced her back against an ornate post that supported the porch overhang, her mind stubbornly returning to the troubles at hand. She had to find a way to keep the ranch—she just had to!

Noble groaned in his sleep, hugging his pillow to him, his hand caressing it as if it were the woman in his dream. He could feel her skin, smell her sweetness, taste her lips.

"Rachel," he said softly, but she did not answer. She slipped out of his arms, her mouth pouting as she stood naked before him. "Let me hold you, Rachel," he said with urgency.

She disappeared into a mist and he sat up in bed, his eyes open, feeling the agony of his loss.

"Dammit!" He slid out of bed and moved to the window. He should suffer; he deserved it, he told himself. He'd committed the unpardonable by taking Rachel's virginity. If she hated him for it, who could blame her? He rubbed the back of his neck and flexed his shoulders. His nerves were raw, and he wanted her so damned badly, he could think of little else.

"That woman is either going to kill me or cure me," he said to himself. "I think she'll kill me."

He watched the rising sun top the trees and quickly dressed. His dream still occupied his thoughts as he went downstairs and out the door. At the stable, he saddled his horse and rode away, hoping to put Rachel out of his mind. What he really wanted to do was ride over to the Broken Spur, take Rachel in his arms and force her to listen to him.

What could he say to her? "Your sister, Delia, never meant anything to me." Oh, Rachel would really fall into his arms if he said that.

It was early afternoon when Noble returned to the ranch and noticed the wagon pulled up to the house. He recognized Jess McVee, and suspected that he'd be the recipient of more home-baked desserts from Mrs. McVee.

He dismounted and strolled toward the house; then he noticed the woman Jess lifted from the wagon. She was slender and petite, and wore a green gown and carried a matching parasol. The parasol was held at an angle, which blocked his view of her face. The woman definitely wasn't Mrs. McVee, who was not nearly as slender or petite.

As Noble neared the wagon, Jess smiled. "I've brought you a present," he said blithely. "You'll like this one."

The woman turned toward Noble, and he judged her to be less than twenty. She was blond, elegant and beautiful. A stranger to him, and yet there was something familiar—

The young lady snapped her parasol shut and held her arms out to him. "Is this all the welcome I am to expect from my own brother?"

His heart opened up and a tide of feeling rushed through him. She looked so like their mother, her eyes huge and the same deep blue, her face the same shape, the same dimples dancing on each side of her mouth.

"Saber?"

She laughed and twirled around for his inspection. "It's I—all grown up." Then her face became serious. "I've come home because we need each other." She looked at him adoringly, the way she had as a child. "At least I need you, Noble."

He crossed the distance that separated them and enfolded her in his arms. "At last we are together. You don't know how much I . . ." He laughed, and for the first time in many years, he felt lighthearted. "The last of the Vincentes," he said, sliding his arm about her slender waist and guiding her toward the house. "Let's go inside to get you out of the sun." Remembering his manners, he glanced over his shoulder. "Join us, Jess."

"No. The two of you need to be alone. I'll just have some of your hands help me unload Miss Saber's belongings." Jess chuckled. "It appears she brought the whole of Georgia with her."

"Did you travel alone?" Noble asked, with a slight reprimand in his voice.

Saber Vincente peered up at her brother through her thick lashes. "Yes. But don't scold me. There's a good reason for it. Auntie wouldn't accompany me until next spring." She laid her head against his shoulder. "I couldn't wait that long to see you."

His heart melted. "Well, you're here safely. That's all that matters."

Once inside the house, Saber turned toward her brother's arms. "I have missed you so desperately. For so long I have wanted to come home, but our father forbade it. Then when I got the letter that he had died, I blamed myself for not being with him."

Noble held her away from him, shocked that she had experienced the same guilt he'd felt. "But you shouldn't feel guilt, Saber. Our father knew that he was dying and he wanted you safely away from here."

Her eyes were brimming with tears. "I know, but I wanted to be with him." She laid her head on her brother's shoulder and found a measure of comfort there. "I miss him so desperately."

Sorrow clouded Noble's vision, and his tone revealed his anguish when he said, "We have each other."

Saber smiled through her tears. "Yes, my dearest brother, we do have each other."

Then he asked, "Was it hard on you—the war, I mean? I know much of Georgia was devastated by the Yankees."

"Yes." She pondered his question. "They burned the plantation house, so I was forced to live in the overseer's cabin with Great-aunt Ellen. Everything was destroyed. All the beautiful furniture

Grandfather had purchased in France. The paintings—everything."

"I am so sorry for what you suffered." Noble drew his sister protectively into his arms.

"It was horrible at the time. But I never intended to live in Georgia. I'm Texas born and bred, and Texas is in my blood as it is in yours." She removed her lace gloves and placed them on the hall table and went back into his arms. "However, I do grieve that the Yankees burned the house where our mother was born and raised."

"Yes, I know," he said, his chin resting on the top of her head. "So Texas is in your blood, is it?" He could remember how he'd felt when he came home to find this house in shambles. "All things change," he said lightly. He held her away from him. "And you have changed from a child to a beautiful young lady."

Saber made a face at him and gave him a mischievous glance. "I was always a lady. But you say I am beautiful. Now that is what a woman likes to hear—even from her brother." She stood back and looked at him musingly. "I'll wager the ladies can't resist you."

He arched an eyebrow. "One of them manages to."

She laid her hand on his shoulder. "Well, this lady loves you, Noble."

He kissed her smooth forehead. "Welcome home, little sister."

* * *

There was a great celebration at Casa del Sol as the vaqueros and their families gathered to welcome Señorita Saber home. There was much happiness, and food was served in abundance. After eating, everyone gathered to celebrate the homecoming of a Vincente. The night was filled with the sound of Spanish guitars and the tapping shoes of the dancers, who whirled about in their colorful costumes.

Saber tapped her foot and then rose out of her chair to join the dancers. She was graceful and lovely as she clapped her hands and whirled to the Spanish dance she'd learned as a child.

Noble soon joined the dancers. His feet tapping out the rhythm, he wove gracefully among the other dancers. The shadows of loneliness had lifted, but not all the way.

After the revelers had gone to their own quarters, Saber linked her arm through her brother's. "What's wrong?" she asked, sensitive to his mood.

"Nothing," he answered, smiling down at her. "I was just thinking how Mother and Father would have enjoyed tonight."

"That's not all you were thinking." Saber's gaze fastened on his. "Who is the woman who makes you so melancholy?"

Noble gave her a half smile. "Am I that transparent?"

"To me you are," Saber replied kindly, placing her hand on his. "Who is she, Noble? Do you love her very much?"

"It's not worth talking about. And I wouldn't say I love her. I admire and respect her, and I owe her." He was reluctant to speak of Rachel, even to his sister. "She has good reason to hate me, so no fault can be laid at her door."

"Then you must be speaking of Rachel Rutledge."

He looked amazed. "How did you guess?"

"Because she believes that you killed her father."

"She knows I didn't now."

Saber looked puzzled. "And yet she still will not have you. I do not understand." Then her eyes became teasing. "You must be the foremost catch in all Texas. How can anyone resist you?"

"Let's not talk about me. Tell me about yourself. How many young Georgian gentlemen are going to come rushing to Texas to ask me for your hand in marriage?"

She blushed prettily. "He's not from Georgia."

"So am I to lose you so soon after we have been reunited?"

"No. At least not right away. Matthew is to be transferred to Montana Territory. He wants to be established before he sends for me."

"He's a soldier?"

"Yes. He's Major Matthew Halloway."

Noble guided her into the parlor and seated her beside him on the light blue sofa. "Tell me about him."

She studied the tips of her black kid slippers.

"He's a Yankee." She raised her searching gaze to his. "Do you mind?"

"Not if you love him, and he loves you."

She looked relieved. "I've been so afraid to tell you about Matt because I didn't know how you'd take it. He was afraid too that you would hold it against him that he fought for the North."

"Saber," he said, taking her small hand in his, "I believe I can say with assurance that Father would ask if the man loved you and if he was honorable. After that, he wouldn't dwell on the man's politics, and neither will I. All I want is for you to be happy."

He kissed her cheek and she threw her arms around his neck.

"Will he make you happy, Saber? And is he honorable?"

"Oh, yes. He's wonderful! He wants to come to Texas to meet you, if you will allow it."

"Allow it? As your legal guardian, I insist on it. I will see this Yankee for myself." Noble stood, bringing Saber up beside him. "Now it's off to bed with you. I'm sure you are exhausted. We'll talk more tomorrow."

"Will you tell me about Rachel?"

"I've already told you about her."

"You say that you don't love her, and yet you have all the symptoms of a man in love."

He tweaked Saber's pert little nose. "And just how would you know about what a man feels for a woman?"

She smiled. "A woman is born knowing. We all have the gift. Didn't you know?"

"God help me, I hope one woman I know can't read men as well as you say. Although I'm sure she can."

"Why should that worry you?" Saber looked inquiringly at her brother.

"You seem to have all the answers. Perhaps I should ask your advice before I go courting."

"You could do worse," she said, smiling. Then she became more serious. "I always liked Rachel, Noble."

"I like her too. But if she didn't hate me enough before, she will now."

"What did you do?"

Noble shook his head. "Interfered in her life. Paid most of her taxes, although I took pains to cover that up. It won't take her long to understand what I did, though. And you can take this for the truth—it wouldn't be unlike her to come gunning for me." He laughed when his sister's face became serious. "Don't worry; she wouldn't actually shoot me—I don't think."

"If you and Rachel are meant to be together, it will happen, Noble."

"Perhaps."

She yawned and he steered her toward the stairs.

"To bed with you."

She nodded and walked away from him, turning at the first step. "It's good to be home."

"You can't know what it means to me to have you back here. It's been lonesome without you."

She gave him the devilish smile that he remembered so well from her childhood. "You need me to put your house in order. Tomorrow I'll begin to rearrange every room. This house needs a woman's touch."

"I'll be glad to leave it all in your capable hands. But I want it to look much as it once did, if that's possible."

"I know. Me too."

He was leaning on the stair post and she was halfway up the stairs. "Good night, Saber. Sleep well."

She blew him a kiss. "Night."

After she had disappeared into her bedroom, Noble walked outside and glanced up at the sky. Something wild and wonderful was stirring within him. The river called him. He wanted to get on his horse and ride as fast as he could to see if Rachel was waiting for him there, but he knew she wouldn't be.

He went to his bedroom and lay down without undressing. He would embrace sleep, because perhaps he would dream of Rachel again. Perhaps he could hold her, kiss her, make love to her, even if it was only a dream.

Soon his eyes closed, and visions of Rachel whirled through his head. Her arms were outstretched, and the proud, haughty beauty belonged to him alone.

At least in the softness of the velvet night.

Chapter Twenty-three

The sky was a smoke-colored gray, and there was a definite nip to the air as Rachel stepped off the porch and walked toward the barn. She'd swallowed her pride about selling to the Yankees. She'd sell her stock to the Devil himself if it would help pay her cowhands.

Her mind raced ahead of her as she calculated how many head of horses she could sell and still have enough to run the ranch efficiently. Good cutting horses were always easy to sell, but not to the army—they had no need for horses with that particular endowment. Her neighbors were in the same trouble as she—they certainly couldn't buy her horses; in fact they had stock of their own to sell.

It was hopeless. If she sold every horse and her entire herd of cattle, she still wouldn't have enough money to pay her taxes. Tomorrow was the deadline. Her spirit raged. How could she walk away from the Broken Spur, as many of her neighbors had been forced to do with their ranches? But she would need money to pay her hands, feed everyone through the winter, purchase more cattle in the spring. Nothing could save the Broken Spur. She ached inside as she pictured loading up a wagon with her belongings and leaving the Broken Spur for the last time.

How would she be able to bear it?

As she entered the barn, she lit a lantern and walked past each stall until she came to Faro's. She reached out her hand and laid it on the mare's shiny black coat. She would get a good price for Faro. The banker had been wanting to buy her for his wife; his offer had been a generous one.

Rachel laid her face against Faro's. "How can I sell you? You're . . ." What was Faro, and why couldn't she part with her? She had been more than just a horse. She represented a time in Rachel's life when everything had been beautiful.

The door suddenly slammed shut and the lantern went out, casting the barn into darkness. Rachel made her way to the front of the barn, thinking the wind had blown the door shut and put out the lantern as well. Pushing against the door, she was astonished to find it stuck. Zeb took pride in his work, and he had certainly done himself proud when he made the barn door so sturdy. No matter how hard she pushed against it, it wouldn't budge.

It appeared to be locked from the outside. But that wasn't possible.

She called out to Zeb, before she remembered that he and all the cowhands had left early that morning, driving the herd to town to be sold at the stockyard.

No one could hear her if she yelled.

She laughed aloud, wondering how she had gotten into this predicament. She wasn't really concerned, but she wondered how long it would take Winna Mae to come searching for her.

Her eyes had grown accustomed to the dark by now, and she reached for the lantern to relight it. A noise from the loft caught her attention; she assumed it was one of the cats that lived in the barn to keep the mice away.

She still wasn't concerned, merely wondered how she'd ever explain how she came to be locked in her own barn. She finally lit the lantern and placed it back on the hook. Most of the barn was cast in shadows, with only a tiny circle of light cast by the lantern.

Again she heard a sound above her, and she made her way toward the ladder that led to her hayloft. She heard the door in the loft slam shut, and the sound of the pulley grinding as if someone was riding it downward. The horses were getting restless, whinnying, while some of the more spirited animals kicked against their stalls.

"It's all right," she called out, thinking her voice would calm them. But why was her pulse racing, and why did she feel that someone had been in the barn with her? She smelled the smoke before she saw the flames, and her heart slammed against her chest.

Someone had locked her in the barn and set it on fire! The loft would be her only escape because there was no lock on the upper door. She had to make it out in time to save the horses!

She ran toward the steps that led upward, but a streak of fire seemed to dive at her from above, the dry hay only serving to feed the blaze until it was an inferno. In no time, the loft was a blinding wall of flame.

With her hand in front of her face to protect it, Rachel climbed the first step, but the heat from the flames drove her backward. Now the horses were fear maddened and they thrashed and kicked against their stalls, trying to get free.

Without thinking, she ran to the stalls, fumbling until she unlatched each half door, then throwing them open. Her lungs were filling with smoke, and she stumbled toward the front of the barn. That would be her only route of escape, because the loft was now totally enveloped in flames.

In spite of the intense heat, Rachel felt a chilling sensation—like a snake winding itself around her heart and squeezing. The smoke rolled toward her like a dark, ominous beast, stinging her eyes and stealing her breath. A great wall of fire lunged forward, devouring everything in its path.

With wild terror she banged on the door, crying as loud as she could, knowing the thickness of the door muffled her cries, and Winna Mae was too far to hear her anyway.

The heat was so intense that she couldn't breathe, and smoke made it impossible to see. She dropped to her knees, breathing the air from the crack at the bottom of the door. Coughing, she couldn't catch her breath as three barn cats circled her legs, mewing, pushing, circling in fear. This time, whoever had been trying to kill her would probably succeed, she thought, her arms falling limply at her sides and blackness engulfing her.

Winna Mae wondered what could be keeping Rachel. The noon meal was laid out on the kitchen table and the stew was ready to serve. She walked to the front porch—something was making her feel uneasy.

That was when Winna Mae saw flames crackling from the roof of the barn, climbing, swirling serpentine toward the sky. "Rachel!" she cried loudly. "Where are you?"

No answer.

Winna Mae realized that Rachel would undoubtedly rush heedlessly into the barn to save the stock and would need her help. She ran across the porch, down the walk and toward the barn. She was out of breath by the time she reached the barn door. She paused for only a moment, wondering why the wooden bar lay across the double doors, locking them into place. She could hear the shrill, unnerving sound of terrified horses and shoved the bar aside, swinging the doors open.

The sudden rush of air drew the flames like a magnet toward Winna Mae. She saw Rachel lying so still that she feared she might be dead. Grabbing both of Rachel's arms, she dragged her outside. Three barn cats scampered ahead of the five terrified horses stampeding into the open air.

Winna Mae bent over Rachel, feeling for a pulse at her throat. She bent low and felt her warm breath on her cheek. Relief washed over her when she felt the strong beat of Rachel's heart. She turned her on her side and rushed to the well, wet her apron and rushed back to Rachel.

Winna Mae washed the soot from Rachel's face and shook her gently. "Rachel, Rachel. Open your eyes."

Nothing.

"Rachel," she said forcefully, lightly slapping her on each cheek. "Wake up!"

Rachel's eyelashes fluttered, and she took in a gulp of air, and then another, bringing color back to her face. She wanted to tell Winna Mae she was all right, but the words clung to her dry lips and she could not utter a sound.

"Rachel, breathe deeply," Winna Mae instructed her. "That's right. Now more."

Rachel coughed and gasped. Her parched lungs were hungry for pure air. After a fit of coughing, she finally sat up with Winna Mae's help and drew more precious, life-giving air into her lungs. They both watched silently as the barn exploded outward, then collapsed into ashes and flames.

Rachel turned to Winna Mae and had to try several times before she could find her voice. Even then it was little more than a throaty whisper. "The horses?"

"I don't know. I hope they all got out."

"Faro?"

"I don't know. Hush now. Don't try to talk."

Rachel shook her head and tried to rise, but fell back. Her mouth felt so dry. She attempted to swallow, and by the third try she was successful. "Someone . . . tried . . . to—"

"I know," Winna Mae said incredulously. "Someone locked you in the barn and set fire to it." She took Rachel's trembling hand. "Do you think you can walk with my help?"

Rachel nodded. But when she stood on shaky legs, she sagged toward Winna Mae and leaned heavily against her. Walking slowly, they finally made it to the porch. Rachel turned to look back at the barn, which was only smoking embers. Her gaze searched frantically for Faro, but she didn't see her.

Winna Mae assisted her into the house and seated her at the kitchen table while she poured milk into a tin mug.

"You . . . saved my—"

"Hush. Don't talk just now," the housekeeper told her, adding a liberal amount of honey to soothe Rachel's throat. "Drink this." She extended the mug to Rachel. "Later we will talk. Tomorrow, perhaps."

Wetting a cloth, Winna Mae wiped more soot from Rachel's face and was relieved to find that her skin wasn't burned. Then she saw the redness on Rachel's hands and doused them in a pan of water. There were burn blisters on both palms and on her upper right arm. Winna Mae deftly covered them with ointment and then wrapped them in white gauze.

"Winna Mae, who would want me dead?" Rachel asked worriedly. "Who would—"

"I don't know," Winna Mae interrupted her again, her tone uneven. "But it's time we found out."

After Rachel had drunk the milk-and-honey concoction Winna Mae mixed for her, she found her throat didn't hurt quite so much. But Winna Mae insisted she go to bed, and Rachel agreed, after making Winna Mae promise that she would find out if Faro had gotten out of the barn safely.

Although Rachel didn't think she would be able to rest, she was so exhausted, her eyelids fluttered shut and she fell into a deep sleep.

She did not know that Winna Mae stood over her with a troubled frown. Someone was definitely trying to kill Rachel, but who? Winna Mae tried to think who would hate Rachel enough to lock her in the barn and then set fire to it.

Winna Mae reached out and laid her hand against Rachel's cheek. "Sleep easy. I will watch over you."

That night the much-longed-for rain came. Lightning dove across the sky on jagged wings like a fire-breathing dragon. Intermittent wind gusts bowed the trees, and rain capered across the land, settling the dust and washing down the gullies toward the Brazos River, filling the river to its banks. The storm tore across the land, downing trees and cutting a path through the tall, dry grass.

Rachel awoke to the patter of rain against her window. She thought she must be dreaming. Could it really be raining?

Lightning pulsed, streaked, illuminated the land, but the rain had come too late to help the ranchers who had lost their spreads, and it had come too late to help Rachel.

She heard movement and turned her head to see Winna Mae sitting beside her bed, a rifle across her lap.

"You should get some sleep," Rachel said. "Don't worry about me. The men will be home day after tomorrow."

"I'll go to bed directly." Winna Mae had no intention of leaving Rachel tonight, but she knew Rachel wouldn't sleep if she thought she was staying up on her account. "Faro's fine."

Relief resounded in her voice. "You found her?"

"No, she found me. She came to the back door stomping and noisily demanding attention. I led her to the corral and gave her hay and water, then latched the gate."

Rachel let out a grateful sigh and closed her eyes. "It's raining."

"Yes, it is."

Rachel slept peacefully while jagged streaks of lightning played tag with boisterous thunder that made the ground tremble. The long-awaited rain pelted against the cracked and scarred land, which thirstily soaked up the deluge, and began to heal.

Rachel walked toward what remained of her barn, which was now just a hideous dark thing that smelled sickeningly of wet ashes. She reached up and touched her throat; it was still dry and hurt like the devil. Even the rain that had come in the night, ending the drought, brought her no joy. With a heavy heart she entered the corral where Faro waited for her.

After examining the mare closely, Rachel was satisfied that she'd escaped injury. She patted her horse's sleek neck, and gave her a carrot.

Her saddle and all the tack had burned in the barn, so she formed a makeshift bridle out of leather rope and slipped it over Faro's head; then, clutching her rifle, she bounded onto the mare's back.

"Let's go round up the other horses," she said, leaning close to Faro's head. She shivered when she thought of how close she'd come to losing this creature that was so dear to her.

Winna Mae called out to her, but Rachel was too far away to hear. The housekeeper shook her head. "That Rachel," she mumbled to herself. "Someone tried to kill her yesterday, and today she thinks only of the horses."

She entered the house and placed the coffeepot on the back of the stove. The men wouldn't be home until tomorrow. Until then, she wanted to be sure that Rachel was safe. But how could she protect her if she went riding about the countryside as if she didn't have a care in the world?

Rachel held her rifle across her lap, her eyes sweeping the terrain ahead of her. Someone wanted her dead, and she didn't know who it was. But she wasn't going to hide in the house like a witless coward.

She just had to be more careful from now on, and trust no one but Zeb and Winna Mae, and maybe Tanner.

She tried to think who could want her dead. Delia? No, not her sister. She knew Delia had faults— she drank, and deep down she was unhappy—but Rachel also knew that her sister loved her and would never hurt her. Could it be Whit? Perhaps. He was capable of anything. But she doubted he would go as far as trying to kill her. What about Noble? Her breathing closed off and she experienced a stabbing pain in her heart.

"Please don't let it be Noble," she said aloud.

Chapter Twenty-four

The weather had suddenly turned bitterly cold, and dark thunderheads dominated the western sky, while the eastern sky had an eerie yellow glow.

Rachel stepped off the porch and watched the cowhands ride in with Tanner at their head. She allowed her glance to linger on each face, wondering if one of the men who worked for her had locked her in the barn and then set it on fire. She decided that none of them would have committed such a heinous act. Besides, they had been in town with Tanner and Zeb.

The cowhands stared in dismay at the charred remains of the barn; then each turned his gaze to their lady boss. They noticed that Rachel's hands were bandaged, and they looked even more puzzled.

"We had a fire," she said, stating the obvious, unwilling to explain what had really happened when she wasn't even sure herself. Later she would explain to Tanner and Zeb what had happened, and they could warn the others to be on their guard against any strangers who showed up at the ranch.

"Lightning must've struck the barn," Tanner said, dismounting and moving toward the blackened ruins for a closer look. "Did the animals get out, Miss Rachel?"

"Yes," Rachel answered. "All of them."

Zeb reached down and picked up the hinges from the ashes and studied them for a moment. Then his canny gaze swung to Rachel's face and to her bandaged hands, which she'd kept clasped behind her. He read more from what she wasn't saying than from what she'd said. "I knew I shouldn'ta gone into town and left you alone. There's too many strange calamities been happening lately." He closely examined the twisted hinge and scratched his head reflectively. "Any fire hot enough to melt this weren't nature made. No siree, it was a man done this—'less I miss my guess."

Winna Mae met the old man's eyes, sending him a silent confirmation of his suspicions.

Meanwhile Rachel drew Tanner aside, while the other hands strolled toward the bunkhouse, anxious to put the coffee to brewing before Zeb set his hand to it.

Tanner looked down at Rachel's hands. "You got that in the fire?"

Rachel nodded. "I'll tell you about it later. How much did you get for the herd?" she asked.

The roughness of Tanner's face smoothed out and he smiled. "I brought you some good news, Miss Rachel."

"What?" She could use some good news, she thought.

"I sold the cattle at the stockyard like you said. And as we suspected, a Yankee sergeant bought them all for the army."

"Is that supposed to cheer me up?" She shifted from one foot to the other, while trying to follow his reasoning. "I didn't want to sell to the Yankees, but what choice did I have?"

"They're offering even less than we figured," Tanner continued. "Three dollars a head and not the four we wanted. But I took it like you told me to."

She sighed inwardly, calculating the total. "It's not nearly enough. Did you pay the men?" That was her first concern.

"Yes, ma'am." He gazed back at the charred remains of the barn. "Then I took myself over to the tax assessor, thinking I might be able to talk him into taking part of the taxes now and the rest after spring roundup."

Rachel's eyes brightened with hope. "Tanner,

are you telling me he agreed to wait until spring for the rest of the taxes?"

"Nope. Better than that. He said they'd made a mistake in your tax assessment. Said your taxes were only two hundred and fifty dollars. I paid him right then, knowing that was what you'd want me to do." Tanner looked pleased. "I didn't know those tax people could make mistakes. 'Specially not such a whopper."

Instead of looking pleased, Rachel's eyes became like sword points. She felt her heart plummet and she was overwhelmed by agony. For a long moment she stood like a statue while her mind whirled. "They don't make mistakes, Tanner," she exclaimed.

Before Tanner realized what Rachel was doing, she jerked the reins out of his hand, crammed her booted foot into the stirrups and swung onto his saddle. "Tell Winna Mae not to worry about me. I'm going to see Noble Vincente."

"Miss Rachel," Zeb called, hurrying after her, "the river's up. Could be flooding by now. 'Sides, I feel a coldness in my bones—there's worse weather on the way—could be one of those blue northers coming. Don't go riding off anywhere."

Usually just the words *blue norther* struck fear in the heart of anyone who had ever felt the effects of the uncommon storm. Rachel merely looked at the old man for a moment and then urged the horse into a gallop, leaving Zeb to eat the horse's dust.

Tanner watched Rachel ride away astride his horse. If he lived to be a hundred, he'd never understand women—especially not that pretty little filly. He'd thought Rachel would be pleased about the taxes. But she sure as hell hadn't been. What bee was buzzing around in her bonnet? he wondered. He turned to Zeb and shrugged, noticing that the old man looked worried.

Tanner wanted a cup of coffee to warm him. It had dropped at least ten degrees since they'd ridden in.

Zeb had been right about the river. It was full to its banks and running swiftly, with uprooted trees and other debris being swept downstream. Unmindful of the danger, Rachel plunged the horse into the swollen current, and after being carried downstream, they made it safely across.

Rachel set her eyes on the distance while anger gnawed at her. She hadn't a doubt in her mind that Noble had paid the bulk of her taxes. Yes, and he had concocted the story that the tax assessor had told Tanner. If he thought she would be grateful to him, he was mistaken. She would rather lose the Broken Spur than take Noble's money.

Wet and bedraggled, Rachel dismounted and hurried up the walkway to Noble's house. Knocking on the door, she braced herself, ready to do battle with him and wishing she had the money to throw in his face.

Margretta opened the door and smiled brightly

when she saw Rachel. "Pardon, Señorita Rachel, *el patrón*"—she hesitated, trying to find the words in English—"is away. Please to . . . enter."

"*Gracias*, no," Rachel replied in frustration. "Tell Señor Vincente that I want to see him at once."

Margretta looked puzzled. "Pardon, señorita?" She looked behind her and motioned for someone to come forward. Her husband, Alejandro, appeared at her side. His lips curved into a smile when he saw Rachel.

"Come in, señorita," said Alejandro, who had a better command of English than his wife. "You are welcome in this house."

"Is Señor Vincente at home, Alejandro?"

"No, señorita. He will not be back until afternoon."

Rachel had torn the bandages away from her hands before she entered the river, and they were cold. She reached into the pocket of her heavy coat and removed her gloves. Impatiently she worked her fingers into them, wincing at the pain from her burns. "Tell Noble when he comes home that I want to see him."

"*Sí*, I will tell him, Señorita Rachel. But he will be sorry to miss you. Will you not come inside and wait? I am sure that Señorita Saber would be glad to see you."

"Saber has come home?" Rachel asked, knowing if it were any other time, she would be happy to see Noble's sister.

"*Sí*, Señorita Rachel." He stepped away from the door to allow her to enter. "Come in."

As much as Rachel would have liked to see Saber, she was too angry for pleasantries. "Just give my message to your *patrón*." She turned away and mounted her horse.

With a troubled expression, Alejandro watched her ride away. As he glanced at the clouds, his anxiety deepened. There was a storm brewing, and it looked as if it would be a bad one. He hoped the señorita would reach home before it struck.

As often happened in West Texas, the blue norther struck without warning, making Zeb's prediction come true. The temperature plummeted to below freezing within minutes. Snow fell eastward, slowly at first, and then with blinding intensity. The wind whipped across the land, bending trees, its howl sounding like a woman's scream.

Rachel had not yet reached the Brazos when she was surrounded by a world of swirling, bone-chilling cold. The snow was so heavy, she couldn't see past her horse's head. She knew that she had to find shelter soon or she would freeze to death. She became disoriented. Frantically she glanced behind her, wondering which direction to take.

Huddling in her coat, she had never felt so cold. Why hadn't she listened to Zeb? If only the wind would stop blowing, she might be able to hear the river and gauge her direction.

A strong gust drove snow into her face, and it

felt like tiny needles pricking her skin. She had known people who had been caught in a blue norther and had barely escaped death. Six years ago, Hamp Whitlock had frozen to death while looking for strays. When they found him, he was less than a hundred yards from his house. It was said that he'd lost his direction in the blinding snow and couldn't find his way.

The horse stumbled over a slippery spot and went down with Rachel on its back. She managed to free her left leg, which was wedged beneath the horse, and slide out from under its bulk. She grasped the reins and pulled. "Come on. You have to get up or you'll freeze to death."

The poor animal attempted to rise, but made an agonizing sound of pain. Rachel quickly examined the horse's right front leg and she realized, in horror, that it was broken. She had left in such a hurry that she had neglected to bring a gun, so she was unable to put the animal out of its misery.

Unsure of what to do, she sat down near the thrashing animal, wondering who would find their bodies when the storm cleared. No man would go out in this storm to look for her, because it would mean his death as well.

She didn't know how much time passed, but the horse lay quieter now, only making occasional soft whinnies. Her teeth chattering and her body trembling from cold, she dropped her head on the horse's neck, needing to feel close to another living creature. She tried to guess her location, but nothing looked familiar. She was still on the Casa del Sol side of the Brazos because she hadn't crossed the river. Would Noble be the one to find her dead body?

Visions of his face flashed before her, and she cried out to him. "Noble, help me. Please help me." She had always heard that one called out for one's beloved at death, and she had called for Noble. Until now, she hadn't known the extent of her love for him.

She felt as if a weight pressed in on her chest, and she had never been so cold. With death beckoning to her, she could be honest at least with herself. "Noble, I love you," she said between trembling lips. But her cry mingled with the snow and was lost on the wings of the howling norther.

Rachel didn't know how much time had passed, but the horse lay completely still. She tried to rake the snow off the poor animal, but it was falling too heavily. Ice had formed on Rachel's lashes and in her hair. She hardly felt the cold now, only numbness. The air seemed to freeze in her lungs and throat. A sensation not unlike swimming in the river came over her and she closed her eyes, giving herself over to the lingering comfort it offered.

Sleep, that was what she needed—sleep. It hurt to move, it took effort for her to open her eyes, and it took all her strength just to breathe.

*   *   *

Noble spoke quickly to Alejandro. "Tell me again what Rachel said." His eyes went to the window, but he could see nothing past the blinding snowstorm.

"She said she wanted to see you, *Patrón*. And when I told her you were not here, she went away. I asked her to wait, that there was bad weather coming, but she went anyway."

Noble reached for his wool-lined coat and lifted his rifle from the gun rack. "I must look for her. She couldn't have made it home in time to avoid the norther."

"But *Patrón*, you will get lost in the snow," Alejandro argued, his dark eyes filled with concern. "If you go, I will go with you."

Noble walked to the door, and stopped as if he were listening to something. "Did you hear that?"

"I heard only the wind," Alejandro said. "What did you hear?"

Noble shook his head. "Nothing. I thought for a moment that someone—that Rachel called. No. It's probably only the wind."

Noble opened the door, and the wind was so strong it almost drove him and Alejandro backward. An urgency gripped him as he swung into the saddle and rode in the direction Rachel would have taken. If she had stayed in a straight line, he might find her, if not—no, he wouldn't allow himself to think about that possibility.

Alejandro stayed close to his side, fearing they would be separated in the storm.

317

Noble felt the moment the wind shifted from the north to the east and died down somewhat, making it easier to see. His face was grim as he searched right and left. If Rachel had been lost in this storm, they had to find her soon, or it would be too late.

Perhaps it was already too late. His heart clenched like a fist and hammered against the wall of his chest. No, he would know it if Rachel were dead.

Rachel moaned and tried to shut out the persistent voice that kept calling her name. She just wanted to be left alone. Go away, she thought. Had she said it aloud? She couldn't be sure. Then again, she might be dreaming.

She felt warmth cover her and spread throughout her body. Then she thought she heard a shot and a faint whinny from Tanner's horse. Had someone put the poor animal out of its misery? But then again, she might be delirious.

Rachel tried to open her eyes but it took too much effort. She had the sensation of being lifted onto a horse, and someone was holding her against his body. She buried her face against the person's neck and drifted away again.

"Rachel, stay awake—stay with me. It's just a short ride to the line cabin."

She clearly heard Noble's voice, or had she conjured him up in her need for him?

"Rachel." Noble shook her this time. "Don't go

318

to sleep. Talk to me. Come on." His voice was insistent. "Talk to me, Rachel."

"I called for you," she said without opening her eyes.

"I know you did, Rachel." He was too concerned that she might die to wonder how he had heard her calling him all the way from Casa del Sol.

"You're falling asleep on me again, Rachel. Fight the sleep. You can do it."

"No." She batted his hand away. "I don't want to."

"Think of how angry you are with me, Rachel," he told her. "Think about the reason you came to Casa del Sol when you knew a storm was coming."

"Yes, angry." It was such an effort to speak, but she wanted to tell him how she felt before she surrendered to the arms of peaceful sleep. "You hurt me."

"Tell me what I did."

She could feel the horse moving beneath them, but everything was so fuzzy. Darkness hovered over her like an ominous cloud. Why wouldn't Noble let her sleep?

Noble looked down at Rachel with fear in his heart. The strands of her hair were frozen and matted with ice. He brushed snow from her face, hoping his horse knew where the hell it was going, because he couldn't see ten feet ahead of him. The line cabin was in the vicinity, but in such a storm he could easily miss it.

His worry at the moment was to keep Rachel

awake or she might succumb to the cold. He knew enough about her temperament to realize that if he made her angry enough, she would certainly fight back.

"Rachel, only a very foolish woman would venture out in such weather."

She did not respond.

He tried another tactic. "Have you no heart? Don't you care about the people who are worried about you? What about Winna Mae? She must be beside herself with worry. You are selfish, Rachel."

Still she gave no response.

"Rachel, have you considered Zeb? He's set himself up as your faithful watchdog. Think how worried he is at the moment."

No reaction.

He had to make her angry so she would respond to him. "Rachel, I thought your father taught you better than to come out in such weather. He would be disappointed in you at the moment."

With effort, she dragged her eyes open and glared at him. "I despise you, Noble."

He laughed and held her closer. "Despise me, hate me, my dearest Green Eyes, but keep talking to me—come on, talk! Tell me how much you loathe me."

She moaned and pushed his hand away. Why wouldn't he leave her alone so she could sleep?

Noble spoke close to her ear. "Talk to me, Rachel. You can't go to sleep because you may never wake up."

"You . . ." She tried to shake her head, to push him away again, but she was too weak. "Sleep. I need—"

She had gone limp in his arms, and he shook her violently.

"God, no, Rachel. No!"

Chapter Twenty-five

Rachel floated on a cloud of warmth and didn't want to open her eyes. For several minutes she just listened to the sounds around her, trying to identify them. She heard the crackling of a fireplace, the sound of sleet peppering a window, someone moving about quietly so as not to disturb her.

She opened her eyes halfway, peering through veiled lashes. She lay on a narrow cot in some kind of crude cabin. The walls were made of unfinished logs. Her hands brushed against and identified a woolen blanket that covered her. Whoever was here with her—she couldn't see who it was—placed something hot on the blanket next to her feet, and the delicious warmth worked its way up her legs.

Now the person stepped into her view and she recognized Noble, although his back was to her. He lifted a stone from the embers of the open fireplace with iron tongs and wrapped it in heavy cloths. When he turned toward her, she quickly closed her eyes. He placed the stone at her back, and the same warmth she'd felt at her feet spread through her upper body.

His footsteps moved to the side of the bed, and her eyes swept open to focus upon a pair of black Spanish boots. Her gaze went to his face and he smiled down at her.

He knelt beside her, placing his hand on her shoulder. "You had me worried for a time. How do you feel?"

Her eyes slid shut, and nothing could have induced her to open them. She floated on boundless warmth, drifting somewhere between reality and dreams.

She sighed in her sleep, and the worried frown on Noble's face eased. Rachel seemed to be sleeping naturally. She really was going to be all right. He sat beside the fire, his booted feet propped on the iron grate, his eyes on Rachel. When had she become so important to him? Why did he feel such an empty void, as if he were not a whole man unless he was with her? He'd been frantic when he thought he'd lost her in the storm. Did he believe in love, the lasting kind? He knew that his feelings for Rachel were strong, although he was not ready to call it love.

A slight smile curved his lips. She was like no other woman he'd ever known, obstinate, proud, sometimes foolishly rushing into danger with no thought for her safety. She could be fierce and deadly, like the time she defended him in Tascosa Springs, or she could be stunningly beautiful, like the night of the dance. Then she could be soft and desirable, like the night they made love by the Brazos and she matched his lovemaking with an equal passion.

Memories of that night swirled around in his head, and he closed his eyes. He must not dwell on that—not now. He had to find something for her to eat, something hot to heat her inside.

On a dusty shelf, he found several tins of beans, so he heated them in the iron pot suspended above the fire. He ladled some into a chipped blue bowl, and approached Rachel.

"I have something for you to eat, Rachel." He went down on his knees beside her. "Come on, wake up."

She opened her eyes and looked at the bowl. "What is it?"

He shrugged. "I'm afraid all we have is beans. But they will at least be hot and nourishing."

She pushed his hand away. "I don't want any."

"Nonetheless, you must eat." He raised her with one arm while balancing the bowl in his other hand. Although he supported Rachel, her head fell forward against his chest. He set the beans aside and held her close to him.

"I hope you realize what a damned foolish thing you did today, Rachel."

She wanted to push him away from her, and she wanted to stay snuggled against him. She remained in his arms. "I seem to recall your voice telling me how foolhardy I was." She pulled back to look at him and sighed. "Or did I dream that too? I'm not sure what's real and what isn't. I don't even know if I'm dreaming now."

He shook with laughter. "This is not a dream." He nodded at the cabin. "Surely, if you were dreaming, you'd imagine someplace better than this."

She pulled away from him when she remembered the reason that she had gone to Casa del Sol. "Did you pay the taxes on the Broken Spur?" she asked pointedly.

She felt him stiffen. "We'll talk about that later. Right now I want you to take at least two bites of beans and then I'll let you sleep all you want."

"Why is it that everyone always seems to want me to sleep?" she inquired with irritation.

"I can think of several reasons," he said in a teasing voice—so much like the old Noble she'd known. "You can't talk when you are asleep."

Instead of laughing at his light banter, she met his eyes questioningly. "What happened to Tanner's horse?"

"I shot it, Rachel."

It was her fault that a beautiful animal had had to be destroyed, and the guilt weighed heavily on her. "Thank you."

After that, she dutifully took several spoonfuls that he poked at her, wrinkling her nose after every bite. When she lowered her head to the mattress, Noble arranged the covers about her shoulders.

Noble rose to his full height and gazed down at her. "The storm let up just before we found you. Alejandro rode to the Broken Spur to let everyone know that you are safe." He looked toward the window. "It's stopped snowing for the moment, but the wind is still blowing."

She nodded gratefully, forgetting that she was supposed to be angry with him.

He walked to the small window and stared out into the encroaching darkness. The clouds had moved away as quickly as they had come, but there were other storm clouds hovering in the east. A dazzling sunset tinted the snow bloodred.

Rachel was docile for the moment, but after a rest she would be herself again, and unleash her anger on him. He should have known she'd find out that he'd paid her taxes. His lips thinned. He thought he'd been so clever in instructing the tax assessor just what to tell her. Apparently she hadn't been fooled for a moment.

He turned back to find her watching him. "Sleep," he said gently.

And she did.

Noble sat beside her, watching her sleep. Seeing that she still wore her gloves, he gently worked her fingers out of them. When he saw the angry burn marks, he lifted one hand, examined it, and then did the same with the other. Troubled, he wondered what kind of accident had happened to her. He touched his lips to one small palm and then pushed it gently under the wool blanket.

His eyes clouded with speculation. It seemed to him that too many accidents had been happening to Rachel lately.

Rachel felt the heat of the fire, and rolling, scorching smoke closed off her breathing. She tried to run, but her legs wouldn't move. She heard the sound of the terrified horses as the flames approached their stalls. She wanted to go to them and open their stalls, but again, she couldn't move.

She reached the barn door and banged against it with her hands, but no one could hear her.

"Help me," she cried. "The barn's on fire. For God's sake, help me!"

Strong hands caught her flailing arms and clamped onto her wrists. She was pulled against a hard body and she fought even more.

"Rachel, you're all right. It's only a dream. You are safe."

She heard Noble's voice and she clutched at his arm. "Noble, help me—help me!"

One arm held her close while his hand moved up and down her back soothingly. "Rachel, I'm here. I won't let anyone hurt you."

She grasped his shirtfront, her breathing labored. "Someone is trying to kill me," she whispered, still in the grip of her nightmare—not asleep anymore, but not yet awake.

Noble picked her up and carried her to a chair in front of the fireplace and sat down with her on his lap. His lips touched one closed eyelid and then the other, as he held her as tenderly as a baby. "No one can hurt you now, Rachel. I won't let them."

Rachel snuggled closer to him, needing his warmth and the assurance that his strong arms gave her. She drifted in and out of sleep. At last she opened her eyes. The cabin was in shadows since the lamp had burned out, and the fire in the hearth was only smoldering ashes. It took her a moment to realize she was in Noble's arms.

"It was only a dream, wasn't it?" she asked, seeking his eyes. "I had a nightmare, didn't I?"

"I don't know, Rachel." He lifted one of her hands and looked at the burns. "It seems to me that your nightmare was born out of some kind of reality. Was it?"

She pulled her hand free, feeling embarrassed. "How long have you been holding me?" She was now fully awake.

He shifted her weight to his left side. "Long enough for my arm to go numb."

She attempted to rise, but he pulled her back onto his lap. "Don't leave. I like you just where you are."

Slowly Rachel raised her gaze to his, and she melted beneath a pair of dazzling brown eyes. "I am always so confused when I'm with you, Noble," she admitted.

He touched his lips to the dimple in her cheeks, his voice deep with meaning. "Are you, Green Eyes?"

She drew away from him, looking mischievous. "Who can fault me for that? It seems every time we're together some disaster or another happens." She thought he would laugh—he didn't.

"Let's talk about those disasters."

"Which one?" she said with a twist to her lips.

He reached around her and managed to throw two large logs on the fire, making sparks fly up in an arc. Soon the dry wood ignited and he settled back. "Begin with what happened to your hands. It doesn't take the expertise of Dr. Stanhope to know that they were burned. How did it happen?"

Rachel's eyes went to her hands, and although it was painful, she balled them tightly in her lap. "It was nothing that should concern you."

His mouth settled in a firm line and his gaze probed hers. "Indulge me."

"My barn caught on fire."

"I see. And with your usual reckless disregard for your own safety, you ran inside the burning barn to save the horses. That's what happened, isn't it?"

She suddenly wanted to tell him about all the strange things that had happened to her lately. "No. I was in the barn at the time the fire started."

"So you kicked over a lantern?"

"No." She lowered her gaze because she could no longer look into his eyes, thinking how unbelievable her account sounded. "Someone locked the barn from the outside and set it on fire."

She could feel his chest expand when he took a deep breath. "Who was home at the time?"

"If you're thinking any of my men set fire to the barn, you're wrong. They had driven my herd to Tascosa Springs." She stared at her hands and trembled at the memory of that day in the barn. "I was fortunate that Winna Mae saw the smoke. And luckily, all the animals were saved. I was worried about Faro, but she's fine."

Noble knew that Rachel was not a woman given to exaggeration—if anything, she'd smoothed over the truth. If she said she'd been deliberately locked in, then that was exactly what had happened. "What other disasters have befallen you, Rachel?"

"I . . ." Her eyes grew frightened. "I found a diamondback coiled on my bed. When I discovered the hideous thing, it was right at my hand."

His arms tightened about her as if he could hold her fear at bay. "Your bedroom is on the second floor, isn't it?"

"Yes."

"I see."

She thought about the night Whit came into her room and tried to force himself on her. That incident she would never tell Noble. She stole a peek at him, and he was staring at the flickering flames that danced in the hearth. Did he think she was just a hysterical woman who saw trouble where there was none?

Noble already knew about the snake; Zeb had told him. But it was best to keep this knowledge to himself. Someone wanted Rachel dead—but who? His mind went back to the day she'd been shot. He'd always supposed the bullet had been meant for him. Now he wasn't so sure.

"Rachel, if you had an enemy, who would it be?"

"You."

His gaze dipped to her face. "I don't think you believe that."

Her lashes swept across her eyes as shame tinged her cheeks. All he had ever tried to do was to help her. "No. I don't think you would harm me. But I don't need your help, Noble."

He laughed and stood up to carry her to the bed, where he deposited her beneath the blanket. "Lord knows, you aren't doing very well on your own, Rachel. As I told you before, someone has to look after you."

She leaned on her elbow and gave him an impassioned glance. "And you think you are that someone?"

He watched her for so long and with such a soul-stirring expression that she wondered what thoughts were hidden behind those dark eyes.

"If not me, then who, Rachel?"

"You paid the taxes on the Broken Spur, didn't you?"

"Why would I do that?"

She got to her knees, her glorious red hair swirling out about her. "Dammit, Noble—stop answering my questions with questions! Did you or didn't you pay the taxes on the Broken Spur?"

He turned away and moved back to the warmth of the fireplace. "If I did, Rachel, we could call it a loan if it will make you feel better."

She slid out of bed and went to him. "I could never repay that kind of money." Her breasts rose and fell with each breath. "Did it ever occur to you that I don't want your help?"

"It occurred to me."

She felt suddenly dizzy and the room began to spin, so she reached out to steady herself against his arm. "Noble, who gave you the right to interfere in my life?"

He saw her turn pale, and in a move that surprised her, he lifted her in his arms and carried her back to the bed. "What's wrong, Rachel?" he asked gently, going down on his knees beside her. "Are you in pain?"

She pressed her hand over her eyes and licked her lips, while clutching the blanket so tightly in her fists that her knuckles whitened. "No. No pain. I . . . feel dizzy," she admitted.

His arm slid across her shoulder. "Why do you think you have to fight the whole world alone, Rachel? You are just one small woman. Let me take care of you."

She nodded. "You can start by lying beside me to make the room stop spinning."

He laughed and eased his weight down beside her, pulling her body against his. "Never was I issued an order so easy to carry out."

Although the blanket was between them, she could still feel the heat of his body. It didn't matter. She felt safe, and the room had almost stopped spinning now. She closed her eyes, her head falling against his shoulder.

"Sleep, Green Eyes. I'll battle all your demons for you."

She snuggled against him and closed her eyes, feeling safe and oh, so weary.

Chapter Twenty-six

Rachel awoke quickly, sat up and listened, her heart beating with fear. The wind howled and she could hear sleet hitting the window. The cabin was completely dark now and she felt her fear intensify.

"Noble!" she cried, reaching into the dark void. "Where are you?"

A firm hand took hers. "I'm here, Rachel. I just went outside to get more wood. Wait until I build a fire and I'll be with you."

His hand slid away from hers and he disappeared into the darkness. She could hear him laying the wood, and she held her breath until she saw a small flame ignite.

Noble was nothing more than a shadow that reflected bigger than life on the cabin wall. "There," he said at last, when he was satisfied that the fire would take hold. "The cabin should be warm before long." He moved back to her. "I fell asleep and allowed the fire to go out," he told her. "Are you all right?"

She saw him shiver, and realized he was cold. "You must be so tired, Noble. Come under the covers with me," she said, not thinking past giving him some of her warmth. After all, he had seen to her comfort, without any thought for his own.

He stepped back. "I don't know if that's a good idea."

The room was now softly illuminated by the flickering flames. "Don't be silly. You'll catch your death if you don't get warm. Besides, it makes sense that we share the bed. You can't very well sit up all night."

He looked hesitant, then sat down on the edge of the bed and removed his boots.

"Just the boots," she said quickly. "You must sleep in your clothing."

He said nothing as he slid under the covers with her, but Rachel noticed that he kept to the edge of the bed. Even so, the mattress was small, and he was a tall man, so he couldn't avoid body contact with her.

"You have taken care of me, Noble. Move over by me and let me get you warm. We're both grown people."

He drew in his breath. "That would be the problem, wouldn't it?"

She laughed softly. "Are you afraid of little ol' me?"

Without hesitation he said, "Terrified."

Noble finally moved closer, she suspected to keep from falling off the bed. Rachel slid her arm around him, lending him her warmth.

"Are you really afraid of me, Noble?"

"I am. Did I not hear you say that you can shoot a silver dollar out of the air before it hits the ground?" he said, repeating the words she'd uttered that day at the Brazos when she'd pointed his own gun at him.

He turned to face her and found her smiling.

"I was awful that day, wasn't I, Noble?"

"You scared the hell out of me."

"You didn't seem to be afraid."

He chuckled. "For that matter, you scared the hell out of Harvey and his friends in Tascosa Springs that day you held your rifle on them."

"Go to sleep, Noble. I'll battle all your demons for you," she said, throwing his words back at him.

Noble watched the way the firelight played across her flaming hair. "There is no woman to match you, Rachel Rutledge. My life was so uncomplicated when I had only the Yankees to fight. Then I came home and met with a much superior force."

"Little ol' me?"

"Uh-huh."

"Good night, Noble."

Even though they were both dressed, he could feel her soft body against his. "How can I sleep when . . ." He moved away from her just a bit.

He could feel her body shaking and he realized that she was laughing.

"Good night, Green Eyes."

Rachel awoke sometime later to find that the logs had burned low. She felt Noble beside her, his arm resting around her waist. The clouds had drifted away and bright moonlight streamed through the window, while the persistent wind howled outside the cabin and the branch of a tree scraped against the roof.

Glancing down at Noble, she saw that he slept. The moonlight fell upon him and she could see the tired lines etched on his face. Her heart swelled with love for him. Once again he had saved her life. He could so easily have been lost in the blizzard himself. But that hadn't kept him from searching for her.

She wanted to touch his face, to kiss those lips, to— What was she doing? Suddenly she knew she had to put some distance between them. She didn't like the way her mind was beginning to work.

She shook him gently. "Wake up, Noble. The fire's about to go out again."

He stirred and opened those wonderful dark

eyes, staring at her for a long moment. Then a slow smile touched his mouth and he pulled her closer to him. "Who needs a fire when they have you?"

"If you don't lay more wood on the fire, we'll both freeze to death. I don't want your death to be on my conscience," she said bitingly to cover up her true feelings.

His laughter filled the cabin. "You have enough fire in those green eyes to keep this cabin warm from now on."

"Are you going to stoke the fire or not?" she asked, pressing her back to the wall to avoid contact with him. Now she was sorry she'd asked him to share the bed with her.

"Let the fire go out, Rachel. We can keep each other warm with our bodies."

She knew he was teasing her again. "You have all the heat you are going to get from me. I suggest you put more logs on the fire."

"There are no more logs unless I chop some, and it's too dark to go outside." He raised her face to him. "Rachel, have no fear that I'm going to ravish you. Do you trust me?"

She trusted him, but could she trust her own wayward heart, her own passionate longing that plagued her whenever he was near? She nodded, though she still kept her back pressed against the wall.

With a weary sigh, he turned his back to her, and before long she could hear steady breathing that told her he was asleep. Slowly she reached out and laid her hand against his back and allowed it to move up to his shoulder. This moment belonged to her, and she might never be this near to him again. She dared to move closer to fit her body against his, and the now familiar burning started in the pit of her stomach. She ached for what they had shared together by the river.

Tensely, almost shyly, she moved her head so her face lay against his back. She planted a small kiss there—he would never know.

Suddenly he turned over and gripped her chin in a painful clasp. "If you continue to torment me, Rachel, I can't answer for the consequences."

The tattered cloud moved away from the moon and the cabin was illuminated. Rachel and Noble stared at each other for a long, poignant moment.

He sucked in his breath. "I said you could trust me, and I'll keep my promise." The words seemed to be torn from his throat. "You almost died out there, Rachel. What kind of beast do you think I am to take advantage of you now?"

"I'm so frightened," she admitted.

"Are you frightened of me?"

"No. Of something—someone. I don't know."

"With all you've had to face, you sure as hell don't need me complicating your life."

"I want you to hold me, Noble." Her voice sounded like the cry of a lost child. "Please."

In a sudden rush, the restraints he'd been exerting on his feelings snapped. With a strangled cry, he pulled her into his arms, his lips moving frantically across her face, kissing her eyelids, her cheek, then settling on her mouth in a kiss that stole her breath.

"If only I could keep you like this for always and never allow anything to hurt or frighten you again." His arms cradled her gently, lovingly. "But you don't want anyone's help, do you?"

Without answering, Rachel put her arms around his neck and pressed against him, wanting to feel him inside her, making her feel alive and reborn again.

"Green Eyes"—he moaned—"why do you torture me so?"

For her answer, she opened her lips to invite his kiss. His mouth was hot against hers and she welcomed his probing tongue. Her hands frantically unbuttoned his shirt, then moved over the dark hair on his chest.

"I didn't want this to happen," he said, rolling her over. "I wanted to show you that I could be near you and not . . ." He pulled away. "I meant it when I said you could trust me." He turned away from her, and his feet hit the floor when her voice stopped him.

"Make love to me, Noble," she said softly. "I want you to."

He turned back to her; his hand moved from her shoulder to slide tenderly across her breasts, and she could feel him tremble.

"Are you sure you want me, Rachel?"

"Yes. I am sure."

In a frenzy of passion, they both undressed, and soon their naked bodies were pressed together, fitting like a tight glove. Noble hardened and swelled against her, and Rachel thought she would faint from longing.

He kissed and caressed her until she was shaking inside. In a bold move that surprised them both, she rolled on top of him, and eased herself down so he slid into her moistness.

Noble threw his head back, closing his eyes and absorbing her in his mind as she absorbed him into her body. Her silkiness closed around him, and he tried to hold his leashed passion in check. Gripping her hips, he moved her up and down, drawing a trembling gasp from her.

They were swept away on a tide of sweet breathlessness. He shifted their positions so he was on top, and plunged into her over and over.

Rachel felt like a flower opening to a brilliant sun. For this moment he was hers. She was a part of him, and he was a part of her. No matter what happened afterward she would have this to remember. She arched her hips to meet his forward thrusts, biting her lip to keep from moaning.

Again and again her body trembled with sweet eruption, and soon he joined her in climax.

When their bodies cooled, their need to touch each other was still strong. She nestled in his arms while his hand rested against her stomach. She didn't want to move because it might break the enchantment that held them together. She wondered what he was thinking as his hand moved up to caress her breasts. She closed her eyes and sighed, wishing she could stay in his arms forever.

Noble stroked her long hair, loving the feel of it sifting through his fingers.

Her hand slid up his arm and their fingers laced together—first one hand, and then the other.

At last Noble said, "We are good together, Rachel."

"You have had many women," she said, wishing she had not stated the obvious.

"Not like this." He raised her chin and stared into her shimmering eyes. "I want you to understand me, Rachel. I have never felt like this with anyone else, and never will."

She pressed her smooth cheek against his rough one. "And yet this is all we can ever have."

"You said that before."

"Fate was kind, giving us this unexpected time together."

He couldn't find his voice for a moment. "Why, Rachel?"

"The river between us is too wide."

"You said that before, and yet you crossed that river."

Her eyes became sad. "I came not for love, but to tell you to stop interfering in my life. I still feel that way. I suppose I always will."

Noble pulled back and stared at her, his gaze touching every feature of her face. "If this is to be our last time together, give yourself to me once more." His voice held a tone of uncertainty. "Will you?"

She moved forward and pressed her lips to his cheek in breathless anticipation. Could any woman resist Noble when he turned those dark eyes on her? She wasn't able to. The rush of tenderness Rachel felt for Noble came as no surprise to her. She offered him her lips, surrendering to him. For a moment Rachel felt like the helpless Samson being pulled toward quicksand. But what a glorious feeling.

His mouth hovered only a breath away from hers. "I can't seem to get enough of you," he whispered against her lips. "I will always feel this way."

She swept her fingers through his midnight hair. "I know. I feel that way too."

The urgency stirred within him, making him quake. "What have you done to me, Green Eyes?" His question needed no answer. Her softness beckoned him, and he sank into her. As ecstasy overtook them he closed his eyes and wondered if paradise felt anything like possessing Rachel.

"I want you to become my wife," he said, as warmth spread through him.

"I don't think so, Noble. I can never marry you."

"If you speak of the river that separates us, we'll build a bridge across it."

"No, not the river."

"Delia."

"Yes."

He stared at her for a long moment, trying to decide how to answer her. "I assume you haven't spoken to your sister about us."

"No. I can't seem to talk to her about you and me." She closed her eyes. "I don't really know why."

Noble brushed a silken curl from her face. "You are afraid of what she will tell you." He placed his hands on each side of her face. "Look at me, Rachel. I never touched your sister. I've never had the desire to. Beyond that, you will have to decide if you believe me or your sister."

"I can't. Don't ask me to choose. I'll have to choose my sister."

He sat up and refused to look at her. "So that's your answer?"

Rachel clamped her hands over her ears. "Don't do this to me, Noble."

"I'm not doing anything to you. I offered to marry you. I've never asked another woman to be my wife."

"You feel honor-bound to marry me," she admonished, watching his face carefully. "Well, my answer is no. What happened between us was my fault, and you know it. I absolve you of any blame."

He shrugged, knowing anything he said at the moment would be misunderstood. "Here's something you need to think about, Rachel. Sooner or later you are going to have to decide if Delia is telling the truth or if I am." His dark gaze hardened. "Just make certain you choose the right one."

He slid out of bed and quickly dressed. After he'd slipped into his boots, he stood over her. "I can either take you home now, or I'll go to the Broken Spur and get Zeb or Tanner to come for you. If you ride with me, it'll have to be double. Which do you prefer?"

"Zeb."

"Very well." He didn't even look at her.

Rachel watched him leave, and a short time later she heard him chopping wood. When he returned to the cabin with an armload of logs, he still didn't look at her, but went about laying a fire.

"This should keep you warm until Zeb comes for you."

Without another word, he left. The cabin felt so empty without him. Rachel lay back, fighting tears.

He'd asked her to marry him, and she wanted nothing more than to be his wife. But Delia would always stand between them. And she was certain that he'd only asked her to marry him because he felt duty-bound to do so.

Well, he owed her nothing. She had been the one who had seduced him. Her cheeks burned with shame. What must he really think of her?

She slid out of bed and a blast of cold air almost drove her back under the covers. Her mind rushed ahead of her and she quickly got dressed. It was time to demand answers from her sister. Time to find out if it was Delia or Noble who'd woven a web of lies.

Rachel moved to the warmth of the fire. There was something else she had to do. She had a strong suspicion that Harvey Briscal was somehow tied in with the accidents that had been happening to her lately.

She was determined to find him and discover the truth. She would not live her life glancing over her shoulder in fear, or waiting for the next accident.

When Zeb arrived two hours later, she met him at the door.

"You had us right worried, Miss Rachel."

She mounted the horse and glanced at him. "What do you know about Harvey Briscal?"

Zeb merely shook his head, wondering what wild scheme Rachel was hatching this time.

Chapter Twenty-seven

Three weeks later, Rachel was aboard the Robert E. Lee stage line, on her way to El Paso with Zeb as her traveling companion. When they first started out, the weather was bitterly cold. But the closer they got to El Paso, the warmer it became.

Rachel had but one purpose in mind, and that was to find Harvey Briscal. Tanner had asked around town and discovered that Harvey had been seen in El Paso the previous week. Rachel hoped he'd still be there when she arrived; she intended to force him to admit what he knew about the snake in her bedroom and the fire in her barn.

Rachel stared out the window at the desolate countryside. Tumbleweeds rolled about at the discretion of the persistent winds. In the distance, the whiteness of the salt flats reflected the sun and stung her eyes. Occasionally she saw the skeletal remains of cattle and oxen. The wind never ceased, but it was warm, even if it did taste of salt.

She dismissed the discomfort caused by the stage's bouncing and jostling over the rutted road. She was angry that someone was trying to kill her, and she was determined that before she left El Paso, she'd know the culprit.

She glanced across from her and met Zeb's gaze. The dear old man hadn't disputed her decision to make this trip, but he had doggedly insisted she would not leave his sight for a moment.

Her mouth felt dry and it had nothing to do with thirst. Everything was coming to a conclusion, and she feared what would happen when she reached El Paso.

Noble read the note that had been delivered to him by one of the hands from the Broken Spur. He'd hoped it would be from Rachel, but when he began to read, his lips thinned. It was from Winna Mae. She was concerned because Rachel had gone off looking for Harvey Briscal with only Zeb to protect her. In Winna Mae's opinion, Harvey was the one who'd put the snake in Rachel's bedroom. The note went on to beg Noble's help.

With long strides Noble stalked to the stable, where Alejandro and one of his sons were bridle training a dappled gray stallion.

"*Patrón*," the *gran vaquero* said with pride. "This horse is ready to ride."

Tomas ran his hand down the smooth flank of the magnificent animal. "*Patrón*, this one is worthy of a king."

"Alejandro, I need to locate a man who probably doesn't want to be found. But I suspect he still has friends in Tascosa Springs—friends who would be unwilling to talk to me. How would I go about finding a man who doesn't want to be found?" Noble asked, crushing Winna Mae's note in his fist.

Alejandro pondered for a moment, studying the bridle in his hand. Then he said, smiling and pushing his son forward, "I would send my son, Tomas, into town to listen and learn. You would be surprised what someone will talk about when a Mexican is standing right next to him at the bar. It is like we are invisible and do not have ears and eyes. If anyone in town knows about the man you want, my sons will find out for you."

Noble nodded. "The man is Harvey Briscal."

Alejandro gripped Tomas's shoulder. "You heard the name of the man the *patrón* wants you to find. Ride to town. Go to the saloon, where you will listen and learn."

The young Mexican smiled, pleased to be entrusted with such an important mission for the *patrón*. "*Sí*, Papa, I will listen and I will learn about this man." His eyes shifted to the man he'd grown up respecting. "If Señor Briscal can be found, I will learn of it, *Patrón*."

Noble was troubled. "Harvey is a coward, and that makes him dangerous if he feels threatened. If you meet with any trouble, I want you to forget about Harvey Briscal and come home at once, Tomas."

"Do just as the *patrón* has told you. And as your father, I shall add one more thing."

"*Sí*, Papa."

Alejandro's hand tightened on Tomas's shoulder. "You will order a drink, but you will sip it slowly. Do you understand?"

The dark eyes showed disappointment. Tomas said in a deflated voice, "*Sí*, Papa."

"If you have to stay long at the saloon, you must not make yourself suspicious. Order a second drink. Make a show of drinking it, but do not. Your mama will carve out my heart if you come home drunk."

"*Sí*, Papa. I can enjoy one drink but no more."

Alejandro's eyes softened. "See to your safety. I would go, but everyone knows me, and they would not talk so easily if I were with you."

Tomas turned to his horse, and had his boot in the stirrup when Noble stopped him.

"Tomas, throw your saddle on the gray stallion. He's yours."

The young Mexican's eyes widened with disbelief, then brightened with joy. "I shall take the best of care of him, *Patrón*." While he spoke, he was already loosening the cinch on his horse, and he hefted the saddle onto the back of the gray.

"Have you nothing more to say to the *patrón*?" his father asked, his voice chastising, his eyes narrowing. "Have you forgotten your manners?"

Tomas quickly removed his wide sombrero and rolled the brim in nervous fingers. "I thank you for the honor of the horse, *Patrón*."

Noble laughed and clapped the young Mexican on the back. "You will earn him before you get back, Tomas. Look to your father's advice. Make yourself inconspicuous and listen well. But most of all, look to your safety."

Tomas swung into the saddle, his head at a proud tilt. "I will not disappoint you, *Patrón*."

Noble and Alejandro watched the young man ride away.

"He's a son to be proud of, Alejandro."

"*Sí, Patrón*. My sweet Margretta gave me fine children."

"I should like to have a son," Noble said, surprising himself when he put the sudden realization into words.

"How is Señorita Rachel?" the *gran vaquero* asked with feeling.

"Not much gets past you, does it, my friend?"

"I have known you too long, *Patrón*. I have never seen you care so for a woman before. I know where your heart lies."

"Then pity me, Alejandro, because it would be easier to tame a wildcat than to conquer Rachel Rutledge."

"Ah, but to have such a woman for your wife would be worth the trouble, no?"

"Her husband—God help him, whoever he may be—will never know one day's peace."

"*Sí*," Alejandro agreed with the experience of a happily married man who is not entirely in control of his own life. "When a man loses his heart to a spirited woman, he needs much divine guidance." Then his eyes sought the *patrón*'s. "You worry that she is in danger, do you not?"

Noble nodded. "And well I should."

Rachel stood outside the hotel room, trying not to think about the stench that came from the filthy place. It had not surprised her that Harvey would frequent such an establishment. There had been several half-clad women downstairs, and the hotel clerk had looked at her suspiciously when she had told him that she was Harvey's sister.

Zeb stepped in front of her and rapped on the door.

They could hear movement inside, but no answer. Again Zeb knocked, but still no answer.

Rachel set her chin and drew in a deep breath. The door looked flimsy enough. "Move aside, Zeb," she said.

"Now what're you doing, Miss Rachel? We know he's in there, but he ain't gonna open the door to you. We'll just wait downstairs—er, no, we'll wait across the street in that nice little hotel till he comes out. He has to eat sometime."

"I said move aside!" she repeated more forcefully.

Zeb did as she asked, but he stayed close to her should there be any trouble.

With one strong kick, the flimsy lock gave way and the door splintered. Rachel stepped inside and faced Harvey. He lay on the rumpled bed trembling like a coward. The gun he pointed at Rachel wavered. He swallowed once and then again before he found his voice.

"You! What're you doing here?"

Rachel ignored his gun and concentrated on the man's small, greedy eyes. "It's simple, Harvey. I have some questions and you have the answers."

"He's with you, ain't he?" Harvey's eyes darted fearfully to the door.

"Who?"

"That Spanish bastard."

"No. Only Zeb's with me, Harvey. What are you afraid of?"

"Not you."

"I want to ask you some questions." Rachel moved closer to him. "I want to know who you work for."

"I don't have to talk to you. Get the hell out of my room."

By now, Zeb had maneuvered his body so he stood between Rachel and Harvey. "If'n I was you, I'd tell her what she wants to know. She can be powerful fearsome when she's all het up. But you saw that in town that day with the big fellow." The old man's gaze became pointed. "Now tell her what she wants to know. And keep to decent talk. Miss Rachel's a lady."

Harvey licked his lips and slid against the iron bedstead. "I could shoot you both dead and claim it was self-defense. You broke into my room."

Zeb seemed undaunted by the threat. "You could get me right enough, but you'd never see me bleed, 'cause if'n you'll recall, Miss Rachel's a deadly shot."

Harvey scooted off the rumpled bed, his gun dipped, and he seemed to cringe. "It wasn't my idea to go after you, Miss Rachel. I didn't want to."

She stepped to Zeb's side. "Who hired you, Harvey?"

"It was—" His eyes widened in horror as he looked beyond her. "No, no. I wasn't gonna tell her. Don't shoo—"

A shot rang out. Rachel and Zeb watched Harvey go limp and slowly slump to the floor.

In an instant, Rachel turned to see the huge man who filled the doorway. His cruel mouth twisted, his gun still smoking in his beefy hand. It was the redheaded man who had attacked Noble that day in Tascosa Springs.

Red smiled. "I don't expect you to thank me, little lady. But I did save your life. Harvey had a gun."

Rachel quickly went to her knees beside Harvey.

"Who hired you, Harvey?" she shouted, grasping his shirtfront. "Tell me!"

Harvey tried to say something, but a thin stream of blood flowed from his mouth. He stiffened and his eyes rolled back into his head. He was dead.

Rachel stood up slowly and turned to Red. "You shot him deliberately because you didn't want him to tell me who he works for."

Red dropped all semblance of pretense. "Yeah, I did. What're you gonna do about it? You left your gun on the floor beside poor Harvey." He ran his hand over his mouth. "I owe you something, little lady. You made me look bad, and I don't take to people who make me look bad."

Zeb, who had been easing forward, raised his gun. "You forgot 'bout me, didn't you?"

Red fired so quickly that it took Zeb by surprise.

Rachel cried out as she watched Zeb crumple, his gun hitting the floor before he did.

Tears blinded Rachel as she bent down to the dear old man. "Oh, Zeb, Zeb," she said, softly touching his face. "Why did you do it?" She saw the dark stain on his shirt, and anger overwhelmed her. She quickly ripped a strip from her petticoat and pressed it against the wound. She couldn't tell how badly he'd been hurt. But he couldn't die—he just couldn't!

Golden sunset filtered through the dirty windowpane and streaked across Zeb's face. He tried to rise, but Rachel pushed him back.

"I can't . . . help you none. I failed you when you

needed me." Sadness clouded his flickering gaze, and he lost consciousness.

Rachel lunged forward to reach for Zeb's gun, but Red was there before her, kicking it out of her reach. She inhaled quickly, too angry to be frightened. She was never so brave as when she faced her own fears. Drawing in a steadying breath, she stood, staring at Red. "If Zeb dies, you die."

"I don't think so, lady." A slow grin etched Red's features, his eyes running down her body with a suggestive leer. "I'm gonna enjoy your body; then if you're nice to me"—he shrugged—"who knows? I may let you live."

"You are a disgusting coward. I'd rather die than have you touch me."

"Have it your way. But you just ran out of defenders, and you just ran out of time."

"It's you that's run out of time, Red," said a cold granite voice just behind him.

Rachel felt a sob rising in her throat. "Noble!" She looked from him to Red. Red had just shot two people, and now his gun was pointed at the man she loved!

"Step away from her," Noble commanded.

Red threw his head back and laughed. "Well, you see the problem here is that you're gun's holstered and mine ain't. It was kinda like when you was facedown in the streets of Tascosa Springs. Only then you had the little lady here to protect you."

Noble stepped closer to the man. "I don't need a gun to outsmart you."

Red cocked his head with a look of puzzlement. "What do you mean?"

"No, Noble, don't do it," Rachel cried.

Noble's hand rested on the handle of his gun, and he didn't dare take his eyes off Red, who stepped closer to Rachel and placed his gun barrel against her temple. "Do you need to hide behind a woman for courage, Red? Some cowards do."

Rachel shuddered at the feel of cold steel against her skin. She realized that Noble was trying to distract Red's attention from her. She glanced at Zeb's gun, which was halfway under the bed, out of her reach.

Red looked undecided and then angry. "No man calls me a coward and lives." His eyes drifted to Rachel and then back to Noble. "I can kill her now," he threatened. "And I will without regret if you don't drop your gun."

Noble unbuckled his gun belt and let it drop to the floor. Red wouldn't hesitate to shoot Rachel if he didn't do something quickly. "If you are as tough as you say you are, get rid of your weapon and fight me like a man," Noble challenged, taking another step forward. He was baiting the man—playing to his ego—hoping to tear his attention away from Rachel. "Are you afraid to face me from the front, and without help? You're a big man, Red, probably stronger than me. Drop your gun and let me see what you're made of."

Red stared at his gun, and then crammed it into

his holster. "I'm a better man than you'll ever be, big landowner."

Amid muscle and sweat, the two men clashed—Red the larger, more muscular—Noble more agile and more intelligent.

Rachel was all but forgotten now, so she inched toward the gun. At last, her hand closed around the cool handle and she raised it toward Red. She couldn't fire or she might hit Noble. Intuitively, she realized that she was no longer a part of the battle between the two men. Noble had a score to settle with Red, and he would not welcome her interference.

A crowd had been lured into the hall by the sounds of gunfire. Several people watched with interest as the two men came together in a clash of fury.

Red's hand clamped across Noble's face, forcing it backward, while he worked his fingers around, trying to gouge out Noble's eyes.

With a swift uppercut, Noble caught Red in the jaw and the big man went reeling backward, slamming into a chair and tumbling over it onto the floor. Pure rage made the big man's eyes bulge, and he gained his feet and made a mad lunge at Noble.

Noble was ready for him and agilely side-stepped the charge. Red hit the wall with such force, he had to brace himself against the bed to keep from falling.

"You had enough?" Noble asked.

Dazed, Red shook his head to clear it. Sweat and blood ran down his face, blinding him for a moment. With the swipe of a huge hand, he wiped his eyes and located Noble.

Then, charging like a maddened bull, Red landed a fist on Noble's jaw that sent Noble reeling backward. Noble slammed against the wall, but he didn't lose his balance or his calm. He merely smiled.

"Not bad, Red. But if that's the best you can do . . ."

Laughter came from the group of onlookers. Red realized he was being humiliated once again— just like in Tascosa Springs. His anger made him more cloddish and clumsy.

Red was at a definite disadvantage, Rachel thought as she watched the two men battle. Noble remained coolheaded and in control.

This time Red charged Noble straight on. Noble deftly stepped aside and Red hit the iron bedstead, looked stunned and collapsed to the floor.

He didn't move. He was out cold.

Chapter Twenty-eight

Winter retained its grip on West Texas, and the north winds blew almost daily, sweeping across the plains with frigid air.

Zeb had never had so much attention. He was recovering in a bedroom at the big house, where Rachel and Winna Mae saw that he had everything he wanted.

Of course, they didn't make the coffee as strong as he liked it, but it was drinkable. The custard pies Winna Mae served him, because they were his favorite, more than made up for the coffee.

Rachel came downstairs carrying Zeb's lunch tray. She entered the kitchen to find Winna Mae kneading bread dough. "There is nothing wrong with Zeb's appetite. He ate everything."

Winna Mae paused and pushed a lock of gray hair from her cheek with her arm, taking care not to get the sticky dough in her hair. "The old fraud is well enough to get up." Winna Mae laughed. "But he isn't any trouble. I'm just glad he survived his wound."

"I don't know how I would have lived with the guilt if anything had happened to Zeb."

"He worships you, Rachel."

A knock came at the front door. Rachel placed the tray on the table and went to answer it. When she opened the door, she found Noble and another man standing there.

"Come in," she said, wishing she'd put on a gown that morning instead of trousers.

Noble smiled at her in greeting. "How's Zeb?"

"Enjoying a life of ease."

Rachel looked at the man who accompanied Noble, expecting to be introduced. Rachel judged that he wasn't much older than herself. His hair was shiny, black and shoulder-length, but neatly tied away from his face. He looked uncomfortable in the black suit and wool greatcoat he wore. She met his eyes and saw something like anxiety reflected there. That was when she realized that he had the features and high cheekbones of an Indian.

"May we see Winna Mae?" Noble asked.

Rachel was puzzled, but said, "I'll get her."

Moments later she returned with Winna Mae. The housekeeper had removed her apron and smiled at Noble with genuine friendliness.

Noble looked uncertain for a moment. Then he took Winna Mae's hand and led her to the young man, who had not spoken a word. "Winna Mae, I'd like you to meet your son."

Noble felt Winna Mae's hand tremble and she stumbled backward. A gasp escaped Rachel's lips and tears swam in her eyes.

The young Indian man's eyes softened and he went to Winna Mae and said in perfect English, "Mother, you look just as my father described you."

Winna Mae reached out and touched his face tenuously, as if she were afraid he wasn't real. "Silent One, can it be you?"

"It is I. But my name is now He Who Walks Tall," he said with pride. "At the white man's school they called me Robert Tall."

"You look so like your father," she said, wanting to take him in her arms, but knowing an Indian warrior would not welcome such a show of affection from his mother. "Is your father—"

"Five winters ago, he died. We both thought you dead."

Winna Mae inched closer to her son, wanting so much to put her arms around him, but still she dared not.

He Who Walks Tall took the decision out of her hands. His strong arms slid around her shoulders and he brought her to his chest. "Mother, I thought I had no family, but now I have you."

Noble took Rachel's hand and led her toward the parlor so mother and son could become acquainted.

"Noble," Winna Mae called after him softly.

Noble paused and turned back to the housekeeper.

"I can never thank you for—"

Noble held up his hand. "There is no need to thank me."

He moved Rachel out of the room, and she stood for a long moment with her back to him. When she turned to him, she was crying softly. "Do you know how wonderful you are?" She held her hand out to him. "I am so grateful for all you have done for us. But mostly for this—for making Winna Mae happy. Did you see how happy she was?"

"Don't," Noble said, stepping away from her before she could touch him. "I didn't want your gratitude."

Rachel stared into his melting brown eyes, becoming reacquainted with the many emotions he brought to life within her. "Is something the matter?" she asked, wondering why he acted so distant.

"No, why should you ask?"

She offered him a chair and asked if he would like something warm to drink, but he declined. She seated herself on the edge of a chair and raised her gaze to his. "How did you find Winna Mae's son?"

"I can't take the credit, Rachel. My lawyer in New Orleans hired a man who knew where to look. This morning he brought the young man to Casa del Sol. It seems what was left of the tribe was imprisoned on land in Oklahoma Territory. He Who Walks Tall was sent to a school back east, where he was well educated. That's about all I know."

"You are much too modest. None of us would have known how to find him." She made a pretense of straightening her sleeve. "Winna Mae's son won't have to go back to the reservation, will he?"

"No. He can either stay here or I'll find a place for him."

"I'm sure he won't want to be separated from his mother after all this time."

Noble still seemed withdrawn; she had never seen him so controlled. "Are you sure you don't want something to warm you? Have you eaten?"

He drew in his breath slowly, patiently. "Rachel, I don't want anything. But I do have a bit of news for you."

She waited for him to continue.

"As you know, the sheriff in El Paso put Red in jail to await his trial."

"A good place for him."

"Someone shot him through the bars, Rachel. He's dead."

She paled. "Who . . . why?"

"That's what I'd like to know. I believe it was

Harvey and Red who had tried to kill you. I thought Red shot Harvey to keep him from naming him as a partner in the scheme. Now it seems someone shot Red to silence him."

"What do you mean?"

"I mean the danger isn't over, Rachel. Whoever hired them is still out there somewhere."

"You're scaring me, Noble. I had begun to feel safe. Now, if you are right . . ."

"All I am saying is that you must be particularly careful. Don't go riding alone, and don't take any unnecessary risks."

"I can't think of anyone who would want me dead."

He rose to his feet. "Someone does."

Rachel stood and moved restlessly about the room. "I don't want to talk about that now, Noble. I want to tell you what's on my mind. This needs to be said, so please hear me out without comment—until I finish."

He swept his hand toward her in a gesture that told her to continue.

"This isn't easy for me." She walked to the window and then back again. "You were aptly named, Noble, by your mother and father. When I think how I have wronged you, and how much I owe you, I feel sick inside. Can you ever forgive me?"

He studied her carefully. "There's nothing to forgive."

"Oh, but there is. If you only knew how I feel about you. I . . ."

"Yes?"

"I admire you."

"Anything else?"

"I . . ." She dropped down on the sofa, unable to put her feelings into words.

"Perhaps I should tell you how I feel about you, Rachel."

She ducked her head. "I know, I know. You think me unladylike, riding about the country dressed like a man, always getting into trouble." She stared at the ceiling for a moment until she could speak again. "I'm not at all a lady."

He smiled. "Not prim and proper, but I never cared for that sort."

"I can't sew; I don't like to mend. I'm an awful cook. I can make a good cup of coffee."

He pretended seriousness. "A woman who can make a good cup of coffee has much to recommend her."

"Don't tease me."

He sat down beside her and took her hand. "Rachel, I don't think you understand what you've done for me. You gave me back my life. When I returned to Texas, I was a haunted man, with no purpose and no direction. Then you burst back into my world and tilted it a bit. You gave me a reason to get up in the morning—a reason to live."

Tears gathered behind her eyes and rolled down her cheeks. "You are much too generous. I have caused you nothing but trouble."

His dark eyes glistened and a thin smile curved his lips. "You have done that."

"I wouldn't be surprised if you never wanted to see me again."

His gaze touched each feature of her face. "Would you like that?"

"No! No, I wouldn't."

He placed his hands on each side of her face. "I can't take a breath without thinking about you. When I see a sunset, I wonder if you are watching the same beauty at the same moment. You are always with me." He seemed to be searching for the right words. Finally he blurted out, "Will you marry me, Rachel?"

Her head fell onto his shoulder. She wanted more than anything to be his wife. "You haven't said you love me, Noble."

He kissed her forehead, then just held her close. "What do you think I've been saying?"

She drew back, studying his eyes. Yes, she saw softness there, and something more. The hand that rested against her back was unsteady. Could it be that he loved her? *Oh, please let him love me as much as I love him,* she said silently. "Noble, I do love you. I have for a long time."

She watched as a slow smile lit his whole face.

"I wondered what it would take for you to admit you loved me. I was sure you did."

"How could you know?"

"Because we are so good together. And I love you so much, how could you not love me?"

Happiness filled her heart, and a warm blush climbed up her cheeks as she felt her body responding to him even now. But there was still the matter of Delia.

"Will you allow me to speak to my sister before I give you my answer, or at least before we make it public?"

"Because you still believe that I made love to your sister?"

"No." She touched his face, wondering how she had been so fortunate to win the love of such a man. "I know you didn't, because I now know the kind of man you are. You would never desert a woman as Delia was deserted by the father of her child. Whoever the man was, it wasn't you." She blinked her eyes to see through her tears. "The only reason I want to see Delia first is to tell her that I love you. Can you understand that?"

"Yes, I understand. But do it quickly. I want you for my wife."

He bent his head and kissed her until she broke away, trying to catch her breath, and she saw that his eyes were bright with passion.

"And I want you in my bed," he murmured, raising her hand and kissing her palm.

She laid her head against his chest and listened to the drumming of his heart. "I will go to Austin by the end of the week."

"No. I don't want you to leave the ranch." He forced her to look at him. "Invite your sister to come here."

"Why should I—"

"Because I will worry about you if you don't."

She nodded. "I suppose I must get used to taking your orders. I'll write to Delia, asking her to come at once."

His laughter filled the room and he stood, drawing her up with him. "A cat cannot lose its stripes, and you will never be subservient to any man, not even me." He hugged her tightly. "Stay the way you are. I would have you no different."

Rachel was puzzled, remembering the time he'd told her he didn't like other men seeing her in trousers, and wondering if he still felt that way. "Beginning today, I shall never wear trousers again."

He arched his brow. "Do you mean it?"

"It's a promise I make to you. I always keep my promises."

His hand clamped on her arm as a strong feeling of possessiveness took hold of him. "Now," he said, moving away from her. "I must leave you. I want to speak to Zeb and then to Tanner."

"You are leaving?" she asked in disappointment.

"If I stay around you any longer, I may forget where we are."

Rachel looked horrified and then intrigued by the idea.

Noble's laughter carried him out the door and up the stairs to see Zeb.

In that moment, it occurred to Rachel that Zeb was not staying in the house because he liked being pampered. He remained because Noble and Winna Mae wanted him nearby to keep watch on her. No doubt Tanner was supposed to watch her when she left the house.

Suddenly a chill took the edge off her happiness. If Noble was right about Red and Harvey, then some nameless, faceless person might still try to get to her. Apparently Noble and Winna Mae thought so.

She was not a coward, but her mouth went dry and her chest tightened painfully.

She sensed that whoever it was, he would try again.

Chapter Twenty-nine

The sky was cloudless, and it was an unusually warm day for January. The snow from the previous week had melted, and a mild wind sweetened the air.

Delia had arrived the previous day and now occupied the overstuffed chair in the parlor as a queen would occupy a throne. She looked beautiful in a pink gown with white lace at the collar and cuffs. She daintily sipped tea from a cup belonging to the porcelain tea set she'd given Rachel for Christmas.

"Rachel, I can't believe it. Winna Mae finding her son after all these years." Delia placed the teacup on a low table and looked pensive. "Having a son agrees with that old woman. She actually smiled at me this morning. But it's a little unsettling to have an Indian in our midst, even if he does sleep in the bunkhouse."

Rachel set aside her own teacup, frowning. "It's not Winna Mae I want to talk to you about."

"No. I thought not. You want to tell me about you and Noble, don't you?"

Rachel glanced up in surprise. "How did you know?"

"I'm your sister. I'd be a fool not to know that Noble loves you, and that you love him."

"It's more than that, Delia. I want to marry him."

"Has he asked you?"

"Yes."

"And you want my blessing?" Delia's voice had a hard edge to it. "You want me to sanction the marriage?"

"I'd like that, yes. But mostly I want you to tell me what you know about the day Papa died."

"You don't believe that it was Noble's child I carried, do you?"

"I did for a while, but not now."

Delia let out a pent-up breath and leaned her head back against the chair. "I have relived that day over and over in my mind." She lifted a trembling hand to her face and seemed visibly to shrink. "When I told Papa that I was going to have a child, I thought he was going to strike me." Her gaze went to Rachel. "He never loved me like he did you. I had hoped he would be a father to me just this once, and have pity for me. But he didn't. He raved about how I was no good and he'd always known I'd disappoint him. Then he insisted on knowing who the father was. I never meant any harm to Noble or Papa. I thought if I said it was Noble, Papa would let it drop, because Noble was already engaged to some woman in Spain."

"You loved Noble."

"What female didn't love him? He's not the kind of man you can keep from loving. And once you love him, you never get over it."

Rachel reached for her sister's hand, finding it cold and unyielding in hers. "Who was the father, Delia?"

"I can't tell you. But it wasn't Noble." Delia's voice rose hysterically and she jerked her hand away from Rachel and stood up, going to the window. "The man meant nothing to me. It just happened. Anyway, that awful day, Papa grabbed up his rifle and headed for Casa del Sol." She buried her head in her hands and sobbed. "I never saw him in such a rage. He said Noble would marry me or he'd never see another sunrise." She turned to her sister. "I died a hundred times that day, as I tried to imagine Noble denying that my baby was his. I was humiliated, and I thought Papa would come home, knowing I'd lied to him." She walked back to the chair and slumped into it. "I wish whoever killed Papa that day had killed me instead. I have paid for my mistake every day since."

Delia raised her head. "You want to know the

Constance O'Banyon

ironic twist in all this? Noble kept my secret. Even when he was accused of killing Papa, he never told anyone that he wasn't the father of my child. If I know him, he was even reluctant to tell you, wasn't he?"

Rachel felt warmed by the honor of the man she loved. "Noble always insisted I ask you what had happened between the two of you. He did finally tell me, but only because it was destroying our love for each other."

"That's as I suspected. I'm so sorry."

"That's not important any longer." Rachel gripped her sister's hand. "But who could have killed Papa and planted the evidence against Noble, Delia?"

"I didn't know for a long time." She bent her head as if she had the weight of the world on her shoulders. "Lately, I've had my suspicion, but I don't know for sure."

"Tell me!"

Delia suddenly acted as if she were detached from her surroundings. Her eyes held a blank stare and she stood up, teetering, and walked toward the stairs. It was obvious that she'd been drinking. "I need to lie down."

"But Delia—"

Delia waved her away and left the room.

Rachel heard her sister's unsteady footsteps on the stairs. She stared into space for a long time. What did it all mean? Who was the father of Delia's baby, and who had killed their father?

374

Rachel needed to get out of the house and breathe fresh air. Talking to Delia had brought back horrible memories of that awful day their father had been killed.

Rachel went to the new barn that had been hastily constructed, and saddled Faro. Galloping away from the ranch, she found herself riding in the direction of the river—the one place where she could think undisturbed.

When she reached the Brazos, she wished she'd brought a coat, because the wind had shifted to the north, bringing an ominous chill. She dismounted and sat on the riverbank, reliving the moments she'd spent there with Noble. Her mind shied away from the day she'd been shot.

"Well, well, look who we have here." She hadn't heard Whit approaching. She watched him dismount and walk toward her. She felt a prickle of uneasiness at being alone with him. "I thought you were in Austin," she said, getting to her feet. Her gaze flew to the saddle holster, where she'd left her rifle. "What are you doing here, Whit?"

He moved closer. "Can't I visit my beautiful sister-in-law if I've a mind to?"

"I told you to stay away from me."

He drew so near she took several steps backward.

"I can't seem to stay away from you, sister-in-law. You have a way of getting into a man's blood."

Raw hatred flowed through her. "I despise you for what you are doing to my sister, and for what you tried to do to me. If you don't leave me alone, I'll tell Delia that you tried to force yourself on me. I'll do it, Whit."

He grabbed her by the arm, dragging her resisting body forward. "I've known I had to have you the moment I saw you and Noble frolicking naked." He nodded to the river. "It was in this very spot that you went into the river with him."

"You!" She struggled against his tight grip. "You're the one who shot me that day!"

His smile was pure evil, tightening the skin around his thin lips. Bringing his brows together across the bridge of his nose, he glared at her with hatred. There was nothing boyish or appealing about him now.

"Yes, I did it. I couldn't stand the thought of Noble taking you like he took my loving wife. He's always had everything, while I had to work for what I have."

Rachel's heart beat wildly with fear. "You killed my father!"

"Yes, I did that too," he admitted. "I'd come to call on Delia that day. Neither she nor your father knew that I overheard them talking about the baby. It was a hot day and the windows were open. I stood on the porch and listened to every word. I'd always hated Noble, but nothing like the hatred I felt for him that day. I slipped away and waited for your pa to cross the river."

"But how did you get Noble's gun?"

Whit seemed willing to tell her everything, and

she knew then that he'd never let her leave the river alive. She had to keep him talking, and hope help would come.

"That was the easy part. I followed your father to Casa del Sol, hung back in the bushes and listened to him talk to Noble. I had it in mind to kill Noble, but another plan came from their talk. Of course our golden boy denied ever being with Delia, and your father, like a gullible old fool, believed him."

Rachel's fear gave way to rage, but she had to control it for now. She took a deep breath and asked, "How did you plant Noble's gun beside my father's body?"

"That was the brilliant part. Noble had laid his holster aside while he'd been talking to your father. When both men left, Noble forgot to take his gun. I helped myself to it and followed your father. You can guess the rest. Your father never knew who shot him. It was a clean shot right through the heart. I dropped Noble's gun beside his body and simply rode away."

Nausea coiled inside her stomach like a slithering snake. "You are a monster." Tears stung Rachel's eyes and clung to her lashes. "How could you kill my father? He never harmed you."

"I wanted Delia, and that was the only way I could have her. She needed a father for her baby, and I was willing to take her any way I could get her. I was glad when she lost the Spaniard's brat, though. I didn't relish raising another man's child. Especially not Noble's."

"Delia didn't love you."

"No, she loved the golden boy, the Spaniard. But she didn't get him, did she?"

Rachel struggled and fought to get away from him, but he was too strong for her. She tried to ignore her growing panic. She needed to keep him talking. "Was it you who locked me in the barn and started the fire?"

Whit smiled. "How clever of you to figure that out." His eyes hardened and his jaw went slack. "I hired those fools, Harvey and Red, to get rid of you, but they mishandled everything. Red was supposed to get rid of Noble, but he failed in that too." He blinked his eyes and grinned. "Red did me the favor of shooting Harvey so he wouldn't talk, and I shot Red for the same reason." He laughed, but the sound was without humor. "No one will ever suspect me of the deaths." His hand slid to Rachel's slender neck. "And no one will blame me for your death, either. I am clever, don't you think?"

"You're a monster."

A shot rang out, and Whit was so startled that he loosened his hold on Rachel long enough for her to twist out of his arms. Delia stepped from behind the trunk of a cottonwood tree, her gun trained on Whit.

"You killed my father and now you threaten my sister." Delia was crying, but her hand was steady and her aim did not move from Whit's chest. "I won't let you hurt Rachel."

"Sweetheart," Whit said in a silken voice. "I did it all because I love you."

"Don't take another step, Whit. I knew you were ambitious and unscrupulous, but I never thought you were a monster." Delia shuddered, thinking of his hands on her after he'd killed her father. "You are going to confess everything to Sheriff Crenshaw."

"Delia, think about what you're saying. We have a future in this state. You aren't going to throw it away now. If Rachel were out of the way, you would inherit the Broken Spur, and I'll one day be governor. We could have everything."

"Do you actually think I'd hurt my own sister? You are mad, Whit. I won't rest until I see you hang for my father's death."

He took another step toward her. "Give me the gun, Delia. You know you'll never use it."

"Won't I?" A river of tears streamed down her face. "I'm sorry, Rachel, that I ever exposed you to a man like Whit. I swear to you that I never knew that he . . ." She wiped blinding tears from her eyes. "I watched you ride away, and then I saw Whit following you at a distance. Suddenly everything came together in my mind. It was as if I knew all the time, but didn't want to believe it. I knew Whit was going to try to kill you, so I got a gun and followed him. I'm glad I did."

Whit was inching ever closer to Delia. "Your sister's no better than a harlot, lifting her skirt for Noble just like you did. I saw her with my own eyes."

Delia shook her head. "I was never with Noble, Whit. The baby I carried in my body—the baby you made me get rid of—was your brother's baby. Your sod-busting, dirt-under-his-fingernails brother. I didn't mean for it to happen; it just did. I didn't want to marry Frank, so I could never tell anyone that he'd fathered my baby—not even Frank."

Whit let out a furious yell and lunged for Delia. She closed her eyes, waited for the impact and pulled the trigger.

Rachel watched trancelike as Whit's knees buckled and he crumpled to the ground, his chest gushing blood. He held his hand out to Delia, clutched the hem of her gown and raised his head to her.

"I . . . did love you, Deli—" His hand slipped from her gown and his body twitched as he drew his last breath.

For a long moment there was only silence. Then Delia glanced at her sister. "I had to do it, Rachel. He killed Papa, and he would have killed you." She stood unblinking, averting her gaze from her dead husband. "God forgive me. I had to do it."

Rachel ran to her sister and took her in her arms. "I know you had to do it, Delia. It will be all right. Everything will be all right now." Rachel pried the gun from her sister's stiff fingers and led her toward the horses.

"It's all over now; Papa's killer is dead," Delia said in a daze. "Why did he kill Papa?" she asked, looking puzzled. "Why?"

"I don't know." Rachel hugged her sister's trembling body. She feared it would be a long time before Delia recovered from this day.

"Delia, I was the one who vowed at Papa's grave to avenge his death. But you are the daughter who kept that promise. Papa would be proud of you."

"Would he?"

"Yes, very proud. Come, let's go home now."

Word swept through Texas about the tragedy that had happened by the Brazos River. Delia didn't have to go to trial, due to the circumstances, and because of Sheriff Crenshaw's compassion. She vowed never to return to Austin, to a life that had not made her happy.

Noble had been beside Rachel and Delia through the whole ordeal. Rachel suspected that he had a lot to do with the kindness their neighbors showered on Delia.

Since the tragedy, Delia kept to her room a lot. Surprisingly enough, Winna Mae took care of her, and finally convinced her to turn away from the past and start to live again. Delia never drank spirits now. Rachel suspected it had been Whit who had encouraged her to drink in the first place.

Tanner was also a help. Not a day passed that

he didn't bring a clump of wildflowers, a pretty ribbon, some sweetmeats, or a gift for Delia.

Soon Delia was laughing again, flirting and looking at Tanner with shining eyes. Rachel wondered if Delia and Tanner were falling in love. Tanner would give Delia the respect and kindness that Whit never had.

Not now—not this soon—but someday, they might marry. She could see the two of them living in the big house, here at the Broken Spur. Whereas Delia had despised the ranch before, it had now become her sanctuary.

Chapter Thirty

The night before Rachel's wedding, she was so happy she couldn't sleep. She tiptoed downstairs, thinking a glass of milk might relax her. She found Winna Mae sitting at the table, a cup of tea in front of her.

"I thought you might come down so I waited for you, Rachel."

"You know me too well."

"Yes."

"Winna Mae, although I'll be leaving tomorrow, I want you to know that the Broken Spur will always be home to you and your son."

The housekeeper was quiet for a moment. "We won't be staying here after you leave."

Rachel felt crestfallen. "You aren't going away? What would I do without you?"

Winna Mae gave Rachel one of her rare smiles. "I'll only be moving across the river to Casa del Sol. Noble has asked me to be the housekeeper there. His vaqueros are going to train my son to work on the ranch. Robert Tall has already moved into the bunkhouse at Casa del Sol."

Rachel's hand covered Winna Mae's. "I'm glad you will be with me."

Winna Mae took a sip of her tea. "You know that Zeb's been given the job of looking after Noble's horses."

"Yes." Rachel imitated Zeb's gruff voice. " 'Noble, I'll be coming across that river when Miss Rachel does. She can't do without me, nor me without her. We're kinda family-like.' "

Winna Mae and Rachel laughed; then Rachel became silent while she traced the flower pattern on the tablecloth with her finger. "I'm afraid, Winna Mae."

"Why is that? You are marrying a man you love, and he loves you. What have you to fear?"

"That I'm too happy, that it won't last, that something will go wrong."

Winna Mae patted her hand. "Live each day as if it were a gift from God. You have had a hard time, Rachel. I've watched you struggle to keep this ranch going. I saw you cry when you didn't know I was watching. It's time you looked to your

own happiness and treasured the love you and Noble have for each other."

Rachel's eyes swam with tears. "I will, Winna
Mae. All I want is to make him happy."

Winna Mae nodded. "If I ever saw a happy man,
it's Noble Vincente when he looks at you."

A warm spring breeze scattered colorful wildflowers across West Texas. The day dawned bright and
clear as the population of Madragon County gathered at the church to attend a wedding.

As Rachel and Noble exchanged their vows before the priest, a mockingbird trilled outside the
window, serenading their union.

Rachel looked into Noble's dark eyes and felt his
love wrap around her with a warmth and protec-
tiveness that took her breath away.

After they were pronounced man and wife, they
accepted the congratulations of their friends and
family.

Noble's sister, Saber, kissed Rachel's cheek.
"Now I have a sister. I'm almost sorry that I'll be
leaving this afternoon for Montana Territory to
marry my sweet Yankee."

Rachel hugged her tightly. "I only hope you will
be as happy as I am at this moment."

"I shall be." Saber moved to her brother, who
swallowed her in his embrace.

Rachel reached for Delia's hands. "Will you be
all right at the Broken Spur?"

Delia smiled, her whole face alight. "I have

come home at last, Rachel. In a year, perhaps more, Tanner—" She broke off and actually blushed. "He's nothing like Whit, and that's in his favor." She laughed happily. "Well, we'll see."

Mrs. McVee went about proclaiming to everyone who would listen that she'd known all along that Rachel and Noble would get married.

Noble pulled Rachel into his arms. "Alone at last."

Rachel pressed her face against his chest, knowing that this was where she belonged. "I am too happy to speak," she said, her arms sliding about his waist.

He lifted her chin and brushed her lips with his. "Green Eyes, my wife." He tested the title and experienced the pleasure it brought him. "I like the sound of that."

"Rachel Vincente. I like that."

He lifted her into his arms and carried her up the stairs. When he reached the bedroom, he set her on her feet. Several lamps illuminated the room. She had expected that he'd take her to his room, but this one was larger, and she could see a sitting room through the open door.

"This is not your bedroom—not the one I occupied when I was recovering from the bullet wound."

"No. This is the master suite. But if you would prefer something smaller . . . ?"

"No. I love it here."

Rachel knew Saber must have had a hand in

decorating. Lovely Spanish furniture, massive and yet delicately carved, graced the room. Maroon and cream hues blended in harmony that was pleasing to the eye.

Noble led Rachel to the huge mahogany bed, with peacocks carved into the wood. "I was born in this bed," he explained. "I want our children conceived and born here as well."

She melted against him, loving the thought of giving birth to his child. "I love you so, Noble."

He touched her cheek, his eyes soft and loving. "You have had my heart for a long time. There was never anyone but you for me, although I didn't always know it."

She asked, womanlike, "When did you first know that you loved me?"

"Looking back, I believe it was that day you watched me break Faro. When I looked into your eyes, I was thunderstruck. Of course, you were too young at that time, and I tried to control the feelings I had for you. I admit that while I was away, I had no conscious thought of you, other than sadness because you believed that I killed your father."

"Let's pretend that never happened." She laughed, snuggling against him. "I remember well the day you gave Faro to me. It was the first time I had ever had the feelings of a woman, and it frightened me."

Noble gripped her shoulders and his eyes

probed hers. "Did you ever have those feelings for another man?"

"No." She swept her fingers over the frown on his forehead. "You are the only one."

He walked around the room and extinguished all the lamps but one. Then he returned to Rachel, his hands going to the fastening at the back of her gown.

She closed her eyes, wanting to remember this moment forever. She was coming to him as his wife. They would always be together. She had wronged him in so many ways, but she would make amends now. She would be a good wife to him.

Soft Spanish guitars were strumming in one of the courtyards below, and a beautiful voice blended with the music.

Noble smiled, and opened the window so she could better hear the music. "The vaqueros sing for the new mistress of Casa del Sol," he said, coming back to her. "Their gift to the *patrón*'s lady."

His dark eyes softened as she'd never seen them before. She stood on tiptoe and kissed his lips, trembling with anticipation at the thought of lying in his arms as his wife. This time they would not have to be parted. She could go to bed beside him and wake up in his arms.

No shadows loomed over them now.

Noble expertly unhooked the back of her wedding gown and it soon slid down her body and billowed to the floor at her feet. His clothing quickly followed and he picked her up, kissing her while carrying her to the bed.

He lowered her onto the mattress and joined her there. Their bodies fit together, like silk against leather, soft curves against hard muscle.

"My Green Eyes," he murmured, embracing her in his warmth.

Her lips traveled along his neck, and she remembered the day at the well when she had wanted to do just that. Then, she'd had no idea that she would one day wed the beautiful Spaniard who had stolen a sixteen-year-old girl's heart.

She raised her head and looked deeply into his eyes. "You are an extraordinary man, Noble."

He smiled, more interested in her creamy breasts, which were cupped in his hands. "Where did you get such a notion, Mrs. Vincente?"

"From you," she said, closing her eyes and trying not to think about his mouth kissing the tips of her nipples, and then his tongue sliding around one, sending a thrill all the way to her toes.

She threw her head back when she felt him swell against her. She was only moments away from ecstasy. She would tell her husband later how wonderful he was. But for now . . .

Only an occasional sigh or a murmured word of love could be heard above the strumming of the guitars.

* * *

389

Much later when Noble held her in his arms, they both watched the moon make soft patterns through the lace curtains.

His hand rested across her stomach, and her head nestled against his shoulder.

"Our courtship has been a strange one," she said, pretending seriousness.

"In what way?" he asked, kissing her cheek.

"I had trouble deciding if I should shoot you or kiss you."

Amused laughter escaped him. "I'm glad you decided on the kissing, knowing your deadly aim."

Rachel's thoughts went back to the day he'd first come home and she'd aimed her rifle at his heart. She shuddered and pressed closer to him. "I love you so much," she whispered. "So very much."

"Do you want to hear about the first time you ingratiated yourself into my life?" Noble asked, shifting her weight so his arms went around her and he pulled her tightly against him.

"If you want to tell me." She nipped thick lashes that were so long they made shadows on his cheeks. She nuzzled his ear and kissed along his jawline.

He looked at her with softened eyes. "If you continue to do that, I won't be able to talk."

She settled against his shoulder and folded her arms, smiling. "You have my complete attention."

He shook with tender laughter. "Have I?"

"Oh, *sí*."

He seemed to be reaching back into the past,

because his wonderful eyes took on a faraway look. "You may be surprised at how young you were at the time."

She raised herself up on her elbow and looked at him quizzically. "How old was I?"

"I was aware that your mother had delivered a second daughter, of course. The whole county knew your father was wishing for a son."

She smiled. "I know."

"I saw you from a distance quite a few times, but thought nothing about it. After all, an eight-year-old boy has no interest in a baby, and a girl child at that."

She was becoming more and more intrigued. "You aren't going to tell me that you've loved me since I was a baby."

"I said nothing about love, Rachel. I was talking about how you ingratiated yourself into my life and never let go."

He was quiet for a moment as if remembering. "Before they built the new Methodist church behind the bank, it was located across the road from the Catholic church that my family attended."

"I remember." She looked at Noble. "I'm a Methodist, and you are Catholic. Will that make any difference to you?"

"Not to me."

"And not to me. We have conquered tougher differences than our religions."

Noble smiled. "Yes. We have." He pulled her closer to him and continued speaking. "One Sunday, it was in the spring, and you must have been about a year old at the time." He nodded thoughtfully. "Yes, no more than a year old."

"Go on," she urged.

"Our respective families had arrived to attend services at our different churches. Our mothers, being friends, met halfway in the road. My mother reached out and took you in her arms."

"I don't remember your mother very well. She died not long after my own mother."

"I believe you are right." He spoke softly. "What first drew my attention to you that day was the sight of your red-gold curls. I ambled closer to my mother to get a better look at you." He laughed as if at a private joke. "You were like a cherub, an angel, and I had never seen anyone so beautiful. I wanted to reach out and touch the curl that hung over your forehead—but I didn't."

"No?"

"No. I looked into that chubby, perfectly formed face and you gave me the biggest smile. I was captured by your eyes—green eyes, like I'd never seen before. Then, to my surprise, you held out your arms and made a dive for me. I had to catch you because you had left my mother's arms and fallen into mine. After my first shock, I realized you had laid your head on my shoulder and one dimpled hand rested on my cheek. At first I was afraid some of my friends would see me holding you and make fun of me, but when you raised your head and pressed your lips to my cheek—I was lost. Green Eyes, I called you that day, and you giggled, patting my face with both hands. I won't say that love grew that day, but every time I met you afterward, I would seek your eyes. I'm still fascinated by them. And somehow I felt that they took on a special glow when you looked at me."

"That's because you are so handsome." She smiled provocatively. "So you like my eyes, hmm, *Patrón?*"

An expression of pain flickered across his face. "The first day I saw those eyes look at me with hatred was the worst day of my life."

She wanted to hold him, to wipe away the memory of that day and the many others that followed. She wanted to stand beside him against the whole world if he needed her. "Noble, I'm so sorry about . . ."

His dark mood faded and his hand drifted across her breast, then circled the silken mound. "Recently I have come to admire other things besides your eyes."

"Such as?"

His mouth lightly touched hers. "This." He ran his fingers through her hair. "Your sweet-smelling hair." He stroked his long, lean fingers down the side of her cheek. "The texture of your skin." He kissed the tip of her nose. "And this." His head moved to her stomach and he softly planted a kiss there. "This." His hand drifted across her thigh and moved her legs apart, and he caressed her until she moaned. His voice was deep with emotion now. "And this."

"I love all of you." He kissed her deeply, lingeringly, until her eyes were bright and her body softened against him.

"It's time for you to hang up your rifle," he said, half serious, half in jest. "I'll take care of you from now on, Green Eyes."

The Snow Queen

ANNE AVERY

When Boston-bred Hetty Malone arrives at the Colorado Springs train station, she is full of hope that she will soon marry her childhood sweetheart and live happily ever after. Yet life amid the ice-capped Rockies has changed Michael Ryan. No longer the hot-blooded suitor Hetty remembers, the young doctor has grown as cold and distant as the snowy mountain peaks. Determined to revive Michael's passionate longing, Hetty quickly realizes that no modern medicine can cure what ails him. But in the enchanted splendor of her new home, she dares to administer the only remedy that might melt his frozen heart: a dose of good old-fashioned loving.

_52151-2 $5.99 US/$6.99 CAN

ELAINE BARBIERI

Purity, Honesty, Chastity—They were all admirable traits, but when they came in the form of three headstrong, spirited, sinfully lovely sisters, they were...

Dangerous Virtues

From the moment Purity sees the stranger's magnificent body, she feels anything but what her name implies. Who is the mysterious half-breed who has bushwhacked the trail drive she is leading? And why does she find it impossible to forget his blazing, green-eyed gaze?

Though Pale Wolf attacks her, though he is as driven to discover his brother's killer as she is to find her long-lost sisters, Purity longs to make him a part of her life, just as her waiting softness longs to welcome his perfect masculine form. There may be nothing virtuous about her intentions toward Pale Wolf, but she knows that their ultimate joining will be pure paradise.

___4272-X $5.99 US/$6.99 CAN

DANGEROUS VIRTUES:

ELAINE BARBIERI *Honesty*

Honesty, Purity, Chastity—three sisters, very different women, all three possessed of an alluring beauty that made them...DANGEROUS VIRTUES

When the covered wagon that is taking her family west capsizes in a flood-swollen river, Honesty Buchanan's life is forever changed. Raised in a bawdy Abilene saloon by its flamboyant mistress, Honesty learns to earn her keep as a card sharp, and a crooked one at that. Continually searching for her missing sisters, the raven-haired temptress finds instead the last person in the world she needs: a devastatingly handsome Texas ranger, Sinclair Archer, who is sworn to put cheats and thieves like herself behind bars. Nestled in his protective embrace, Honesty finds the love she's been desperately seeking ever since she lost her family—a love that will finally make an honest woman out of her.

_4080-8 $5.99 US/$6.99 CAN

WINTER LOVE

NORAH HESS

"Norah Hess overwhelms you with characters who seem to be breathing right next to you!"
—Romantic Times

Winter Love. As fresh and enchanting as a new snowfall, Laura has always adored Fletcher Thomas. Yet she fears she will never win the trapper's heart—until one passion-filled night in his father's barn. Lost in his heated caresses, the innocent beauty succumbs to a desire as strong and unpredictable as a Michigan blizzard. But Laura barely clears her head of Fletch's musky scent and the sweet smell of hay before circumstances separate them and threaten to end their winter love.

_3864-1 $5.99 US/$7.99 CAN

PASSION'S TIMELESS HOUR

VIVIAN KNIGHT-JENKINS

Bestselling Author Of *The Outlaw Heart*

Propelled by a freak accident from the killing fields of
Vietnam to a Civil War battlefield, army nurse Rebecca Ann
Warren discovers long-buried desires in the arms of
Confederate leader Alexander Random. But when Alex
begins to suspect she may be a Yankee spy, the only way
Rebecca can prove her innocence is to convince him of the
impossible…that she is from another time, another place.

__52079-6 $4.99 US/$6.99 CAN